I0578907

Praise for *ISABELLE*

"My sister, Mary Baird Mayer, has written a wonderful book about our maternal Great Grandmother, Isabelle Dahl Anderson Sletten, who emigrated from Sweden to build a strong and loving family on the plains of the Dakota Territory in the 1880s, and '90s. Isabelle delivered her eight children by herself and Mary writes with pathos about the deaths of four of them, as well as the death of her first husband, Gus Anderson. She highlights the strong and loving marriage between Isabelle and her second husband, our Great Grandfather, Ingvold Sletten. It was this strong bond that enabled her to endure the sufferings and celebrate the blessings of life on the prairie. Together they built a strong family that flourishes to this day."

—**Ruth Baird Pollard,** Author of *Loving Gordon: A Dementia Caregiver's Journey*

"*Isabelle* is an extraordinary story of a woman's faith, courage, and perseverance unlike any I have ever read. I am convinced it should be required high school reading to help every American citizen appreciate the sacrifices made by all the brave souls who settled the land we love so much. Thank you for sharing this soul-stirring, epic story of a mother's love."

—**Mark Johnston,** Author of *The Last Breakup: Finding New Life and True Love Just When All Hope Seemed Lost*

"*Isabelle: Dakota Prairie Pioneer Wife and Mother* lovingly gives life to the tremendous plight of a Swedish pioneer woman, giving us a window into the important roles of women that are often overlooked."

—**Arlo Paust,** Author of *Lina of York,* historic researcher at Mount Horeb Area Historical Society, and the author's cousin

ISABELLE

Dakota Prairie Pioneer Wife and Mother

MARY BAIRD MAYER

Editing by Mark Johnston • Cover design by Rolf Busch

Library of Congress Cataloging-in-Publication Data

Mayer, Mary Baird

Isabelle: Dakota Prairie Pioneer Wife and Mother

p. cm.

Paperback ISBN: 978-1-947708-67-9

Ebook ISBN: 978-1-947708-68-6

Library of Congress Control Number: 2020925312

First Edition, February 2021

CITRINE PUBLISHING

Schenectady, New York, USA

(828) 585 - 7030

www.CitrinePublishing.com

*To all our ancestors who came before us
and the stories of their lives
waiting to be told*

Isabelle Dahl Anderson Sletten
(1851-1921)

Circa 1917

1

1876 - 1877

STANDING IN FRONT OF the man I was about to marry, I knew a whole new chapter of my life was beginning. So much had happened in the five years since I left Eda Parrish, Sweden, and boarded the "Kong Sverre" for the long journey to America. The year was 1871, and I was only nineteen at the time—all alone, scared, and excited about the future. As I boarded the ship, I waved farewell to my mother, Maria, and sisters, Kerstin and Karin, and wondered if I would ever see them again.

My brothers, Magnus, Peter, and Nils, had already departed for America and sent money so I could join them for a better life. They said America was a wonderful place with many opportunities. They had bought farms, married, and started families in Wisconsin, but wanted to go further west to a place called Nebraska, where they had heard the land was more suitable for farming.

After arriving in America, I traveled by train to Wisconsin, lived there for two years, and then made the long journey to Nebraska with my brothers in 1873. We traveled by covered wagons, drawn by oxen. Crossing multiple rivers and walking for days on end, it was a long, hard trip that took six weeks to complete. I helped deliver several babies on the trail. I also cared for many who became ill thanks to the nursing skills I had learned from my mother.

Finally, we came to Hartington, Nebraska, across the Missouri river from Dakota Territory, where my brothers wanted to settle. I helped keep house for them and nearby neighbors. I also nursed their sick children and those of other families in the area.

Then I met Peter. Peter August Anderson. He was called Gus by everyone. He had also emigrated from Sweden. I met him when I was staying with my brother, Peter, who had moved to Meckling, Dakota, and operated a steam boat on the Missouri River.

We were attending service at a small country church near Meckling, called Bergan Lutheran Church, when I first saw Peter. After the service, at a church picnic he came over and asked to sit with me. Of course, I said yes as it was refreshing to talk to someone besides my family. He spoke Swedish, and I was thankful for that. It was easy to talk to him. I soon felt like I had known him my whole life.

That was how our relationship started. After that day, he came to my brothers' home regularly to see me. We took long walks and talked about our dreams for a new life. He had come to Dakota about a year earlier, claimed a homestead, and built a sod house. He had some livestock and a good team of horses, had planted some crops and hoped to put more in next spring. He had also put up a small barn.

Within three months, we knew we were in love. He asked me to marry him one Sunday after church, and I accepted right away. I loved him so and couldn't wait to be his wife. He had taken me to see his sod house, and it was very cozy and warm. It could use a woman's touch for sure, but I was happy it was finished and move-in ready.

We took our vows in the little Swedish church on March 22, 1876. We promised to "love and obey until death do us part." We believed with our love nothing could separate us.

He carried me over the threshold of his house later that night, and we started our life together. We knew life on the prairie could be harsh and there would be many hardships, but we felt we could face anything together.

May arrived with soft rains, and Peter and I started breaking the sod. It was hard work, but we worked together and laughed a lot. He didn't let me do any of the heavy work; he didn't believe that a woman should have to work that hard. I was strong and told him I could keep up with him anytime.

We had calves and looked forward to when they would be weaned so we would have milk cows. With our little farm bursting with new life, we had a wonderful time that summer.

By June, I knew we were expecting our first baby. I was not feeling well and knew my symptoms were a sign of pregnancy. One day after milking our cows, I had to sit down because I was feeling dizzy.

"Belle, what's the matter?" Peter asked. "Are you OK?"

"I'm pretty sure we are going to have a baby," I said. "I have seen the symptoms before and know what they mean. Are you ready for this, Gus?"

He came over and swept me off my feet and swung me around in his arms. "Belle, I'm so happy. A baby in the house will be wonderful.

I'm not getting any younger, so I'm glad we didn't have to wait too long to start our family."

I was twenty-five, which was older than most women who marry. Gus was thirty-six. We were ready for the big family I had dreamt about.

"If my calculations are right, our new arrival should come about February," I said. "I have a lot to do to get ready. I need to knit some blankets and make clothes and diapers. I know babies go through a lot of diapers."

"I'll get started making a cradle, and then a rocking chair, so you can rock our baby to sleep," Gus said excitedly. "Of course, I'll do my share of rocking the baby, too."

He kissed me again. I don't think we could have been any happier. I was floating on a cloud the rest of the day. February could not come soon enough. I hoped for a boy because I knew that was what Gus would want to help him on the farm someday.

On February 19, I delivered our first child, a son. We named him Amil. Gus was ecstatic and insisted on helping all he could. He loved to sit in the rocker and hold little Amil, often singing a Swedish song in his ear. "He is so soft," he said as he caressed the top of his little head. "I have waited for a son and now I have one. Belle, I am so in love with you, and having a child together only deepens our love."

This was just the start of my journey as a pioneer woman in Dakota Territory. I would have many more joys and sorrows, but I knew my life in America would always be better than my life in Sweden. I hoped that someday I would be reunited with my mother and sisters.

1877 - 1878

THE SPRING AFTER AMIL was born was a hard one. We had so much snow that it flooded the bottom land. We could only pray that the water would go down before it was time to plant. It was a very wet spring, but by June the land was dry. We hoped it was not too late to plant the crops.

Peter and I worked side by side in the fields. I had Amil tied in my apron, and he seemed to enjoy being outside with Mama and Papa. We planted wheat and had prairie grass hay for our animals. We milked cows twice a day, so we had plenty of milk and butter. We purchased some chicks that spring and looked forward to fresh eggs by mid-summer.

Gus and I talked about the grasshopper invasion of 1874. He had come to Dakota Territory in 1873 with some neighbors of ours. He lived with them the first year while he put up a sod house and planted crops. The grasshoppers came the next summer in 1874.

"They looked like a dark cloud that covered the whole sky and blocked out the sun," Gus said. "It was quite a sight. They ate all my crops, the wood off the wagons, and even clothes that were hanging on the line. They left nothing in their path. Many people were discouraged—to the point of pulling up stakes and leaving."

"Gus, I know how terrible it was for the farmers!" I exclaimed. "Do you think that will happen again?"

"Well, if it happened once it could happen again, but we need to persist. Someday our children and our grandchildren will reap the benefits of our hard work and sacrifice," Gus said. "We couldn't say that if we had stayed in Sweden. There just wasn't land like there is here. We are so blessed to have this land to call our own. We will pass it down to our descendants, and they will benefit from our work. Just think, Belle, our children will have land to farm, and they will pass it down to their children. Someday, a hundred years from now, someone will still be farming this land where we first broke sod and planted seeds."

That was such an encouragement to me; thinking about our own land being passed down to Amil and perhaps his children too. They could farm and make a good living for their families. That was why we came to America, and I never forgot that.

That fall we had a good crop and stored enough hay for the winter. I planted a small garden, and it yielded enough vegetables to eat in the summer and store in the root cellar for the winter. Our chickens started producing, so we had fresh eggs for break-fast. We were so happy there with our little family. We talked about building a frame house, but our first priority was getting the fields planted and harvested each year. We decided we would build our dream house when we were established. We talked about it often and planned what it would look like.

The next year was a good one with bumper crops, and our cattle herd had increased. Six new calves were born in the spring. Amil was learning to walk and toddled around the yard. He loved the cattle and stuck his little finger through the fence for the calf to suck on. He laughed and laughed.

"Gus, I have news for you," I said one day as we were having breakfast, "we'll have another baby probably around January."

Gus was happy. "I was hoping we would add to our family soon," he replied. "Amil needs a playmate. I was hoping we could have a house by then so you would not have to give birth in a sod house."

"It's not so bad, Gus. I love our little house," I said. "It is cozy and warm in the winter and cool in the summer. I have fixed it up, and it looks quite charming. I love the clock that we got as a wedding present from my family that sits on the shelf near the table. Every time it chimes, it reminds me of our wedding day."

Sure enough, on the first day of January a little son joined our family. He was smaller than Amil, but he thrived. We named him Peter after his father and we called him little Peter. Gus had made a small bed for Amil, so little Peter inherited the honored place in the cradle. Amil and little Peter were almost two years apart. I knew they would be best buddies and envisioned them running in the yard chasing the dog, even though we didn't have a dog at that point.

It was more difficult to help Gus with the field work that summer as Amil was very mobile and little Peter was getting too big to be tied in my apron. We constructed a fenced area where they could play while we worked in the field and kept an eye on them. We were brown as little Indians from the sun.

Speaking of Indians, we saw them from time to time as they traveled from the north to Yankton to trade furs. One day as I was preparing some sandwiches with fresh bread I had baked that morning, I turned around to find a tall Indian standing in our doorway. I suppose he was looking for lunch. When I picked up the bread knife, I heard a noise. When I looked, the Indian was gone. I guess the bread knife scared him. When Gus came in for lunch, Amil could hardly wait to tell him all about the Indian, even though he didn't know many words.

"Papa, Papa" Amil yelled as he ran to Gus. "Big tall Indian scared me! Up, Papa, up!"

Gus picked him up and held him close. "Amil, we don't have to worry about the Indians because they are friendly," Gus assured him. "They were here before we were and helped us learn about the land. So, don't be afraid, they won't hurt us. I think Mama scared them more than they scared you. She can be a pretty scary lady at times," he teased.

Then he picked up little Peter, sat down in the rocker with the two of them, and told stories about the early Dakota years. Soon, little Peter was fast asleep, so I took him from Gus's arms, carried him to the cradle, and tucked him in. I felt so blessed to have our little house, two beautiful boys, and my wonderful husband who cared for us so much. Then we sat down for lunch with our fresh baked bread. What a treat. We bowed our heads and thanked God for all the blessings He had given us.

1880 - 1881

OUR CROPS LOOKED GREAT that year. It had rained at the right times, and my garden was full of produce. I was looking forward to harvest time, even though it wouldn't be easy since Amil was three, and little Peter was just about two. They were busy little boys who were always underfoot, and they just loved to be near Papa. When Gus came into the house, they ran to him to be picked up. Gus was strong enough to lift them without a problem. He would take both of them, one in each arm, and carry them around like sacks of flour. They loved it when he played 'horsey' with them.

By late September, we had a lot of hay in the stacks next to the house, and we brought the pasture cattle into the yard. Half the wheat was harvested, so Gus took it to town to be milled to flour for our winter supply. When the rest of the wheat was harvested, we would have enough for the whole winter. Most of my garden was harvested, but I had yet to dig the potatoes. I was content in our sod house, and ready for the quiet winter to start.

In early October a bad storm came, starting with lightning and thunder. It rained cats and dogs. Amil and little Peter we terrified by all the thunder. Soon snow started to fall.

"What, snow this early?" I commented to Gus. "I hope this isn't what our winter is going to be like. I still have to dig my potatoes and the wheat! What will happen if we can't get the rest of the wheat in?"

"God will help us, Belle. I can't imagine that this snow will stay around for long. The weather has to warm up some so we can finish the harvest. Come boys, you better get tucked into bed so you can stay warm," he said as he scooped them up in his arms.

I was worried when it began snowing so hard that I could hardly see the barn from the window. I wondered, *what about the cattle and the milking cows? How will we reach them to give them hay and do the milking?*

The next morning, the blizzard raged on. Gus tied a rope around his waist, fixed it to the door, and went out to the yard to get some of the cattle into the barn. As he disappeared into the blizzard, I prayed he wouldn't lose his way and never return. He told me to stay inside with the boys and said he would be back in about an hour.

Two hours later, he had not returned. I thought about going after him, but I didn't want to leave the boys alone. They were oblivious to the danger that lurked outside. I was feeding them breakfast when Gus came through the door, covered head to toe with snow. Totally exhausted, he collapsed into a chair and just sat there.

"Gus, are you alright? Did you get the cows milked and fed?"
I asked.

"Belle," he said slowly, "this is one of the worst storms I've seen.
I bet we have three feet of snow already and it doesn't look like it's
letting up. I was able to get most of the cows into the barn, but some
of them are too stubborn and wouldn't move. I did the milking, but
there was no way I could carry the pail to the house; it was just too
windy, and the snow was too high. I will try to get the other cattle
in the barn this evening. I'm afraid we are in for a bad winter. We
better be careful with food so we don't run out. If this keeps up a
few months, we could run out of food."

I helped him get his outer clothes off, and we sat down to eat
with the boys.

"Papa," Amil said, "did you make any snowballs?"

"I made a bunch, Amil. When the snow stops, we'll go out and
throw them. How would that be?" he replied.

We were all sitting by the fire when Gus said, "Belle, I better
try to bring in more wood for us to stay warm. It won't be easy,
but I must try. I tied the other end of the rope to the barn door for
guidance. I hope this storm will give us a little break, so I can get
to the barn and feed the cattle. We have plenty of snow for water
but getting to the wood and hay will be a challenge. If you have a
pail or something that has a cover on it, I think I can bring in some
milk next time. The kids need milk to drink, but I may lose some
as I make my way over the snow drifts."

That afternoon, Gus bundled up again and headed out the door.
The wind and snow blew in and the boys thought it was fun to have
snow in the house. It seemed like it was letting up a little—at least
I prayed it was. Gus made his way back to the house and handed

me a half empty pail of milk. "That's all I could bring because half of it spilled on the way," he said. "I think I'll get the fire wood now as long as I am out here. Don't worry, I can see a little as long as the sun is still up, but soon it will be dark, so I better hurry."

At the beginning of November, the snow finally relented. Gus brought in some unprocessed wheat and moved a little hay close to the house so we could twist it into sticks to burn if we ran out of wood. The cattle in the barn were doing fine since Gus could bring them hay and water. The cattle that refused to go into the barn were covered with snow and ice and showed no signs of life.

That day the boys and I went outside for the first time in almost a month. The snow was blinding but beautiful at the same time. Everything was white and sparkling. The boys had fun playing in the snow and throwing snowballs at Papa. We played for a while, and then I said, "OK, boys, it's time to go back in. You are getting cold and Papa has chores to do."

We all tumbled into the house, took off our wet clothes, and placed them by the fire. It was warm and cozy in the sod house, but I was worried because it was only November. I wondered what we do if the roads didn't open and the trains didn't run. If we ran out of food, we couldn't get anything from town.

I tried to put those thoughts out of my mind, but after a two-day reprieve the snow started again—this time even worse. The wind howled around the house and the snow tried to creep in under the window sills. We were burning wood faster than ever as the temperatures dropped.

I was feeling so tired and couldn't stop thinking about my pregnancy. I told Gus that night while we were eating supper. As usual, he was reassuring and said he was looking forward to my spring delivery. We celebrated in front of the fire.

"The baby should be here next April," I reminded him. "It will give us something to think about this long cold winter. At least the baby has a nice warm place to sleep. Gus laughed as we held each other close.

The snow and wind kept up for another month with only short breaks. All the roads were blocked with snow and the trains had stopped running. One day a neighbor stopped by to see how we were faring. He said even with his team and sleigh the horses had a hard time getting through the snow. He gave us some flour, and I couldn't thank him enough. We did without many things, but the one thing we always had was good neighbors.

The flour lasted for quite a while, and we were able to get more milk to the house when the snow and wind stopped. Gus was able to shoot a few rabbits which helped. To get to the barn Gus had to scoop a path almost every morning; he piled the snow banks higher and higher until I could only see the top of his head. Then he had to dig into the snow banks to reach the haystacks to feed the animals.

We ran out of wood so we kept busy every day twisting hay into sticks. They burned quite well, but they didn't last as long as wood. Sometimes Gus would bring in some dried cow chips, which burned surprisingly well but left a bad odor in the house. It was a small price to pay to keep warm and keep the children from shivering.

The boys were growing, and soon Amil would be four and little Peter three. I dreamed about having a baby girl. I always wanted a baby girl to dress up and fix her hair. But I would be happy with whatever God decided to give us.

Things continued the same through December and January; it would snow for four or five days then clear for one or two. By Amil's birthday on February 19, the snow decreased and there were longer breaks between storms. Gus was happy that he didn't have to scoop snow every day.

By March, the worst of the winter was over. Then it thawed and the snow began to melt. Gus took the sleigh to town with the team. He fixed some large bells he had brought from Sweden to the horse's harnesses and they rang out as the horses trotted away. It reminded me of Sweden and made me homesick. Gus made it to town and returned with food for our family, plus a lot of news.

"The trains were stuck on the track for months, but thankfully some men scooped it out and cleared the tracks," he said.

That night after I fixed our first good meal in months, Gus and I sat by the fire talking about our life in Dakota. Suddenly he grew quiet. When I asked him what was wrong, he told me something that had been bothering him for some time.

"Belle, I have been having some stomach pains the last few weeks. Sometimes it's so bad that I have to curl up in a ball and wait until it quits. I haven't said anything because I didn't want to worry you, especially with the baby coming and all," he confessed.

"Gus, what could it be? It makes me think of my father and how he suffered with stomach pains. He died! Please don't tell me you are that sick!" I started to cry. Gus put his arms around me and assured me that he was not going to die.

"It's probably just something I ate and will go away soon," he said. "Now you better get to bed and get your feet up; I see they are a little swollen."

"I have had a little more swelling, but I attribute it to just sitting too much and not getting out to walk. I think everything will be fine," I said confidently.

As we snuggled next to each other that night, thoughts of what could be wrong with Gus ran through my mind. Could it be an ulcer from all his winter worry? Maybe it was just some indigestion—but that wouldn't cause so much pain. Then I thought back to when my father was ill. I was only five, but I remember how Mama cried and cried when he died. It bought back some painful memories. My little brother died only two months before. I remember how my mother hadn't recovered from his death when my father passed away. Oh, I wonder how she got through all of it. She must have been a very strong woman.

I said a silent prayer that night. *Lord, please be with Gus and make him well; our little family needs him so much. Please be with me, help me to be strong no matter what may happen, and be with me as I bring another baby into this world.*

1881

IN APRIL WE HEARD the Missouri River had flowed over its banks and destroyed most of Vermillion and a lot of Yankton. I was relieved that my brother, Peter, had moved back to Cedar County in Nebraska, so he wasn't affected. Nevertheless, we heard horror stories about whole houses being swept down the river with people crying and frantically waving out the windows. Some of our friends lived along the river, but thankfully they were safe.

Halfway through April we requested a doctor's visit because Gus was having terrible pain and wasn't sure if he could even do farm work in the spring. We didn't get good news. The doctor said given the symptoms and pain, he was sure Gus had advanced cancer. He told us to prepare for the worst, and that we should consider hiring someone to help on the farm.

It felt like someone punched me in the stomach; I just couldn't believe what was happening. After the doctor left, Gus and I just sat in silence, not knowing what to say.

Finally, I said, "Gus, you're strong, and I know you can beat this. You have to! Please tell me that you won't leave me and the children all alone. I just can't stand the thought of losing you."

I let him take me in his arms; his arms were so strong from hard work and yet so tender. We cried together for a long time.

Gus broke the silence and told me what he had been thinking. "Belle, I have worried that something like this might be what's wrong. I will be able to work some, but right now I think we should find someone who can pretty much take over the farming. There is a young man who lives about four miles from here named Ingvold Sletten. His family settled about the same time I did, and Ingvold is looking for work to build a house on his place. I think we should go see him before I get much worse."

"Oh, Gus, I just can't believe that you may not live. It just can't happen. Please say it isn't so," I said as tears streamed down my face.

Amil and little Peter saw all that was going on and timidly walked over to where Gus and I sat. Amil patted my arm in sympathy, and little Peter wanted up on my lap. What would I do with the two boys and another baby due next month? It was just too cruel of God to allow this to happen. *Please, Lord, please don't let this happen!* I pleaded inside.

That night Gus told me he would make sure that we weren't alone with no one to care for us. "I will make sure of that, Belle," he whispered in my ear.

The next morning we made the trip to Ingvold Sletten's farm. There we found him working with some of his cattle and putting up a barn. He had some hay stacked by the barn, and Amil and little Peter headed straight for it.

"No, boys, you must not play in the hay," I called. They came back and hid their faces in my skirt.

Ingvold came over and tried to shake hands with the boys, but they were too shy and hid farther behind my skirt. "I bet you boys are a big help to your Mama and Papa," he said.

I remember his shining, icy blue eyes and kind disposition. I could tell he was a little taken aback when Gus told him about his cancer prognosis. Ingvold confirmed that he was looking for summer work and said he could start as soon as the ground thawed and the fields dried up. It was such a relief to both of us.

When we were ready to leave, Ingvold and Gus shook hands, and then Ingvold tried to shake hands with the boys. They shyly put out their little hands and shook his big hand. Ingvold said, "Now you boys take care of your parents, and some day you will be all grown up and papas yourselves."

They nodded their heads and ran to Gus, who lifted them into the wagon. "If you can come over tomorrow, I will show you what I need you to do," Gus said.

On the way home we both were deep in thought. I was thinking about how long I would have Gus. I just couldn't imagine life without him. How would the boys deal with losing their father? It was too much to think about. I slipped my hand under Gus's arm and enjoyed the warmth. As we rode along, the boys nodded off to sleep, and Gus finally said something.

"Belle, I think Ingvold is a very kind and good man. I think he'll be a great help to me now and after I am gone. He seems very reliable. I will have to depend on him a lot the next few months.

Let's not talk about it too much; we should just enjoy the time we have together."

When we got home, we went to the barn to milk. Amil and little Peter loved being in the barn. It was warm and cozy, and they watched the cows getting milked. Amil said, "Papa, when can I learn to milk the cows? I am big enough, aren't I?"

"You are almost big enough, but in a few more months maybe you can give it a try," Gus said. "How about getting some hay from the loft and throwing it down for the cows? That will be a great help."

Amil climbed up and soon little clumps of hay were falling. "At this rate it will take all night to get hay for the cows," Gus laughed.

"Gus, I love to hear you laugh," I said. "We need to do a lot of laughing now. We need to enjoy each other every day so we will have wonderful memories of our times together. I don't want the boys to be sad when they think about you. I want them to remember the good times."

The next day Ingvold came over and Gus showed him around the farm. They planned what they would plant in the fields and what they would do with our cattle. Ingvold thought maybe we should sell some of the cows that were going to have calves because we could get a good price for them. Gus agreed because he knew that I couldn't care for all the cows. We would keep several milking cows for milk.

The boys really warmed up to Ingvold as they followed the men around the farm. When they came into the yard, Ingvold had little Peter up on his shoulders and Amil was tagging along behind.

"Mama, I got a ride from Ingold," little Peter told me as they ran into the house.

"Well, that's nice of Ingvold to give you a ride," I said, turning to Ingvold. "How about staying for supper tonight? I made plenty."

"Not this time, I need to get back to check on my cattle and work on my barn a little more," Ingvold said. "I hope to get it done before winter and then start on a house. But thank you anyway. It smells mighty good in here."

"She is the best cook east of the Missouri," Gus said with pride.

"OK, Gus, I'll be back in the morning, and we can start sorting the cattle and decide which ones we should sell," Ingvold said. "Bye boys, I know you will be good boys. See you tomorrow."

That night as Gus and I lay in bed, he told me that he had talked to Ingvold about staying on to help with the farm after he was gone. "He seemed open to it, but time will tell. How about a kiss from my sweetheart? I'm bushed from everything that has gone on the last few days."

Before he could even finish his prayer that night, he was fast asleep. I knew he was pushing through a lot of pain. I could see it in his face, and I knew he was worried about not being up to helping with the farm work.

The doctor had given us some pain medication, but Gus didn't want to take it because he was afraid it would make him groggy. He wanted his full faculties for his work. But I knew there would come a time that he would need the medication. I didn't want him to suffer as my papa and brother did. I would do all I could to make him comfortable when the time came.

May 28th the boys were outside riding their stick horses, galloping around, and pretending to be cowboys when my labor pains started. That night the contractions continued and I was unable to sleep much. I would get up and walk the floor as I usually did.

The next day Gus was out working and Ingvold was planting. When they came to the house for lunch, I planned to tell Gus that I needed him to stay close for the rest of the day in case I needed his help. I delivered the boys by myself and had no problems, but I knew there was always the risk of difficulties. I also thought Gus needed more rest, so I planned to ask Ingvold if he would be OK without Gus for the rest of the day.

Between pains I was able to get the lunch meal together and was lying down when the men came through the door with the boys. Ingvold was giving them rides on his big boots, and they were giggling and squealing with delight.

"OK, boys, you need to let Ingvold get washed up for lunch, and you need to wash your hands," I said as I steered them toward the wash basin. "You may have a little brother or sister today."

Four-year-old Amil knew what that meant. "Is the baby coming today, Mama?" he asked.

Gus looked at me with concern. "I think it may not be very long from now," I said. "Ingvold, can you do without Gus this afternoon? I would like him to stay close to the house."

"Sure, Belle, no problem," Ingvold said. "We have almost finished the last of the planting, and I can finish it up myself today. Do you want me to get my brother Ole's wife to come and be with you?" Ole's family lived only about a half mile from our place.

"No, that isn't necessary; I have been through this before with no problems. I just want Gus to be close in case there is a problem, and he can take the boys outside and keep them occupied this afternoon," I said.

"Belle, this meal is so tasty. If I had known you were having pains, I would have told you not to worry about making a meal for us," Ingvold said, as he finished up the last bites on his plate. "Why don't you lie down, and I'll wash these dishes up and get out of your hair."

I reluctantly took him up on his offer, and Gus followed me into the small bedroom off the kitchen. After making me comfortable, he went out to the kitchen and helped Ingvold finish up the dishes and then took the boys outside.

"Come on boys, let's look at the cows in the barn to see if we have any new babies out there too," Gus said. He cherished every minute with his boys as he knew his time was short. As he walked with the boys to the barn, Ingvold walked with them. "You run ahead and check out the cow in the barn. I will catch up with you," Gus told the boys.

"Ingvold, I don't know how much time I have left," Gus said when the boys were out of earshot. "I worry about leaving Isabelle alone with three small children. Will you stay on after I am gone and take care of things around the farm? I know the boys really look up to you, and Isabelle will need a man to do much of the work around here. I know she can sell the farm, but that will take time."

"Things will work out," Ingvold replied. "I will always try to do what I can to make things easier for Belle and the boys. You must spend time with your family now. With the new baby, Belle will need you around the house. I will take care of the field and the livestock. I don't know if you should sell the farm because someday little Amil and Peter Jr. may want to farm. I know they are little now, but they will be growing like weeds."

Ingvold headed back out to the field as Gus entered the barn.

"Papa, Papa, look Papa, Bessie had a baby!" Amil was so excited he jumped up and down with little Peter. Sure enough, there in the stall with Bessie was a new calf, sturdy and strong.

"Is it a boy baby or a girl baby?" little Peter asked.

"It's a little girl baby who will someday give us lots of milk like her mama. What do you boys want to name her?" Gus asked.

Amil piped up, "I think Patsy, because she likes to be patted."

"That sounds like a great name for our new little girl calf," Gus said. After they helped Patsy feed from her mama Bessy, they brought in new hay to make a nice bed for Patsy.

"Can we walk down to the field and tell Ingold about our new baby calf?" Amil asked. Little Peter pulled at his papa's pant leg to get him to go out the door.

"OK, boys, after I check on your mama, we can go tell Uncle Ingvold about our new baby calf."

When Gus entered the house, he could hear me working at birthing the baby. I assured him everything was going well, and he had time to go to the field and tell Ingvold about the new calf. "By the time you get back, the little one should be here," I said.

When they neared the field, Ingvold was just finishing up the last row, and as he came near, he stopped the horses to see what was wrong.

"Is Isabelle, OK? Do you need me to fetch the doctor?" he asked.

"Uncle Ingold, Uncle Ingold, we have a new baby calf, a girl one!" Amil exclaimed as he ran to meet Ingvold.

"You do?"

"Yes, and we named her Patsy, because she likes to be patted. She is so soft and cute!" Amil said. "Papa said she will give us a lot of good milk someday, just like her Mama."

"I bet she will!" Ingvold said.

"I'll check the rest of the cattle and stop by the house before I leave to see if there's something you need," Ingvold told them.

"Yes boys, we best be getting back to the house to see if Mama is feeling better by now," Gus said.

"Bye, Ingold," Amil and little Peter said in unison.

"See you later sweet potaters!" Ingvold called as he headed back to the horses.

When they entered the house, Gus came to check on me after giving the boys crackers and milk to eat. There he found me holding a little bundle of joy.

"Peter, we have a girl! Come look at her, she is beautiful!" I called out. "Get the boys; they'll want to see her too."

Peter went into the kitchen and told the boys to follow him into the bedroom. When they entered, I was in the bed looking different from how they were used to seeing me. I was usually up and fixing supper and cleaning the house; but now I was in bed with a baby in my arms.

"Boys, come here and meet your little sister," I said.

The boys looked in the blanket at the round, red, and wrinkled face.

"Mama, Mama, where did that come from?" Amil asked.

"You know that Mama has had a baby in her tummy; well she came out to meet you," I said.

"Is she our little brother?" asked Amil.

"No, no," I exclaimed, "she is a girl, so she is your sister."

"A thither," little Peter shouted, "a thither!"

"What's her name?" Amil asked. "We could call her Patsy, like Bessie's little baby girl."

"No, Amil, we want her to have a special name, I said. "How about Mary—that's your grandma Dahl's name. Papa and I have decided to call her Mary Augusta. Remember that August is your Papa's middle name."

"I like Mawee, Mama," little Peter exclaimed.

"She is so little," said Amil with a sigh.

"She will need her big brothers to take care of her," I said, pulling the boys up on the bed.

There with my little family, I thanked God for all He had given us and asked Him to give me the strength to get through the coming months.

"OK, boys, we need to have something to eat and head to bed," Gus said. "We need to let Mama and little Mary sleep now. Come in the kitchen and I'll make you some scrambled eggs."

"Oh, Papa, do we have to? We want to sleep here with little sister Mary." Amil was stroking her little cheek.

"Listen to what your Papa said boys, " I said, as I kissed them on top of their heads. "You can see little Mary in the morning. You'll have plenty of time to get to know her."

"Night-night, Mama, we love you and little Mary!" said Amil.

Later that night when the boys were fast asleep in the other room, Gus and I lay in each other's arms. Gus cradled little Mary in his arms and stroked her soft hair.

"She is going to look just like her Mama," he said. "God has been good to us, Belle."

"Yes, he has, Gus. God has led us through many things in our life, and I know He will lead us through the things that are coming," I said.

"I talked to Ingvold about staying on to help around the farm when I am gone," Gus said. "He is such a caring and loving young man, and I know you all will be in good hands with him around. The boys have gotten quite attached to him already."

"Oh, Gus, please don't talk about that now. Let's just enjoy what we have today. I know that God will take care of us," I said.

We drifted off to sleep in each other's arms with little Mary tucked between us.

5

DECEMBER 1881

THAT SUMMER, GUS GOT weaker and weaker and could only milk the cows twice a day before he had to come into the house and lie down. I brought the milk up to the house, separated the cream from the milk, and churned the cream into butter. Ingvold did the field work and cared for the cattle. He was a hard worker but always took time to play with the boys, which they loved. He let them sit on his big boots while he walked around the yard and sit on his horse while he led it around. They loved that and giggled and squealed with glee.

One day in late August as I was churning butter, little Peter ran breathlessly into the house.

"Mama, Mama, Papa is sick, he can't walk! He fell in the cow yard and can't get up. Come, Mama, come quick!"

When I reached Gus, he was totally out of breath from trying to get up.

"My legs just won't hold me," he said. "Go find Ingvold so he can help get me up."

I told little Peter, "You stay here right by Papa until I get back."

"I will, Mama," he said timidly.

Ingvold was making hay about a quarter of a mile away. I jumped on my horse bare-back and rode in his direction. When Ingvold saw me coming, he knew something was wrong and stopped what he was doing and ran towards me.

"Come quick, Gus has fallen in the cow yard and can't get up, and I can't get him up by myself," I said.

To save time, Ingvold jumped onto my horse with me, and we rode off towards the house together. When we got there, Gus had regained some of his strength but was still unable to stand by himself. Ingvold and I each grabbed one arm and lifted him to his feet. Ingvold put his arm around Gus and helped him into the house. After I got him cleaned up and into bed, I thanked Ingvold for his help.

"I don't know what I would have done without you here." I began to weep. "I just don't know how I will manage when Gus is gone."

Ingvold came over to me and put his hand on my shoulder. "I will be here to help you, Belle, which is what Gus wants," he said. "He asked me to take care of you and the kids when he is gone, and I promised him I would."

From then on, I did the milking while Gus stayed in the house with the children. He loved to sit in the rocker and rock little Mary. Of course, the boys also wanted their turn on his lap. Gus was losing weight because he had no appetite due to his pain medicine, which made him sleep more.

Ingvold finished up all the field work by the end of September. He also got the cattle to market as we needed the funds from their sale and knew I wouldn't be able to handle them myself. We kept the milk cows to provide milk for the children.

By November, Gus was in bed most of the time and only asked for water, no food. If he tried to eat even a little, he would get sick and vomit everything. He required the pain medicine around the clock to keep him comfortable, and the doctor said it was just a matter of time.

We had a nice snow at Thanksgiving. Ingvold came over for dinner and played with the kids. They missed him because he didn't come by as often now that the cattle were gone and the field work was finished.

I had missed him too and was glad when he visited. We had formed a close relationship as he helped with the farm. As Gus became less responsive, Ingvold made a point of stopping by every couple of days. One day we were talking about where I could bury Gus. I had no money and had not purchased a plot. Ingvold told me that he had purchased some plots at the new cemetery in Parker, and I could bury Gus there. I was so relieved.

A week before Christmas, Gus was not responding to me at all. He slept all the time, and I turned him and cleaned him several times a day. As the reality of his imminent death began to sink in, I panicked. *What will I do on this farm by myself? I know Ingvold said he would take care of us, but he is young man of eighteen and has his whole life ahead of him. Is it fair to ask him to take on a family of four?* I asked myself.

A few days before Christmas, I knew it wouldn't be long. I asked Ingvold to stop by every day to see if I needed help. He would come by about 10:00 a.m., stay for lunch and leave late in the afternoon. On the second day, Gus showed signs that he was close to death. I sat by him and held his hand, while Ingvold took the boys outside to play in the snow. As I sat there with Gus, I prayed that God would give me the strength I needed in the coming days.

Just before noon, Gus took his last breath. I rested my head on his chest and cried.

Ingvold quietly came into the house and let me lean on him for comfort. The next few days were a blur with the funeral and burial. I had spent much of the winter sewing new suits for the boys and a dress for Mary. After the funeral, I decided I wanted a family picture taken. We hadn't taken one when Gus was alive, so while we were all dressed up in our new clothes, Ingvold took us into Parker to get our first family portrait. It would end up being an important picture that I would cherish long into the future.

1882

THE NEXT SPRING STARTED early in April with blooming wild-flowers and singing birds. The crops looked good, and I was hopeful for a good return. The winter had been a hard one without Gus, but Ingvold was true to his word and stopped by every day to see how we were doing. Little Mary loved to sit on his knee and listen to him sing a Norwegian lullaby. The boys loved him, and I was beginning to feel something more than friendship.

I did as much work as I could. Tying Mary in my apron, I enjoyed taking her out with me to milk the cows. I also helped Ingvold with the field work as much as possible. I looked forward to those times together. He had such a happy outlook on things and was very funny.

One day mid-summer I was out in the field with Mary tied in my apron while the boys played nearby. I had brought lunch with my special apple pie for Ingvold. He stopped what he was doing when I approached. He was so strong and tanned from working in the field.

"Well, if it isn't Belle and her young'uns," he said playfully. My heart jumped when he said my name. I didn't think I could ever love someone again after Gus died, but I believed the Lord had brought Ingvold into my life. The boys ran to him, and he lifted them into the air, which made them giggle with glee. Little Mary was beginning to talk, and she tried to say his name as she pointed with her chubby little arm.

"How is my little Mary girl?" Ingvold asked.

"Better eat while the pie is warm," I said. "When I put the children down for their nap I'll come out and help you."

He smiled and said with a twinkle in his eye, "I'll look forward to that!" His light blue crystal eyes and smile melted me. I found myself not wanting to be apart from him. One day he had taken me to see his house. He acted like he wanted my approval. He was always very careful not to be too forward, but I could tell he cared about me.

After the last of the pie was scooped up, I took the children back to the house for a nap. When they were asleep, I fixed my hair, straightened my dress, and put on a clean apron. Then I went to meet the man I had fallen in love with. Excitement filled my heart as I got closer. He saw me coming and jumped down from his horse. "Howdy ma'am, don't you look pretty!" he said.

I blushed and said, "What do you want me to help you with?"

"Wait, I just want to look at you first," he said with a twinkle in his eye.

"Belle, I have fallen in love with you. I don't want to be apart from you anymore. Will you marry me?" he asked.

This did not come as a surprise, yet I had a hard time believing it was true.

Before I could answer he added, "Of course, I think we should wait until I have my house totally complete and ready for a family."

I heard myself saying "I love you too, Ingvold, and I want to be your wife. You have been such a support this year, and I don't know what I would have done without you." I stepped a little closer, and he took me in his arms and kissed me gently.

Then he stepped back and said shyly, "I think most people around here know there is something going on with us, so let's show them what. Would you like to go to the church picnic with me this Sunday?"

I could hardly keep my heart from bursting. "Yes, Yes!" I said.

I helped with the hay for about an hour before I headed to the house and checked on the children. My heart was bursting with joy. The children were still sleeping soundly, so I knelt by my bed and thanked God for giving me Ingvold. I bustled around to make a very special supper for him, my future husband. I loved the way that sounded so I repeated it. "Ingvold Sletten, my husband."

Sunday could not come soon enough, and the kids and I were ready when he pulled into the yard with his buggy. The boys ran to meet him calling, "Ingold! Ingold!" He scooped them up and placed them carefully on the rear seat. He took Mary in his arms, helped me up, and passed Mary to me. This would be the first time we would be seen as a couple. I couldn't wait to spend the day with him. We chatted on the way, and the boys asked, "What is that?" and "Are we there yet?" a hundred times. Ingvold was so patient with them.

"Boys, have you heard about your mama coming here from Wisconsin, a long way away?"

"Tell us, tell us" they squealed.

"Well, your mama was very brave to come here. There were no houses or trees, and she had to ride in a wagon or walk all the way. It took six weeks to get here. That is a long, long way. Much farther than the trip to the church," Ingvold said.

"Did we ride too, Ingold?" Amil asked.

"No, Mama came here with just her brothers and their families. But she never once complained or asked when they were going to get there," Ingvold said.

"Did you go with her, Ingold?" Amil asked.

"No, but I came with Grandpa and Grandma Sletten and my brothers and sisters. It was a long, long way, but we wanted to get a farm where we could raise our own families. Now, we want to tell you a surprise," Ingvold continued.

"A surprise! What, Ingold?" asked little Peter. I could see their eyes widen as they quietly waited to hear the surprise.

"This is a big, big surprise, are you ready?" Ingvold asked.

"Tell us, tell us!" both boys said in unison.

"I am going to be your new Papa, and you will come to live in my house very soon," Ingvold said.

"When Ingold, when?" the boys asked together.

"As soon as I get my house finished. Then you can have a room of your own. Would you boys like that?" Ingvold asked.

"Yay, yay! We are getting a new Papa and a new room!" They were bouncing up and down in the seat.

"We have arrived at the church now boys, remember to mind your manners," I cautioned.

Ingvold helped them hop down, and they ran off to play with the other children. It felt natural for me to walk arm in arm with him. He stopped to talk to everyone we met and introduced me as his future wife. Everyone was happy for us and offered congratulations. It was a wonderful afternoon.

On the way home, I moved closer to Ingvold, and he put his arm around me, which gave me goose bumps. He stayed until I had the children in bed, and then we went out under the stars, sat on a blanket, and talked about all our hopes and dreams for the years to come.

"Ingvold, when will you have the house finished?" I asked. "I love you so much and want to be your wife soon."

"Well, I should be finished with the house by next spring," he said. "I almost have the exterior done, and I can finish the inside during the winter. I am thinking about March or April, but I will really hurry now. I am as anxious as you are to start our new life," he said, kissing me again. "Now you better get in the house, and I best be heading home."

He walked me to the door and gave me another sweet kiss. I watched as he climbed into the buggy and waved goodbye. I had so much to be thankful for, and I knew God had been with me in both troubled and good times. As I looked up into the starry heaven, I prayed in a whisper, *Thank you Lord for being with me and helping me to find so much happiness again.* Then I went into the house and kissed my sleeping children.

1882

WAITING FOR CHRISTMAS THAT year was hard for the boys because they knew what was going to happen. "Presents, Presents!" little Peter could hardly say it as he hopped on one foot and then the other on Christmas Eve.

"Will Ingold come for Christmas?" Amil asked. "We want Ingold to come!"

"Yes, he is coming, and then we will be going to grandpa and grandma Sletten's for a wonderful Christmas dinner. You will meet some new cousins there too."

"Who, who, who?" little Peter cried.

"You sound like an owl." Amil said. "What new cousins are coming?"

"Your Aunt Caroline from Wisconsin is coming on the train with four of her children. One of them, Christian, is about your age, Amil. You will have a lot of kids to play with," I said.

"Yay, cousins! Yay, cousins!" Peter and Amil chanted together.

Christmas morning dawned bright. The sun-drenched snow looked like a bed of diamonds. I loved the sight of new snow. Just before Ingvold arrived to go to grandma and grandpa's house, I made lunch for everyone. I had made a rag doll for little Mary and a couple of small dolls for the boys as they liked to play with their sister.

Because of all the excitement, the boys had trouble getting to sleep the night before, so they were sleeping late. Little Mary was already up and toddling around the house when I woke them. Within minutes they were dressed and waiting by the window for Ingvold to come with the sleigh. Suddenly the boys let out a scream, "Ingold, Ingold! We see the sleigh!"

They were jumping up and down now, and little Mary tried to jump with them. "Do you hear the bells, Mama?" they squealed. Ingvold had attached the bells Gus brought from Sweden to the horses' harness, and they loved riding in the sleigh as the bells rang.

When I heard Ingvold stomping the snow off his boots on the stoop my heart jumped. I was so much in love I could hardly believe it. I felt so much joy in the past few months. In a few more months he would be my husband, and we would never have to be separated.

The door opened and there he was: cold and rosy cheeked, which made him even more handsome. The boys immediately ran to him and wanted to be picked up. He had a gunny sack over his shoulder and was saying, "Ho, Ho, Ho, Merry Christmas!" He set the bag down, gave all three kids a big hug, and then turned to me. "Merry Christmas, Belle," he said. Then he took me in his arms and kissed me. My knees were weak, and feelings of love overwhelmed me.

"What's for lunch?" It smells great, and I am hungry as a horse," he said.

I teasingly said, "Well, you can't eat this meal I made—all you get is hay! But I guess you are here now, so we better sit down and have a little lunch. The kids have been asking a hundred times when they will get their presents today. Come, children, time to eat, and then you can open your presents."

I made a light lunch since we were going to have a big meal later in the day. We talked non-stop. We were so comfortable with each other. The children didn't say a word and finished eating quickly so they could get right to the presents.

"Well, I think it's time to have the presents now!" Ingvold announced. I brought out the dolls I had made, and right away little Mary took her little doll and rocked it back and forth. The boys were excited to have their dolls too, but they were more interested in the sack Ingvold had brought in.

Ingvold put the sack on the table and let the boys reach into it. Little Peter was first. He pulled out a small wooden stick horse that Ingvold had carved and painted to look like a real horse. It even had reins so the boys could gallop around the room. Amil's horse was black and white like Ingvold's horse Midnight, and Peter's was brown like our horse Sandy. They were happily galloping around the room when Ingvold reached into the sack once more. He pulled out a small box and got down on one knee and said. "Will you marry me, Belle?" He had asked me before, but now it was official.

"Yes, yes!" I could hardly control my happiness. The ring was beautiful! Just a simple band, but it was from the one I loved. He slipped it on my finger and then kissed me tenderly. We enjoyed a moment together before the boys galloped right in between us.

"My horse is beating Amil's!" little Peter exclaimed. They gathered their dolls to sit on the horses.

"We better leave our horses tied up at home when we go to grandpa's and grandma's," Ingvold said. "Come and put on your coats and boots. Old Blue is ready to go and snorting impatiently."

The sleigh ride in the beautiful snow and crisp air was wonderful. Ingvold had made sure that little Mary and I were bundled up and put a big blanket over the two boys in the back. They loved the snow and sang, "Jiggle bells, jiggle bells, jiggle all the way."

Ingvold added a little version of his own: "Oh, what fun it is to ride with my sweetheart by my side."

The boys continued with "Jiggle bells, jiggle bells," and Ingvold added, "Oh, what fun it is to ride with my little family."

We were a family. I didn't think it would ever be that way again after Gus died; but there I was, riding beside the man and children I loved so much. Ingvold had grown to love the kids as if they were his own. I didn't want that moment to end, but soon we were pulling into grandma and grandpa Sletten's yard. It was our first Christmas together with his family. My eyes filled with tears.

"What's wrong, Belle?" Ingvold asked quietly.

"I didn't think I would ever be this happy again! This Christmas has been one of the happiest I have had since I left Sweden. I'm also missing my mother and sister Karin today. I haven't seen them in so long. Since they arrived in America in July, I haven't been able to go see them."

"We will see them soon, I promise," Ingvold said. "You have just had so much happen this year. I know your brothers will take good care of your mom and sister while they stay with them."

The boys were getting anxious to meet their new cousins, so Ingvold climbed down and helped them get untangled from the blanket. They bolted toward the house like a gunshot! Ingvold took little Mary in his arms, "Come little one, today is your first Christmas with your new family."

After helping me down, Ingvold put his arm around me as we walked to the house. The house was filled to the brim with family and many children. The boys were a little timid at first, but before long they were playing "cowboys and Indians" with the other children. Amil and Christian were the cowboys and the others were the Indians. We enjoyed watching them gallop around and around on their make-believe horses.

Ingvold's sister, Caroline, had greeted us at the door with a big hug. She had not been home for quite a few years and was so happy to see everyone, especially Ingvold.

"My, you have gotten so tall, Ingvold, I hardly know you. It looks like Isabelle has been a good influence on you, because you look very happy!" Caroline said. "I'm so happy to meet you Isabelle, and I'm so sorry about your husband. My first husband died at a young age. It is very hard to deal with, but it helps ease the sorrow to have someone else to love and take care of you. I am so happy that you will be my sister-in-law soon. When is the big day, Ingvold?"

"Soon", Ingvold replied. "We have decided to wait until spring so I can finish up the house I'm building. The exterior is done, and now I am working on the inside. Maybe later we can ride over and I can show it to you."

"I would love that! Then I can picture you sitting in your house together with the children underfoot," Caroline replied.

"Dinner is ready everyone!" Ma Sletten announced. "Come and get it before I throw it out!" She and Caroline had been busy cooking and baking and had a wonderful meal prepared. The children were directed to sit at a little table next to the big one.

Sitting together around the big table, I remembered my childhood Christmases. Since my papa and little brother died when I was young, and my older brothers were always away working, I spent most holidays with only my mama and two sisters. We were poor and didn't have a big family like Ingvold's, but Mama always made sure we had Christmas gifts to open. I had always hoped someday I would have a great big family with a lot of love to go around. My dream had come true.

With Ingvold, I was starting a wonderful little family with someone whom I loved dearly. The Lord had blessed me beyond my wildest dreams and, true to His word, He had wiped away all my tears. As we all bowed our heads in prayer to thank the Lord for his bounty, I prayed silently, *Thank you, Lord, for giving me joy in the morning, Christmas morning.*

8

JANUARY 1883

I WAS AWAKENED EARLY A few days later by a soft crying. "Mama, Mama, Mama." It was little Peter again. Probably a bad dream or a tummy ache.

"What is it Peter? Did you have a bad dream again? Mama is here, let me rock you in the rocking chair, you will feel better soon," I said.

"Mama, my head hurts really bad!"

I took him in my arms and carried him to the rocker. Right away I noticed that he was burning up with a fever. *Diphtheria!* I tried not to think the worst. Several of Caroline's older children had come down with high fevers, sore throats, and coughs; she thought they may have contracted something from someone on the train on the trip from Wisconsin. Then the doctor called with the grim news: they had Diphtheria. Thankfully they recovered, but medical resources were limited, and Diphtheria was still ravaging the whole country. Some families had lost all their children to the dreaded disease. *Please Lord, spare my children,* I prayed.

I carried little Peter to my bed, not wanting to disturb Amil, and prepared a basin of cool water. "Go back to sleep, Peter. Mama is here, and I will never leave you alone. I asked God to make you feel better, go back to sleep now."

Placing the cool cloth on his fevered brow seemed to calm him somewhat as he drifted off to sleep. But when the sun came up, he was writhing in pain again. "Mama, Mama, my throat hurts, my head hurts! Where is Ingold?" I knew I had to try the treatment my mother used when I was young. It was quite harsh, and I didn't want him to suffer any further, but it had to be done.

I took a goose feather, dipped it in kerosene, and worked up the courage to swab little Peter's throat. He coughed and gagged as tears rolled down his cheeks. Tears were streaming from my eyes as well. I just couldn't do it a second time.

"Papa Ingvold will be coming later today," I tried to reassure him. As his symptoms worsened, I prayed Ingvold would come earlier than the expected 11:00. I needed to get my son to the doctor if the roads were open. Since Christmas, we had endured one snow storm after another. Caroline had stayed put after her children were better because the train could not get through.

Suddenly I heard a timid knock on the door. *Ingvold!* I rushed to the door and swung it open to find him standing there covered with snow and red-faced from the cold. "Ingvold come in, I have been praying that you would somehow come earlier! Little Peter is sick. I know it must be Diphtheria."

Ingvold came in, took his wet coat and boots off, and put them by the fire.

"It's OK, now, Belle, I had a dream that little Peter was sick, and I had to come." He took me in his arms, and I cried.

"Oh, Ingvold, I didn't know what to do. I prayed and prayed that you would come sooner. Do you think we can get to the doctor? I know there isn't much that can be done if it is Diphtheria, but we have to try."

"Belle, all the roads are blocked. It took me two hours to get here. I don't think there is any way to get the doctor here. I will sit with little Peter now so you can get some rest. Go in with Amil. When he gets up, I will get him some breakfast."

"Oh, Ingvold, I can't sleep with Peter so sick," I said.

"Belle, you will be no good for him if you wear yourself out. I am perfectly able to care for him," Ingvold said. He led me into the other room, and I got into bed and drifted off to sleep.

Before I knew it, I was awake, and the sun was shining brightly through the window. I smelled coffee and heard Ingvold in the other room whistling. Amil was talking non-stop between bites. *Thank you, Lord, for bringing Ingvold,* I prayed as I went to the basin to wash up.

"How is little Peter?" I asked. I expected the worst.

"He is sleeping now," Ingvold said. "I think he is somewhat better. His fever is down, and he is coughing less. Come sit down and have some lunch, Belle, I made my specialty! Pancakes! No one around can make better pancakes than me!"

The pancakes smelled wonderful, and I had a big appetite. As I sat at the table, Ingvold brought me pancakes and kissed me on the cheek.

"We need to talk about a wedding date, Belle. I was thinking about Valentine's Day. What do you think? Will you be my Valentine?" Ingvold asked with an endearing smile.

I had to think about it a little. It was only a a little over month away, and with little Peter's sickness it was hard to see any happiness in the near future. I wondered, *what if Amil and little Mary became sick too? After all, they had been around Caroline's children at Christmas.*

"Oh, Ingvold, I would love nothing more than to marry you on Valentine's Day, but right now, we need to ensure the children recover from this terrible illness. I am so happy that you are in my life, I want to spend all my time with you, and I wish we were already husband and wife. I love you so much and don't know what I would do if anything happened to you. Please tell me you will stay well; I just can't stand the thought of losing you."

"Belle, Belle, don't worry about me," he said. "You need to take care of yourself and the children. I'll be here as much as possible. You and your children mean more to me than I ever could have dreamed."

"Mama, Mama," I heard little Peter's weak voice calling. Ingvold and I rushed to his side to find him burning up with fever again. He had a constrictive cough, like his throat was closing off. His neck seemed to be swelling, and he was fighting for air.

"Mama, Mama, my head!" He was barely able to speak through his gasping breaths and coughing spells

No, Lord, please help me, I prayed. Ingvold and I took little Peter's hands and prayed. "Lord, you know how much we love little Peter. He is just starting his life. Please don't take him from us." I was weeping, and tears were running down Ingvold's cheeks.

Little Peter was slowly being suffocated by the terrible illness, and I was horrified because I could do nothing about it. Only God could heal him now. Knowing God's will is not always our will, I prayed, "God, please don't let little Peter suffer long. I just can't stand to see him suffer!"

All day Ingvold stayed with me and helped try to soothe little Peter. We took turns sponging little Peter off and changing his wet sheets. We both got very little sleep that night, but we were together. I don't know what I would have done if Ingvold was not by my side.

It was about two in the morning when little Peter took his last breath. It had been a terrible night, but Ingvold had stayed by my side. Together we cried over little Peter's lifeless body. Together we washed him and dressed him in his new suit.

When the sun came up, Ingvold thought that he could get to his parents' house to make a small casket for little Peter. We would have to take him to the undertaker where they would keep his body until spring when the ground was warm enough for the burial. It was heart wrenching to think of my little Peter alone at the undertakers until we could give him a final resting place.

Ingvold said he had bought many plots in the small Parker cemetery, and that little Peter could be buried there alongside his father. It was comforting to know my son would rest next to his father, but it would be the hardest thing I ever had to do.

Ingvold departed for his parents, and Amil, little Mary, and I stayed behind. I dreaded telling Amil his little brother was gone. How could I? They were like two peas in a pod; one was never without the other. Seeing little Peter's stick horse tied up to a chair next to Amil's made my heart sink and I prayed, *Oh, Lord, give me the strength to tell Amil that little Peter is gone. I don't know how I can do it.*

Amil suddenly appeared. "Where is Peter?" Before I could answer, he ran to my room calling, "Peter, Peter, where are you?" I rushed after him and caught him just before he went in.

"Amil, you must be very brave, just like you were when Papa died. Amil, your brother was very sick last night, and he died. He is not sick anymore and is not hurting," I tried to explain. It was like someone else was saying those words. I took Amil in my arms and held him tight as I cried softly. "Amil, would you like to see little Peter?"

Amil said, "Yes, Mama, I want to wake him up so he can play with me."

"Oh, Amil, we can't wake him up, just like we couldn't wake Papa up. He will have to be buried in the ground next to Papa when the snow is gone."

Amil started to cry, "No, Mama, no! I want to play horsey with Peter!"

"Little Peter cannot play horsey with you anymore, Amil. Now we need to go in and see your brother and say goodbye to him."

Amil was very brave as we stood in the doorway looking at little Peter. I was worried about Amil having contact with him, so we stayed outside the room. Amil said, "Goodbye, little bruver. I love you. I will take care of your horsey and make sure that sister Mary don't ride him. I will ride him every day and give him hay."

As I led Amil away from the room we held each other's hands tight. Little Mary toddled up and raised her arms to be picked up. I took both into the rocking chair and sang softly, "Jesus loves me, this I know, for the Bible tells me so. Little ones to Him belong, they are weak, but You are strong."

Then I prayed again, *Lord, give us the strength we need today.*

9

FEBRUARY 1883

TWO WEEKS LATER WHILE we were eating lunch, Amil came to my side and pulled on my sleeve. "Mama, my head hurts really bad." He had been coughing a little, but he seemed to be happy playing with his wooden horse. I felt his head; it was burning up. *No,* I thought. *This can't be happening. Not Amil too. What about little Mary?*

I thought I should try the feather treatment I used with Peter; even though it had not helped him, it had saved many others. I hated using such a harsh treatment with my children, but I was desperate. I immediately took him to his bed and started the feather treatment. I grimaced as he coughed and sputtered and cried. When I was finished, I sponged him off with cool water and hoped he could sleep. The next day he was not much better. I wanted to do the feather treatment again, but Amil begged. "Please Mama, not the feather again."

"Amil, it will only take a second. It will help you feel better," I said. When I looked in his throat, I saw no membrane yet. I had also given little Mary the treatment to try to ward off any symptoms.

Late that afternoon Ingvold stopped by as he usually did. I was so glad to see him and I told him about Amil. I was feeling very tired after having spent so much time with Amil. Mary was so glad to see him. She pulled on his coat, wanting to be picked up. After he took his outer clothes off, he swung her up in the air. She squealed and laughed with delight.

"Little Mary, how are you today?" He planted a kiss on her forehead, checking for a fever. "She seems well—no fever. Let me look at Amil."

We entered Amil's room to find him restless, coughing, and still burning with fever. "Belle, bring more water and bathe him," said Ingvold. "I will make a little something for our supper and put little Mary to bed. You need to lie down and get some rest. I will take care of Amil tonight."

"Oh, Ingvold, I hate for you to stay, but I am very happy you are here so I can get some rest. Please call me if anything changes," I said.

"Belle, a team of horses could not drag me away from you tonight. I am here for you no matter what, and I'll stay as long as you need me."

By the time I finished giving Amil a cool bath, he seemed a little better and fell asleep. I didn't hear anything from Mary, so I assumed she was also sleeping. I went into the kitchen and smiled when I saw Ingvold asleep in the rocker with little Mary in his arms. I couldn't have asked for a more caring man. I loved him so much and didn't ever want to be apart from him.

I touched his shoulder. "Wake up, Ingvold, Mary needs to be in her bed." He carried her into her bedroom. As I tucked her in, I said, "Ingvold, please don't leave me tonight. I need you so much."

"Belle, I'll be here with you until morning. I'll listen for Amil if he needs anything. Let's lie down and get some rest," he said.

"Ingvold, will you please hold me as I fall asleep? I need you so much."

Laying at my side, he took me in his arms and said, "Belle, you don't have worry, I'll stay here all night. I love you so much." He kissed me, and I kissed him back. Even though we both knew it was wrong to make love before marriage, we couldn't resist. It was so natural and beautiful. Afterward, we fell asleep in each other's arms.

I woke up to the smell of coffee and the sound of Ingvold whistling in the kitchen again. The sweet memory of the night lingered. Was it a dream? No, it was real—oh, so real. Then I thought about Amil. *Amil! Was he better?* I didn't hear his voice. I quickly dressed, washed my face, and combed my hair.

"Ingvold" I called, as I entered the kitchen, "how is Amil?" I rushed into his room to find him propped up in bed with a cup of warm milk and a piece of bread. "Amil, honey, you're awake and better!"

"Yup! I was hungry so Papa Ingold got me something to eat. I feel better, Mama."

I rushed to his bed and felt his head, it was only slightly warm. "Open your mouth and stick out your tongue, I need to make sure your throat looks OK," I said.

"Mama, please, not the feather again, please, I hate that," Amil cried.

"No, honey, let me see and then we will decide," I said.

As he slowly opened his mouth, the memory of little Peter came rushing back. I was afraid to look. Peter's throat had been almost entirely obstructed by the nasty membrane, to the point he could only breath with fast, labored breaths. I prayed, *Please Lord, please let it not be swollen!*"

Gently I used the spoon he had been eating with to look into his mouth. It was a little red, but there was no membrane. The feather treatment had worked! *Thank you, Lord!* I whispered.

"God maked me better didn't he Mama? Can I get up now?"

"No, Amil, you need to rest more so you can get big and strong again. Maybe tonight you can get up a little," I said, handing him a book and his favorite toy.

I heard Ingvold getting little Mary up and changing her diaper. He was so good with the children; it was like he had done it before. Maybe he had helped with his little sister, Alena.

"Good morning sunshine!" he said, as he walked towards me with little Mary in his arms and a twinkle in his eyes. "How are you feeling today?"

"I'm just fine," I replied shyly. "Oh, Ingvold, Amil is so much better! I just can't believe all this is true."

"God is good, isn't He? I heard Amil coughing early this morning, and when I checked on him, I couldn't believe how much better he looked. He was hungry so I got him some warm milk and bread. Belle, little Mary has shown no sign of illness. She is just as strong and healthy as ever. Now you and little Mary need to eat. I made some oatmeal this morning; it is Mary's favorite."

"O'meal, O'meal!" Little Mary cried.

As we sat and enjoyed our breakfast, the memory of last night lingered in our minds. "I love you so much, Ingvold; when can we be married?" I asked.

His light blue eyes twinkled. "The house should be move-in ready by the first of April, if the weather holds out. How about we get hitched on the seventh of April?"

"Oh, Ingvold, I would love that! That will give Amil time to get stronger and ensure Mary's wellness. I just can't wait for you to be my husband," I gushed.

"Belle, last night was wonderful for me, and I am anxious to make you my wife. We will be together soon. I'll work hard to make our house a home for you and the children. Kiss me."

He leaned over and kissed me softly on the lips. My feelings for him were so strong that I just grabbed him and embraced him tightly for a long kiss.

Little Mary clapped her hands and said, "Kiss, kiss!" We gave her a big kiss on each of her cheeks.

The next time Ingvold came he had bad news. His sister's little son, Christian, had died of Diphtheria. Ingvold told me he became ill shortly before Amil had. Caroline was so despondent she could hardly be consoled. Ingvold went on to say Christian would be buried in several weeks in the old Norwegian Cemetery down the road, where her father and mother would eventually be buried.

There was so much sorrow everywhere that I found it hard to be happy. I reminded myself, *the Lord wants us to be happy; we need happiness along with sorrow. That is what life is about. We take the good with the bad. The Lord gives and He takes away. But we need to trust Him every day.*

The next month passed quickly but still seemed like forever. I couldn't wait for Ingvold to be my husband so we could be together in our own little home with our children. God had blessed me so much. I thanked him often.

Amil grew stronger each day and was soon galloping around the kitchen with his stick horse. One day he announced, "Mama, Papa Ingold said we are moving into a house! With windows and rooms!"

I knelt down next to him and said, "Honey, you don't need to call him Papa Ingvold, just Papa. He is your Papa now. We will never forget your Papa Gus, but Ingvold wants to take you as his son and Mary as his daughter. That means he will be your true Papa from now on. Is that OK?"

"Yes, Mama. I love Papa Ing—I mean Papa so much. He is a good Papa," Amil said.

"I love him too; we are going to get married soon. Will you like that?"

He tilted his head. "What is 'getting married'?"

"When two people love each other very much, they get married and live together as husband and wife," I explained. The sound of it made my heart skip a beat. Just a few more days and Ingvold and I would be husband and wife. He had taken us to see the house the day before, and it was so beautiful. There were big rooms with large windows and three bedrooms, which would be filled with children one day—if I got my wish.

"Come now, Amil, we need to pack our belongings for the new house," I said. Meanwhile, little Mary was unpacking boxes as fast as I packed them. She loved to unload baskets of clothes or things from the dresser. I decided to wait until her nap time to finish packing.

MARCH 1883

W HEN INGVOLD CAME BY a week later, he said the cemetery ground had thawed enough to bury little Peter and
Christian.

"Oh, Ingvold, I will feel much better when little Peter is in his
resting place next to his father," I sighed. "I have greatly enjoyed
getting to know your sister; living so close has allowed us to form a
deep bond I will cherish the rest of my life. She is like a sister to me."
I put my arms around his neck and gave him a big kiss. "Ingvold,
have I told you today how much I love you?"

"No, you haven't, but I will never tire of hearing it. Belle, I
should have the house finished by the first of April, we will be
married on the seventh, and then we will be a family. I talked to
the undertaker, and he said he can have both graves dug by the end
of this week. How does it sound to have both burials on Saturday?
Caroline thought that would be OK. We will first go to the Old

Norwegian Cemetery for Christian's service, then to Parker for little Peter's service."

"Yes," I agreed. "I will rest much easier when the burial is over."

I was tired and hadn't been feeling well. I wondered if I was expecting again. 'Time will tell' is what my mother used to say. If I was pregnant, I hoped Ingvold would be happy since he had said he 'wanted a big family with lots of little ones running around.' I had been waiting for the right time to tell him.

Two days later we gathered at the small Pioneer Cemetery with Caroline and the rest of the family. It was a sunny day, and the smell of spring was in the air. Ingvold and I stood next to Caroline as Christian's little casket was slowly lowered into the ground. I put my arm around her waist and let her weep. I was crying too for all the sadness we had shared through the winter. A deep feeling of sorrow came over me, and I reached out for Ingvold's hand. With him at my side I knew I could endure with strength from God.

Next, we all went to the cemetery to say goodbye to little Peter. There I saw Peter's little grave with the casket sitting next to it. Oh, if only I could see him one last time! If only I could hold him again! I grabbed Ingvold's hand, and suddenly a wave of nausea and dizziness flowed through me. I thought, *how can I do this? I just can't let him be put into the ground. Lord, please give me strength!*

Another wave of nausea came over me, and I felt like I was going to faint. Ingvold put his arm around me to steady me. Suddenly I knew the meaning of it all. As little Peter's casket was being lowered into the grave, I prayed to the Lord, You *have taken one of my dear children Lord, but now you have given me a new child to add to our family. Thank you, Lord, for Your ever-faithful love.*

That night after little Peter's burial, everything hit me. The day had been very taxing. We had to say goodbye to little Peter as well as Caroline and her children before they boarded the train. I was happy she was heading back to Wisconsin and her family, but her departure would leave a big hole in my life. I would miss our long talks and good cries. I had only known her a few months, but it felt like a lifetime.

I held her tight before she boarded the train. "Caroline, how I will miss you!" I sobbed on her shoulder. "Please come again and bring your whole family with you."

"I will visit again. I need to come and see little Christian's resting place," Caroline said. "It's so hard for me to leave him here, but it would be impossible to take him back to Wisconsin. You will visit his grave often, won't you, Belle? It comforts me to know you and Ingvold can watch over his resting place for me."

We wept and held each other until the train whistle blew. She boarded the train with her girls, and they waved out the window with their handkerchiefs. "Bye, Uncle Ingvold, bye, Auntie Belle, we love you and will miss you. Bye, Amil and little Mary," they cried out the window. Then they were gone.

There are no words to express how lonely I felt at that moment. It was like I had experienced a whole lifetime in the last year. I was totally exhausted, and all I could think about was sleep.

11

SPRING 1883

THE SEVENTH OF APRIL was a warm and sunny day. Most of the snow had melted but the roads were pretty muddy. I readied myself and the children and could hardly wait for Ingvold to come with Ole and his wife and his brother, Martin. We would be married in the old sod house. His parents' would also be here.

Ingvold's brother Ole was the Justice of the Peace and would be our officiant; his brother, Martin, and Ole's wife, Caroline, would stand up for us. I was sad that none of my family could attend, but they lived far away in Nebraska and the roads were just too bad. When the weather got better and we were settled into our new home, I planned to invite them out. They had met Ingvold the previous summer and loved him from the start.

"Papa, Papa is coming!" Amil cried as he and little Mary ran to the door. I ran with them. I was so happy to see Ingvold climbing down from the wagon; he was so tall and handsome in his suit and top coat. Soon everyone had arrived and we were ready to become husband and wife.

The ceremony was perfect but passed quickly. Before I knew it Ole had pronounced us husband and wife.

Little Mary got the most attention as she toddled around the room. She was the happiest girl with such a sweet disposition. I hoped and prayed she would grow up to be a strong woman of faith.

After the wedding, when everyone was gone and we were alone for the first time as husband and wife. I looked around our old Soddy, which had been my home for the last six years. That snug little home was filled with happy and sad memories, and I would miss it. After loading our things in the wagon, we were off to our new home with the bells ringing, just like it should be on a wedding day. Ingvold and I sat with our arms linked while the children dozed in the back, bundled up against the early April breeze. Life was so good, and I knew God was with us. We could face anything with each other and with God. *Thank you, God! Thank you!*

Later, as I lay in bed in our new home with Ingvold by my side, my mind was too restless to sleep. Suddenly Ingvold said. "What's wrong, honey? Can't you sleep?"

"Ingvold, I have something to tell you," I said. "You know I have been very tired lately and have had some dizzy spells the last few days. I have waited to tell you until I was sure. Honey, we are having a baby! Are you excited about it?"

"A baby! Really?" He took me in his arms, and we held each other tight. "Oh, Belle, I am more than excited!" he said joyously.

"It happened the night Amil was so sick," I said. "I had been waiting to tell you until I was sure. Our baby will arrive about October or November. Next Christmas we will have a family of five. I think the Lord has given us this baby to help ease the pain of losing little Peter. Oh, Ingvold, I have such sorrow and joy at the same time."

"I feel the same way Belle. I didn't think I could feel such pain when little Peter died, but I am overjoyed about the new baby. Belle, we will be so happy together, and I know we will have many more children to love. Now let's get some sleep." Then he kissed me, and we drifted off to sleep in each other's arms.

The next morning as we all sat around our new kitchen table, I was struck by how much change we had endured in the last two years. Listening to Amil and little Mary chatter with Ingvold reminded me of how blessed we were to be together. It was a new beginning, a new day, and a new family member would be joining us soon. I prayed, *thank you, Lord, for everything you have given us and whatever the future holds. I know you will be with us and never leave us.*

April brought more blessings with plentiful rain, and by early May the prairie flowers were in full bloom. I loved opening the windows to smell the fresh breeze. Amil took his little sister outside, and she picked some flowers. She handed them to me and said, "See, Mama, flowers!"

I said, "Why thank you, Mary. I will put them in a vase on the table. They will look so pretty there, don't you think?"

With big bright eyes she clapped her hands and said, "Pretty, Mama, pretty!"

Later that morning, Ingvold went into town to file the necessary paperwork for the sale of my farm, which Gus left to me and our children. A couple was interested in it, but we had to wait until it went through probate to sell.

Ingvold had been given guardianship of Amil and Mary after our marriage, and he wanted to put most of the proceeds into a trust fund for them. A few days earlier while we were lingering at the table over a cup of coffee, he spoke up. "Belle, I think the money from the sale of your farm should go into a trust fund for Amil and Mary. I want them to get a good education, and they will need money for that. I never had an opportunity to go much further than sixth grade in school, and I want our children to have a good education so they can get good jobs. In this country, you can't go very far on a sixth-grade education."

"Oh, Ingvold, that is such a wonderful idea," I said. "I never went to school in Sweden since they didn't require it, so I had to work for my family since I was seven. I can't even write my own name. I suppose I will have to sign some papers with the sale of the farm. What will I do? I always wished I could teach. I know you don't want me to work, but sometimes I feel like I am not doing my part."

"Belle, just put that thought right out of your mind. You have done so much for our little family," he said firmly. "I never feel like you need to do more. We are doing fine. All you need to do is keep the house clean and take care of all the kids we will have! As far as signing your name, people are allowed to just make an 'x' for a signature, so I will witness it is your mark." With that, he winked at me with his twinkling blue eyes.

Oh, those blue eyes! They were the first thing I noticed the day Gus and I met him. His eyes glistened with kindness, compassion, and tenderness. I hoped all our new little ones would have his eyes.

With Ingvold returning from town soon, I tidied up and fixed something for lunch while Amil, now seven, fed hay to the animals and picked eggs. He loved the chickens and treated them like pets.

He really wanted a dog, but we weren't sure about getting one so soon. Amil was getting so big, and Ingvold was teaching him how to ride a 'real horse,' as he called it. Now, his old wooden stick horse sat idle in his room next to little Peter's.

Little Mary was busy playing with her doll when I heard Ingvold coming into the yard. I saw Amil run to meet him. "Papa, Papa, I have all the chores done!" he said. Ingvold jumped down from the wagon, got a box out of the back, and opened it.

When Amil peered into the box he exclaimed, "A puppy, a puppy! My own puppy!" He scooped the puppy up, and it licked him all over his face. "He sure likes you," Ingvold said. "You have to promise to always take care of him, feed him, take him for walks, and teach him to be a good puppy, OK?"

"I will, Papa, I will! I love my puppy. What should I name him? Maybe Licky, because he likes to lick!"

"Maybe Lucky, because he is so lucky to have you as his owner," Ingvold said as he petted the dog's head.

"I like that! Lucky it is," Amil said. "Let's take him in the house to meet Mama and Mary. They will love him too!"

"Well, he can come in once to meet the family, but after that he will need to stay outside because Mama doesn't allow pets in the house," Ingvold coached him.

Of course, as soon as Amil set him down in the house he made a little puddle. "Uh-oh, Amil, that is why we don't allow pets in the house," I said. "Now you have to clean it up because he is your dog to love and take care of."

"Oh, I will, Mama," Amil assured me. "I will do everything for him, and he will play with me and run with me, just like little Peter did… Mama, I miss little Peter so much." Tears rolled down his cheeks as he gazed at me. Thankfully, Lucky was right there to kiss them all away.

Mary ran to see the dog and called, "Puppy, Puppy!"

"His name is Lucky, not puppy," Amil corrected her.

"Well, now it's time to take Lucky outside to the barn where he can be safe and get used to the cows. Lunch is ready, and Papa is hungry as a horse," I said.

"I am too, Mama," said Amil. "I could smell the food a mile away."

After we bowed our heads and thanked God for the meal, Amil added his own prayer saying, "Dear God, thank you for our food, and thank you for bringing me Lucky. He will be my friend now. Amen."

SUMMER 1883

THE SUMMER WAS A busy one as we settled into our new home. Ingvold was done planting, and now he was busy constructing a larger table and a few more chairs for us. I was sewing flour sacks into curtains and still trying to decide what colors our bedroom curtains should be.

"Ingvold, help me decide what color I should make the curtains in our bedroom. I can't decide on blue or green. I think both would look nice," I said.

"Belle," Ingvold said, "whatever you pick will look just as beautiful as the curtains you made for the rest of the house. Why don't you use both colors?"

Then he kissed me and said, "I need to go to town to get a few more things to finish the table. I should be home before supper. I have been wondering if you still love me after I said a little bad word when I hit my thumb this morning! Belle, will you forgive me?"

"Oh, Ingvold, don't be silly," I said. "I know and God knows that you don't mean to swear, but sometimes it just slips out. I will always love you even when you slip up. How about you? Will you love me even if I slip up?"

"Well, maybe just once," he kidded, "but I'll have to find something you've slipped up on because so far you have been perfect. Give me a kiss and I will be on my way."

I kissed him before he even finished his sentence. "Drive safely this morning and watch out for those snipes you're always talking about. I wouldn't want you to have a crash with the horses."

"Don't worry, the snipes aren't out yet. I promise I will be back lickity-split."

I watched as he drove out of the yard. He was so strong and capable and could do anything he set his mind to. I returned to sewing as Amil and Mary played in their room. I could hear little Mary trying to boss Amil around, but he was not taking it.

"Amil," Mary said in her most bossy tone, "you be Papa, I be Mama."

"No Mary, I'm your brother, and I'm *not* going to be your husband," Amil said firmly. "I don't like to play with your doll, so I'm going to ride away on my horse and see what Mama is doing and where Papa went in the buggy."

Soon Amil was tumbling down the stairs with Mary close behind. She thought she could do everything Amil did; and even though she was little she tried hard to keep up.

"Mama, where did Papa go?" Amil asked. "I wanted to go with him."

"Papa went to town to get more wood for the table. He will soon be finished with it, and when he has sanded all the little pieces, you can build your own house from the left-over wood."

"I can't wait for the wood to be sanded; can I sand it? I am big enough to do the sanding, Mama," Amil said.

"Well, I guess you are since you're seven now! Here is a little piece of sandpaper for you to work on your blocks. Papa will be so proud of you for doing such a good job. Mary, why don't you come help me sew? I'll give you some scraps of cloth to make a little dress for your dolly. Would you like that?"

"Yes, Mama," Mary exclaimed, clapping her hands together. "I can make a dress!"

Soon, we were all so busy with our projects we lost track of time. I didn't realize it was time for supper until I heard Ingvold arrive in the buggy. *Oh no, I don't have anything ready and Ingvold is probably hungry as a bear!* I thought.

"Belle, where is the supper you promised me?" Ingvold said with a laugh. "Do I just get hay today? If I only get hay, then everyone must eat it right along with me."

"No, Papa, no hay," little Mary piped up.

"I am sorry, Ingvold, we were so busy that I let the time get away from me. I'll fix something quick. Just give me a few minutes," I said.

"Not to worry, Belle," Ingvold said. "I stopped by the butcher shop and got some fresh dried beef so we can have a sandwich with that wonderful bread you made yesterday. I know that the husband is supposed to bring home the bacon, but today I brought home the beef."

"Ingvold, that will hit the spot," I said. "I have been so hungry lately; I don't know what has come over me. I guess it's because I am eating for two now!"

Ingvold came over and gave me a hug and kiss. "Belle, I didn't want to say anything, but I have noticed you are getting a little round in the tummy section," he said as he patted my tummy. "Now, let's eat, I'm hungry as a bear, not a horse, and I don't want hay. Come children, let's eat."

As we sat down and bowed our heads, Ingvold prayed. "Father, we thank you for the food that you have provided for our little family. We ask that you look over our family and bless us with more children as time goes on. Bless little Amil and Mary and help them to grow up into strong, loving people. We love you and ask all this in Jesus name. Amen."

Amil repeated, "Amen," and little Mary said, "Amen, Papa."

After supper we took care of the milking. Amil was almost big enough to milk a cow by himself, and little Mary put the milk pans out for the kitties.

"Come and get it," Ingvold said as he squirted milk into the pans. The cats trotted right up, and he squirted milk into their mouths.

"Look, Mama, the kitties look so funny when they get squirted," Amil said.

They were soon lapping up the milk as fast as the bowls could be filled. Mary loved the kitties, and she had named all of them.

"Eat, Spotty, eat, Chubby, eat, Minnie," She instructed. She always wanted to direct everything, even the cats.

When the milking was finished and the cattle were fed, we all went to the house laughing and talking about how fun it was to milk the cows together.

I started separating the cream from the milk, and Ingvold called the children to the table for devotions. He insisted on having devotions every night. He had ordered Bible lessons for the kids, and they really enjoyed them.

"OK, now it is time for you little ragamuffins to get into bed. Wash up, and I will tuck you in," Ingvold said.

"OK, Papa," they both said. Soon, I could hear them talking upstairs. "Papa, why did my Papa Peter and little Peter have to die?" Amil asked.

"Well, you see sometimes God has a plan we don't know about, maybe if they had lived, they would have suffered. So, in His mercy, God took them and let them rest. You wouldn't want your Papa Peter and little Peter to suffer, would you?" Ingvold asked.

"No, I am happy they are not suffering anymore and happy that you have come to be our Papa now. Papa, I love you." Amil said.

Little Mary said, "I lub you too, Papa."

With that, he tucked them in, gave them a kiss, and said, "Night, night, sleep tight, and don't let the bed bugs bite."

"We don't have bed bugs," Amil replied, "just June bugs."

When Ingvold came downstairs, I was ready for my kiss goodnight. "Ingvold, you are a natural Papa, I love you for that," I said.

"And I love you for being such a good Mama, even if you do forget to feed me sometimes," Ingvold said playfully. "Now let's tuck ourselves in as we have a busy day tomorrow. I have to do some fencing since one of our cows got out and wandered over to the neighbor's. The cows always think the grass looks greener on the other side of the fence!"

Ingvold fell asleep, but I was wide awake; I couldn't stop thinking about our new baby and how wonderful it was going to be to have a child with the man I love. I had decided to hold off on discussing baby names with Ingvold until I was a little farther along, just to make sure that everything was going as expected. As I was drifting off to sleep, I put my hand in his big strong hand and thanked God for my husband and children.

NOVEMBER 1883

Before i knew it, the summer was over, and we were busy making hay and flour from our abundant wheat crop. Ingvold had made two large haystacks and placed them by the barn for cattle feeding and wood sticks. He had also gone to the river and brought home a large load of wood, though we would probably need more for the long hard winter.

I spent my time making things for our new baby like blankets, little socks, and dresses. I had some clothing from Mary too, so the baby would be nice and warm. Ingvold was so tickled when he saw all the clothing I had prepared.

"Belle, will these fit the baby?" he asked. "They look so small. I don't know if I'll dare hold the baby if it's so small."

"Oh, Ingvold, when it's all wrapped up with blankets you will feel comfortable holding it."

"You liked holding Mary when she was a baby," I reminded him.

"But she was bigger; I didn't see her when she was this small."

"You will do fine. We can practice with a small sack of flour if you want," I said. "I think once you see your baby, a whole team of horses won't be able to tear you away."

"I hope so, Belle. How are you feeling? Do you think the baby will come soon?"

"Yes, I think it will come before the end of November. But we can't hurry this sort of thing. Babies are the ones who decide when they will be born. We just have to be patient."

"Mama, Mama, Mary won't leave me alone," Amil said as he came downstairs. "She bothers me all the time. I wish little Peter were here. At least he was a boy and played what I like. She just wants to play house."

"Don't worry, Amil, I think you'll have a lot of brothers to play with someday, maybe sisters too," Ingvold said.

It was getting cold and several snow flurries marked the start of winter. When the wind blew it seemed to go right through the windows and walls. I missed my cozy, warm sod house, but I loved our new house too. It looked like a home now with curtains over the windows and homemade rugs on the floor. The cradle was ready with new blankets, and Mary loved to rock her dolly in it.

"Ingvold, could you make a little cradle for Mary so she can rock her dolly in that instead of in the baby's?" I asked.

"Sure, I can do that. Mary would you like that?" Ingvold said.

Mary ran to Ingvold and pulled him in the direction he needed to go. "Rock dolly, rock dolly!"

"Good," said Amil. "Now maybe she will leave me alone."

A week later I began to feel some early labor pains, though I wasn't certain because they could be false. Ingvold had gone over to his brother's place to help with something, but he said he would be back before supper. I wondered if I would go into labor while he was gone.

About two o'clock that afternoon the pains were about five minutes apart. I worried Ingvold might not get home before the baby came. A new baby would be quite a surprise for him to come home to. Amil was outside feeding hay to the cows, and Mary was busy conversing with her doll while she put it to bed in the little cradle Ingvold had made.

I thought about lying down to rest, but in no time my pains were only one minute apart, and I knew birth was imminent. Suddenly the need to bear down overwhelmed me. I prayed, *Dear God, help me bring this baby into the world without any complications!* With that, I pushed one time and out came the baby, screaming and pink. Just then little Mary came into the room to see who was crying.

"Mama! Baby?" she yelled.

"Yes Mary, you have a new little brother," I said. After cutting the cord, I picked up the baby, wrapped him in a blanket, and covered the afterbirth with a sheet. "He is a tiny baby, isn't he?"

"Rock baby, rock baby," Mary insisted.

"No, not right now, Mary, maybe a little later," I said. "Have you seen Papa come home? ."

"No, Mama," Mary said.

"Maybe he came home and went right out to the barn. Go to the door and yell for Papa to see if he is home. I need him now. Hurry!"

I heard her little voice calling, "Papa, Papa are you home? Baby, baby!"

I was so relieved when I heard heavy steps on the porch and knew Ingvold was home. "Ingvold, please come in the bedroom," I said.

A few seconds later, Ingvold entered the bedroom very quietly and lit the lamp. Upon seeing his child in my arms his face lit up. "Oh, my! What's this, having a baby without me?"

"It went so fast. I was fine when you left this morning, but then the pains started and just kept coming. Come see your little son."

"A boy? A tiny boy. Belle, he's perfect, isn't he," Ingvold said. He took the baby's hand in his, and the baby wrapped his little fingers around his papa's big rough finger. Tears ran down Ingvold's face as he gazed upon his little son. "Oh, Belle, I didn't know I could love someone so much. He is just perfect. Belle, I love you so much," he said as he gave me a kiss. "Are you OK, do you need anything?" "Maybe you can take the baby to the other room while I get cleaned up," I said. "Mary would love to see him in better light."

"I don't know if I can hold him safely. He is so small."

"You will do fine, just keep his head supported," I said. I had the baby wrapped tightly with a blanket and handed him to Ingvold. "Here is your son, Ingvold."

Ingvold cradled him in his arms and said it felt natural and easier than he thought. "Come, Mary, you can help me rock the baby," he said.

Just then Amil burst through the door. "What's wrong, Papa? What was Mary calling about? I finished the milking, but I can't carry the pail myself," he said.

He stopped in his tracks as he saw the tiny bundle in Papa's arms. "What, a baby already?"

"Amil, come and meet your little brother," Ingvold said. "We haven't named him yet, but we have some names in mind."

"Wow! He is little, isn't he? Why is his head funny?" Amil asked.

"Oh, his head will straighten out, and he will look fine in a couple of days," Ingvold said.

After I cleaned up and changed the sheets, I went to the door of the bedroom and looked out into the living room where Ingvold was holding the baby with both children looking on. The sight warmed my heart. There were the people I loved the most: my new husband, my two children, and a new child with Ingvold.

I felt proud that I was able to deliver all my children without assistance. Then again, my labor was usually short and without much pain. I was very blessed. If they could all be as easy as the latest one, I would be very happy to add more babies to our growing family.

"Belle, we need to name this little one," Ingvold said. "What do you think? We have talked about Peter, in memory of little Peter, but I don't feel right about it. I like the name John. What about you?"

"Well then, John Ingvold Sletten it is," I said, pulling up a chair by the rocker. "John I. Sletten—what a great name. He will surely be a great man one day."

"I think he'll be the preacher of the family," Ingvold exclaimed. "Just think, we are raising a preacher."

"What, a preacher"? Amil said, "He can't preach! He's too little."

"Well, he'll have to grow up, just like you and Mary," Ingvold said. "When he is a man like me, he will be able to preach or do whatever he decides. Amil, what do you want to be when you grow up?"

Amil thought for a while, then responded, "I want to be a farmer and have horses and cows and sheep. I want to be just like my Papa Gus and my new Papa Ingvold."

"That's a wonderful thing to be when you grow up," I said. "But now I think little John is ready to have something to eat. He is trying to chew on his hand which means he's hungry. Ingvold, could you fix the children something while I feed little John."

"Sure enough, Belle," he said as he handed the baby back to me. "Come out to the kitchen, kids. I'll make my special pancakes. How does that sound?"

"Pancakes, pancakes!" Mary yelled. "I love pancakes!"

As they went into the kitchen, I took a good look at little John. He was so tiny, maybe about six pounds, but he seemed very alert and ready to nurse as I put him to my breast. "John I. Sletten, you have brought so much healing to my heart," I whispered in his ear. "Your Mama has suffered a lot in the last few years, but now I have so much joy."

I rocked him as he nursed, and I thanked God for helping me through another delivery and making our baby so well and strong. In the kitchen I heard Ingvold whistling a tune as he fixed his famous pancakes.

1884

AFTER A MILD WINTER and wonderful Christmas with Grandma and Grandpa Sletten, spring came early. Other than a few colds, the children were healthy, and our homestead was a happy one.

I had so much fun getting to know Ingvold's family and creating a long-lasting friendship with Caroline. We stayed in touch throughout the winter, thanks to her oldest brother, Ole, who had the local post office in his home. I hadn't learned to write so Ingvold wrote letters for me. I also kept in contact with my mother and sister Karin, who lived with my brother near Hartington. They had visited once, and we had such a good time reminiscing about Sweden.

One spring morning, I was awakened by bright sunshine and the sound of the cattle mooing for their early morning milking. Ingvold was upstairs getting Mary and Amil ready for the day, and baby John was still asleep in his bed in our room. As I came out of the bedroom, Mary and Amil were coming down the stairs talking to Ingvold a mile a minute.

"Papa, when can I ride my horse all by myself?" Amil was asking.

"Me too, Papa, I want horse too!" Mary added.

"Amil, you are getting bigger every day, but it will be a while before you are able to ride Ben yourself," Ingvold said. "He is a pretty good horse, but it will take time for him to get used to you. I would guess by the end of next summer you will be able to ride by yourself. I will lead him this summer when we go out to get the cattle, and he can get used to you riding him. With Lucky along, we should be able to move the cattle pretty easy. He has become a good cattle dog. I might get some sheep this spring. How about that Belle, would you like to have some wool to make stockings and sweaters for all of us?" he said, turning to me and catching my eye as I walked past.

"I would love to have wool," I said. "I would need a spinning wheel, but if you can shear the sheep, I can card the wool. I think it's a wonderful idea. I miss the sheep in Sweden. It was so soothing to hear their bells tinkling in the country fields. When can we get them?"

"Well, I have the fencing up, and I should be able to go to market in May and get some sheep with little ones; that way we can grow a herd. Amil, would you and Lucky like to take care of the sheep?"

"Yes Papa, we can do that, but I would need to ride Ben," Amil said eagerly.

"Maybe you can ride by the end of the summer," Ingvold said. "But the sheep will be closer to home, so you can walk to the pasture and check on them. Next spring, we'll have many baby lambs, and you'll be able to take care of them. Now, while Mama gets little John up, let's go to the barn and start milking. Mary, you stay here and help Mama with little John."

"I help Mama," Mary said as she ran to the bedroom to see if John was awake. Ingvold kissed me before heading out the door with Amil. "Mama, John wake," Mary said.

"I'm coming, Mary, you mustn't try to pick him up yourself; he is too big and strong for you. He is almost five months now, and he loves his big sister. Look how he smiles when you talk to him."

"I lub my lil' bruver too," she said.

I nursed John while Mary played like she was nursing her dolly. *She will be a good mother someday,* I thought.

After feeding John I put him in his bed, and Mary and I started breakfast. Mary loved helping in the kitchen, and I let her stir the eggs. Ole had chickens so we could have eggs, but I wished I could have my own chickens for butchering. Fried chicken would be great in the winter. I thought about asking Ingvold about getting chickens and putting them in a coop near the house.

I heard the sound of boots stomping on the porch and Amil chattering to Ingvold about riding his horse. "Papa, can you let me ride Ben later in the afternoon, before we have to milk again?"

"Well, we can ride over to Ole's place, and I will lead Ben with you on his back, then we can talk to Uncle Ole about getting some sheep," Ingvold said.

"Ingvold, I would like to get some chickens too," I said. "Do you think Ole has some we can buy?"

"I'll ask him. It wouldn't be too hard to put up a chicken coop. I guess with the kids getting older, it would be good for them to take care of the chickens. Do you think you could pick the eggs?" he asked Mary, as he scooped her up in his arms.

"I like chickens and eggs!" She giggled.

"OK, then we better sit down and eat so we can grow big and strong to take care of chickens and sheep. We are starting to have a pretty nice farm here."

Ingvold sat down next to me, gave me a kiss on the cheek, and dug into breakfast. Between bites he said, "Belle, how is little Johnny this morning? I bet he'll soon be old enough to help with the chores around here. He'll have a big brother and sister to help him."

Later that day when Ingvold and Amil came home, Amil had so much to say he could hardly get all the words out. "Mama! I rode Ben all the way to uncle Ole's, and we are getting some sheep after the mamas have their babies this spring, and uncle Ole has some chickens to sell us, and I'll help Papa build the chicken coop, and the chickens are laying hens, and Papa said we should have little chicks soon, and…."

"OK, Amil," Ingvold gently interrupted. "You better stop talking and help me milk the cows. After supper, we can draw up a plan for how to build our chicken coop. I'm already thinking about what your Mama will make to eat tonight!"

After supper, with Ingvold and the kids around the table and John sitting on Ingvold's lap, the paper and pencils were brought out. Amil tried to draw what he thought the coop should look like, and John tried to grab whatever was on the table in front of him. "OK, Johnny, you will have to go to bed so we can get the chicken coop drawn up," said Ingvold. "Here, go to Mama," he said, as he handed John to me.

It wasn't long before John was fast asleep, and we were all sitting around the table again. Ingvold had drawn up a wonderful plan for the chicken coop, and Amil had added a little door for the chickens to go in and out. Ingvold said he would go into Parker and get the wood on Friday, and they could start building next week.

"It should only take about two weeks to get it finished. Then we can get the chickens from Ole and have eggs soon," Ingvold said.

"OK, kids, it's time for bed now," he continued. "Tomorrow you can help Papa clean up and level the area where the coops will go, so when I get the lumber on Friday, we'll be ready to start."

Ingvold took Mary's hand, and they all went upstairs. I could hear him reading a Bible story to them. They loved to hear him tell stories because he made them so interesting. Tonight, he was telling about how Noah built the ark and had all the animals go in. "Noah was a carpenter like me, and he had to make a place for the animals to go before the big flood. But God helped him know how to build it, just like he will help us know how to build our chicken coop. Night, night now."

After he had tucked them in, we sat by the table and talked about the new animals we'd have on the farm.

"Belle, when I pick up the lumber for the coop, I will have extra material to build some flower boxes for the windows. Would you like that?"

"Oh, Ingvold, I would love to have some flowers! Will you get some flower seeds in town too, along with seeds for the garden I have planned?" I asked.

"I sure will, I'm hungry for some fresh vegetables. When I get the chicken coup done, I will get the garden plot ready for you. No more siting around for you," he teased, as he put his arm around me and kissed me. "Now, let's go to bed, I'm bushed."

1885 - 1886

OUR FARM WAS STARING to look like a real farm. We had cattle, milking cows, sheep, and chickens. They required a lot of work, but I had fun helping Ingvold with the animals, and Amil was getting big enough to help more and more. Mary was big enough now to pick the eggs. She had quite a knack for getting the eggs out from under the chickens without causing them to fuss.

We had a great crop, and I had a good garden harvest too. John was growing like a weed. He would toddle around with Mary watching over him like a mother hen. Just what she needed: someone to boss around.

Early the next spring, a new member would be added to our family. We were excited but hadn't told the children yet. I was glad when the garden was finished and the sheep were sheared. The children were outgrowing their clothes, so I was thankful for the wool. I had plenty of wool to keep me busy making clothing for everyone all winter.

Amil was helping with milking and feeding the animals. He loved working with the animals the most. He took his horse out to the pasture with Lucky and herded the sheep and cattle from pasture to pasture. Lucky was a great herding dog.

I was happy when Ingvold came into the house one evening and announced, "Well, the harvest is done. We finished up at Martin's place today. It's such a good feeling to be done before the winter It won't be long now before the old wind howls and the snow flies."

I had just finished fixing our meal, but the milking still had to be done. "I'll keep things warm while you two get the milking done," I said. Ingvold and Amil put on their jackets and headed out to the barn. I decided to give the little ones something to eat and get them into bed as they were getting hungry and cranky.

"Papa going to tuck us in," John said, as I was tucking him into bed.

"Papa had to do the milking tonight, so it will be too late to tuck you in. I'll send him upstairs to give you a kiss though," I said. I tucked him into the bed he shared with Amil, and then tucked Mary into her bed. "Don't forget to say your prayers, Mary."

"I won't, Mama, I will pray for everyone in our family and the chickens and the cows and the horses and the sheep," she said.

"That should about cover everything. Good night now. I love you and will see you in the morning," I said. As I tiptoed out of the room, I heard Mary dutifully reciting her blessing prayer. She always thought about everyone and everything in her prayers.

That winter was mild, and there was not a lot of snow. I kept busy making clothing for the children and Ingvold tended to the cattle, sheep, and milking. We sat by the fire many nights while he shared stories about growing up. The children loved his stories. He had quite a way of weaving a story to keep the children on the edge of their seats.

One night Ingvold told a story about cattle watching for a farmer when he was thirteen. "I was out in the field, minding my own business, when all of a sudden this huge animal came out of the earth. It was hissing and barking like I had never seen or heard before."

At that, the kids' eyes were as big as saucers and their mouths hung open.

"What was it?" Amil asked. "Was it a bear?"

"Well, I had seen some mighty big holes in the field before, so I had asked what they were," Ingvold said. "I was told they were badger holes, and that I didn't want to tangle with one of those. Well, I took one look at him, and he took one look at me, and down his hole he went as fast as he had appeared."

"Did you ever see another one after that?" Mary asked, as she hung on tightly to his sleeve.

"No, Mary, no, I haven't seen one since, and I don't want to see one either. They are nasty looking things, and I was told they have huge teeth too."

"Do we have badgers here on our farm?" Amil quietly asked.

"Well, I have never seen one, but I have seen their holes," Ingvold said. "Usually they only come out at night, so we probably won't ever see one. Enough badger stories. Now I have a great story from the Bible to read before you go to sleep, so get upstairs and into bed."

"Yea!" Mary shouted, as she and Amil ran up the stairs with John following close behind.

I was glad to have Ingvold put the kids to bed because I was extra tired. March, when our new baby would arrive, couldn't come fast enough. I had most of the little things ready and was in the process of patching some of Ingvold's pants.

After the kids were tucked in, Ingvold and I sat and talked about the day and what name we might give the new baby. I also scolded him for telling such a scary story right before bed time.

"I don't want the kids to have nightmares about badgers. You make it so scary that I'm afraid the children won't be able to sleep tonight," I said.

"Well, I like to let them know there are things out there that might scare us. I told them the Bible story about David and Goliath and showed them how God is with us and will protect us even against the scariest things. We need to trust God to do what is best. They seemed happy with that and were drifting off to sleep by the time I finished the story. Don't worry, Belle, I just like to make things a little more exciting when I tell a story. Sometimes it's fun to get a little scared," he said with a smile.

When he looked at me with his teasing eyes, I just couldn't argue. Life was a lot more exciting with Ingvold. He was so full of life and always thinking about the next thing he could do for our family. Our children loved him so, and he pitched in and helped with whatever needed to be done. He had gotten pretty good at juggling three children at once, and I knew he would be able to handle another.

"What do you think we should name our new little ragamuffin? Maybe Goliath?" he teased.

"I've been thinking about a name. Thomas has a nice ring to it. What do you think?" I asked.

"I like Tom. It sounds very American. I say yes," Ingvold said. "But what if we have a girl? That's a possibility too. Maybe Thomasina? That would be easy. Then we would only have to come up with one name no matter if it's a boy or a girl."

"OK, we can see when he or she gets here. Sometimes a name just seems to fit them, so I like to wait and see what they look like," I replied.

"What? They all look the same: wrinkled and red," Ingvold joked. "But they are all special in God's eyes and to us. It will be great to add another chair to the table. Our family is really growing. Belle, thank you for giving me children; I love you so much for that. You look tired though, so we better get to bed and get some rest."

With that, we headed to bed. With Ingvold at my side it didn't take me long to drift off to sleep. dreaming about our large family eating supper together at our big table.

On March 8, little Thomas was added to our family. He looked a lot like Ingvold but had reddish hair. As was the case with all my children, his birth was uneventful and easy. Ingvold was nearby, but he stayed with the children to keep them occupied.

Thomas arrived in the early evening, so all the children were still up when he made his first sound in our home. Ingvold ushered them into the bedroom quietly and introduced them to their new brother. Mary was the first to say something.

"Mama, I wanted a sister. Now I have another brother," she said.

"Mary, I know you will love this little brother just like you love Johnny. I know you will be a big help to me. You have helped so much with Johnny. I don't think I could have done it without you," I reassured her.

"Well, he is cute, isn't he," Mary said.

"Not so sure you could call him cute," Amil piped up. "He has that same funny shaped head that Johnny had."

"Don't worry," Ingvold interrupted, "Thomas will be a very handsome lad when he grows up. Maybe he'll be president someday. President Thomas Sletten. That sounds about right, don't you think?"

"John, do you want to see your new little brother?" I asked.

Ingvold put John on the bed, and he leaned over and gave Thomas a kiss. "I like little Tom, Mama," he said.

"Well, it's time for bed now. We'll see more of Thomas in the morning," Ingvold said, making a motion toward the door. "Say night-night to Mama and Thomas now."

From downstairs I could hear him telling them the story about when baby Jesus was born and how his mama and papa didn't have a nice house to have the baby in, so Jesus had to be born in a barn with the cattle around.

"Was it smelly like our barn?" Mary asked.

"I am sure it was like most barns," Ingvold said. "They aren't nice, clean places to have a new baby, are they? But God watched over baby Jesus and kept him safe, even when there were bad people who didn't like Him and were trying to get rid of Him. Jesus and his mama and papa were protected by angels who guided them and kept them safe. Now it's time to say your prayers and get to sleep. I'll see you in the morning."

Then I heard Mary saying her blessings prayer, and she included everyone and all the animals too. She ended with, "And bless little Thomas Sletten, who will be president someday, Amen."

That night Ingvold and I said a special prayer for the safe arrival of little Thomas Sletten, the future president of the United States.

SUMMER AND FALL 1886

"MAMA, MAMA, PAPA IS coming down the road fast!" Amil shouted as he banged the screen door open.

"What could be wrong? He doesn't usually drive like that!" Alarm filled my voice, and I ran to the door just as Ingvold jumped from his horse.

"Belle, Belle, there is a fire over at Martin's place!" he yelled. "I need to get the horses hitched up to the plow and plow a fire brake around our house. Help me." He was off to the barn to get the horses hitched up. I ran behind him with fear in my heart.

"Ingvold, how did it start? How bad is it"? I asked breathlessly.

"I don't know what started it, but it's a prairie fire which moves like a wave over land," he said. "It has already burned some of Martin's trees. He managed to keep it from taking the house, but he's still fighting it, so it doesn't come our way. I want you and Amil to get as much water in the horse trough as you can so we can wet down the house. Keep Mary inside with John and Thomas and keep calm. The Lord will help us. Just pray, Belle, *pray.*"

I ran inside and told Mary to stay inside with the little boys. "There is a fire, and Amil and I need to fetch water, so it doesn't get to our house. Don't let little John get outside!"

"OK, Mama, don't worry. I'll watch them, and if they get hungry, I can get them something to eat too," she assured me in a grown-up voice. I was so proud of her. She was five now and was such a little mother and helper. I gathered everything I could use to fill with water and ran back outside.

With dust trailing behind the plow, Ingvold gallantly made a fire break around the house and other buildings. When he was done, he let the horses and cows out of the barn to fend for themselves while Amil and I filled buckets from the well.

After filling the containers with water, I walked to the south side of our house and looked across the field towards Martin's place. My heart raced even faster when I saw billows of thick smoke curling up into the sky. I had heard about prairie fires and how they often burned everything in their path. It had been a dry summer, and now the grass was like flint for the licking flames. Clasping my hands together, I prayed, *please Lord, save our family, our house, and what little crops we have!*

Ingvold headed to Martin's place to help him plow fire breaks and set-back fires to stop the wall of fire from ravaging our land. Soon, I noticed the fire had stopped and wasn't spreading anymore. Sadly, the fire had burned a destructive path across Martin's land, taking many of the young trees he had planted. He had been so proud of those trees after his sister, Alena, and other family members helped plant them. I was relieved to see that many trees had been spared, and I thanked God for saving them.

Soon Ingvold was coming across the field with the horses and plow. He looked like he had been fighting in hell. He was covered with soot, and he could hardly take another step.

"Oh, Ingvold," I said, running to him and throwing my arms around him. "I was so scared! Is it over now?"

"I hope so, but we need to take water over to Martin's to put out hot spots, so it doesn't start up again," he said. "Luckily the wind has died down. We can load up buckets in the buckboard and take them over. We may have to make several trips back and forth." His voice cracked as he talked about how hot the fire was and what a battle it had been.

Amil said, "I can help drive the team back and forth so we can keep water coming. I'm big enough now."

"Yes, Amil, you are almost a man," Ingvold teased, "soon to be ten, aren't you?"

"Yup, in February I will be ten, and I can ride Ben out to get the cows and help Lucky herd the sheep. I think I can drive the team with the wagon without too much trouble!" he said confidently.

"OK, little man, let's get the horses hitched to the buckboard and start loading water. We need to get back to Martin's."

"I wish we had a big hose that stretched from our house to Martin's, so we could just shoot the water right over there," Amil said boldly.

As Ingvold and Amil hitched the horses, I ran to the house and told Mary what was happening. She was huddling with John and Thomas under the table, and they had been crying. "Oh, Mary, you have been so good with the little boys, keeping them in the house and helping them not to be scared. You can come out from under the table now because the fire is under control. Papa and Amil are taking buckets of water to Martin's to make sure it doesn't start up again. How about singing something with John? He loves to sing."

"OK, Mama, what should we sing?" Mary asked, as she and John stood.

"Jesus Loves Me!" he burst out. John would be four in November, and he loved to sing "Jesus Loves Me." Soon they were singing joyfully while John swung his arms like he was directing the choir.

When I returned to the trough, Ingvold and Amil had just departed for Martin's again. As they drove away, I noticed Ingvold was letting Amil drive. Amil was sitting up straight and looked so grown up. He was finally getting his chance to drive the team. I waved and hollered, "Be careful and drive safely!" I knew they couldn't make out my words, but I wanted Amil to know I was looking as he drove away. He was growing up so fast. Soon, Amil would be ten and John would be four.

I walked back to the house and found Mary instructing John about the Bible. She loved to teach, and she was commanding his attention. He was sitting still on the stool, listening attentively. Occasionally a yawn slipped out, but still he listened to his big sister.

"OK, John, you can go play now, I need to get supper started," Mary said in an authoritative voice. With that, she started peeling the potatoes. I sat down in the rocker to rest a little before Amil came back.

Soon I heard the wagon coming into the yard, so I rushed out to help. Amil was looking very important as he came up to the trough and swung down from the wagon. "Better get these buckets filled and back over to Martin's," he said. "I figure we'll need about two more loads."

We worked together to fill the buckets, and Amil drove them back and forth to Martin's. I knew we were finished when I saw Ingvold return with him. They both looked so tired as Amil steered the team into the yard.

After we got the horses unhitched and watered, we all went into the house to get cleaned up. Mary had a good smelling supper ready for us.

"What's this?!" Ingvold exclaimed in delight. "Do we have a new cook in our family? It sure smells nice. I am hungry as a bear. I'll get cleaned up, and we can all sit down to the wonderful supper Mary has made."

Later that night after the children were all settled in their beds and before Ingvold and I got into bed, we prayed and thanked the Lord for helping us stop the fire and gave thanks that everyone was safe.

"Amil really stepped up and was a wonderful worker and helper. He will make a fine farmer someday," Ingvold said.

"I am so proud of him; he has grown so much and takes responsibility without being told. He is a very special boy and reminds me of his father, Gus, so much. He always wants to help, and he's a hard worker," I responded sleepily. Before I knew it, Ingvold was sleeping soundly, and I drifted off thinking about how proud I was of all my children.

FALL AND WINTER 1886

THE SUMMER PASSED WITH no more prairie fires. I harvested a fairly good crop from the garden, thanks to having water from the well that Ingvold dug the previous year. I was putting up some vegetables when Amil came into the house after taking care of the chickens. Mary was following with her little basket of eggs. She had become very good at getting eggs from underneath the chicken without the chicken objecting.

"Mama, Mary wants to follow me everywhere. Can you keep her in the house, so she is not bothering me?" Amil asked. "I just can't get my chores done. Papa told me to finish cleaning the barn and put new hay down for the horses. She is just too little to help me, and I can't work when she is right under my feet," he explained in a grown-up tone.

Seeing him doing the chores and helping out made me proud. I remembered when he was sick with Diphtheria and how worried

I had been. His tenth birthday was coming up in February, and I wanted to do something special for him.

"I understand, Amil. Thank you for all you have done to help around here," I said. "I couldn't do it all myself, and Papa really appreciates having another man around the place."

With that, he puffed up his chest and said, "I better get back to the chores now. I want to have them all done before Papa gets home from the field. I hope next year I can help with the field work. Now, Mary, you stay here and help Mama like a big girl." Then he was out the door.

"Mama, what can I help you with?" Mary asked imitating her big brother's tone.

"Well, Mary, you can help me the most by watching Johnny so he doesn't get into anything that he shouldn't. He has been into everything today," I said. "Just a few minutes ago he found the flour bin and managed to get the top off. Before I knew it, he had flour all over the floor and himself. Oh! I just finished cleaning it up before you and Amil came in. I need to finish canning, so if you can take him into our bedroom and watch him that would be wonderful"

"OK, Mama, I will. Come on Johnny, it's time for your school. I'm the teacher, so you better listen to what I say," Mary said.

"OK, Mary, I go to school," Johnny said, as he followed her into the bedroom.

Mary tried to teach him the ABC's, and they sang at the top of their lungs. John loved to sing, and he had a pretty nice voice. "A B C D E F G, H I J K elemeno P," I heard him sing. Then he would start over. Mary was mostly patient with him.

The rest of the afternoon passed quietly as I finished up my fall canning and placed the jars on the shelf in the pantry. I loved how colorful and orderly they looked on the shelf. It was gratifying to see all my hard summer work turn into wonderful food for the coming winter. Amil came in the house and cleaned up for supper. Ingvold was working later in the field as he wanted to finish harvesting before November came. I started supper.

Meanwhile, John rode his stick horse around the house. He had gotten the OK to ride little Peter and Amil's horses, and he switched between the two. November would be his birthday! I had almost forgotten. I thought about asking Ingvold to make him something. When he was younger, Ingvold made some different stone carvings when he worked for a cattle farmer. He carved hearts, Bibles, and crosses. He had given me a heart carving one Christmas. It was a precious gift, and I still remember him saying, "Belle, this is my heart. I give it to you forever and ever as long as we live." I thought maybe he could give John one of the Bibles he had made. John would feel so proud to have his own Bible.

When we sat down to eat, we heard Ingvold drive into the yard, so we decided to wait for him. Amil ran out to help with the horses. When they came back in Amil was asking him a hundred questions about the field work. Ingvold answered his questions just like he would answer a man. "You know, Amil, we saw a big black snake out in the field today. It had to be at least ten feet long," he said, winking at me.

"No kidding!" Amil said. "What did you do, Papa?"

"Well, I just got down off the hay wagon and took my trusty hoe and killed him before he knew what hit him," Ingvold said. Again, he winked at me and smiled.

"Wow! Were you scared?" Amil asked.

"No, I just prayed that God would give me the courage to get him before he got me! That's what we have to do. Sometimes we are scared of things and don't know what to do, but if we ask God to help us, He always will. Now let's eat! I'm starved."

It was Mary's turn to say the supper prayer. She prayed, "Dear Jesus, thank You for helping my Papa kill the bad snake before he killed Papa," she said. "Keep us all safe this winter and don't let us get lost or hurt in the snow. God bless Papa and Mama and Amil and Johnny and baby Thomas. Oh, and bless Lucky and all my kitties too. Amen."

Soon we were all eating and having a wonderful time telling about our day when Johnny piped up. "Papa, I'm going to have a birthday pretty soon. I will be four!" he said, as he tried to form four fingers.

"You are?" Ingvold said, "I can't believe you'll be that old. That makes me really old then, and your Mama really, really old," he said with a wink. What would you like for your birthday?"

"Weeeell! I want a real horse, like Amil!"

"A horse? That is kind of a big deal Johnny," Ingvold said. "I think you better wait until you are a little bigger. Amil didn't get his 'real' horse until he was about eight. That will be a few more years for you. But I will let you ride my horse with me leading it. I think that might work. How about it?"

"Yes, yes, yes," John said as he clapped his hands together. "I can ride Amil's house horse, he said I could."

"That's nice of him. Thanks Amil for letting Johnny ride your wooden horse; now he has two horses to ride on around the house. Mama, you better watch out or you'll get run over," Ingvold said, as he gave me a peck on the cheek.

"OK, that's enough for tonight, time for bed," I said in a stern voice. "Run and get ready, and I will come tuck you in." Even though I loved them all dearly, I needed time with my husband. Our alone times were getting fewer and fewer, and I missed them.

When the house was quiet and Ingvold and I were sitting together and talking about the day's events, I asked, "Ingvold, do you think you could give one of your carved Bibles to Johnny for his birthday? I think he is old enough to take care of it. Also, I don't really like you telling stories that are not true, like the snake story."

"It was true—I just exaggerated a little to make it more exciting. The kids love that," he said. "What fun would it be if I just said I saw a garter snake and let it go at that? It was just a wee white lie. You still love me, don't you?" he said, as he hung his head as though he was sorry.

"Oh, Ingvold, how many times do I have to say I will love you through thick and thin," I said. "I just want to make sure the kids don't tell tall tales. It isn't a good idea. About two weeks later, it was snowing heavily. It was coming down so hard I couldn't see the barn from the house. I shuddered as I recalled the bad winter in 1881 when Peter died; that year we didn't get a break in the snow for weeks.

Ingvold had strung a rope between the house and the barn so he could get to the animals and feed them and bring in wood for the fire. One morning, Amil went with him to help with the milking. I told them both to be careful and hurry back to the house as soon as possible. After an hour, I started wondering why they were taking so long.

Suddenly Ingvold came bursting through the door, carrying Amil in his arms. "Belle, Amil was kicked by a cow and knocked out. Help me get him into bed. He took a pretty good blow to the head," Ingvold said.

"Oh, no! How bad do you think it is? Has he talked to you at all?" I asked. I couldn't bear the thought of him being injured and us being unable to help. Getting a doctor was out of the question with the blizzard.

We got him undressed and tucked into our bed. His head had a bad gash, and he was bleeding profusely. I tried as best I could to stop the bleeding. As I wrapped strips of cloth around his head, I saw a huge dent in his skull. *No, no God! Please help us to do what we need to do for him.*

I couldn't help but think about the repercussions. Getting kicked in the head by a cow could lead to a brain injury or even death. *No!* I tried to get it out of my mind. He had been so happy that morning, singing with John and Mary. I prayed, *Dear God, I almost lost him when he was six with Diphtheria. I just can't lose him now! I just can't lose him now!*

Ingvold had a serious look on his face and said, "I couldn't believe it. It happened when he walked behind the cow to milk the other one. I should have watched more carefully. Belle, we have to accept the fact that Amil may not recover from this. It's my fault, and I don't think I can forgive myself."

"Ingvold, don't be so hard on yourself; you are the most careful and loving Papa to all the kids," I said. "Amil wouldn't want you to feel bad about an accident. This is something we will just have to face together. I think I better go see how Mary and John are doing. They were pretty shaken up." I could hear them crying in the other room. Mary was trying to comfort John, but she couldn't put on a brave face at a time like that.

I went in the kitchen where Mary and John were sitting and holding each other tightly. They were sobbing, and when they saw me, they jumped right up.

"Mama," Mary asked. "What happened to Amil? Will he wake up and be better?"

"Mary and John, you need to be very brave. Amil was kicked in the head by a cow and is not doing very good," I said. "Getting kicked by a cow is always dangerous, but if you get the hit in the head it can be much worse. I don't know if Amil will live with this injury. It's possible that he will survive, but we have to be ready if he doesn't."

John cried, "Mama, my birthday is tomorrow. Are we going to play in the snow?"

"It will still be your birthday tomorrow. Maybe Amil will be better by then, and you can play in the snow. If not, we have to be brave and ask God to help us," I said.

"No, Mama," Mary cried. "Amil can't die. I can't have another brother die like Peter. Mama, I want to see Amil. Can I?"

"Yes, children, I will take you in to see him, but he has a bad cut on his head," I said. "I had to wrap bandages around his head, and he can't talk to you. Please be quiet when you see him as we don't want him to hear us crying."

I ushered them into the bedroom where Ingvold was sitting on the bed beside Amil holding his hand. He looked so lost; he really had grown to love Amil and hoped that someday he would farm with him.

I tiptoed up to the bed and could see that Amil was fading fast. I let the kids take one look at him and say their goodbyes, then I asked Mary to take John in the kitchen and give him some milk and crackers.

"Ingvold, the time is coming isn't it? He will not recover from this, will he?" I said.

He nodded his head and made a place for me to sit beside him. He put his loving arms around me as I came to the realization that I would soon be burying another son. "Belle, you have to face the fact that Amil will not survive. We have to keep strong for the other children."

"Oh, Ingvold, I don't know if I can do it. Losing a child is the worst heartache a mother can have. You will have to hold me up and help the children, because I just don't know if I can go through this," I sobbed.

"Belle, we'll go through this together, just like we did with little Peter. I will help you be strong, and I have already asked God to give us the strength we need," Ingvold said.

"God!" I cried, "I don't think God cares about us. If He did, He wouldn't have let Gus and little Peter die. He could have stopped it. He could have stopped the cow from kicking Amil too." All my pent-up anger from the loss of my first husband and child came pouring out. "It just isn't fair that I should have to suffer all this sorrow!"

Ingvold started to recite Psalm 23. "Even if I walk in the shadow of death, I will not fear, for You are with me. We have to believe that Belle. We have to trust God," he said.

Soon Amil's breathing became shallower, and the color was leaving his face. *Oh, that face. How I loved it. He was my firstborn. How could I let him go?*

As we sat there beside Amil holding his hands, he slipped away and took his last breath. We held each other for a long time, and then we got up to tell John and Mary their brother was gone. It was the hardest thing I ever had to do. It was the day before John's birthday. I would remember it every year.

WINTER 1886

THE DAY AFTER AMIL'S death was John's fourth birthday. Ingvold gave John one of his carved Bibles and told him, "Johnny, now you are the oldest boy, so I want you to have this little stone Bible. Remember to always trust God no matter what, because He loves all of us more than we know. Losing Amil is a terrible thing, and we can cry about it, and God understands; but He wants us to ask Him to give us the strength we need to get through this, just like He did when little Peter died."

"Papa, I will try," John said through his tears. "I will miss Amil so much."

John and Mary took Amil's death hard, and Ingvold tried to console them. I will never forget the sight of them sitting on their big brother's bed, holding each other and crying. Our little family would never be the same again. I would never again see Amil bouncing through the door, talking non-stop about everything that had happened during the day. He was so full of life and always so kind and considerate. *Oh, I had such plans for him when he grew up. How could I give those up? How could I go on?* I had no answers.

In the midst of my thoughts, little Tommy got my attention. He was nine months old and beginning to pull himself up and walk around. He pulled himself up by my chair and tugged at my skirt. "Mama, Mama!" he said. He was beginning to say a few words like Mama and Papa, but mostly he used sign language to make his needs known. He loved to wave bye-bye when Ingvold left, and he always threw kisses to his sister and brothers.

I took him in my arms and held him close. He was so soft and loved to cuddle. I whispered in his ear, "Oh, Tommy, losing your brothers are the worst things that can happen to a mama, but I will keep on loving all my children and ask God to help me raise them as He wants them to be raised." Tommy patted me with his chubby little hand, as if trying to comfort me.

The next day when the snow had stopped, Ingvold went to his parents' home to tell them the tragic news. They would get the word to the neighbors and other family members.

As word went out, many neighbors and friends stopped by and gave us their condolences. Some of the children who went to school with Amil came with their parents and cried about losing Amil.

"He was a great buddy and we will miss him in school; it just won't seem the same without him," one of the boys said. "He was one of our best softball players."

Ingvold took Amil's body to the undertaker the day after John's birthday. They would keep him until spring and the frost was out of the ground. Again, we had to wait for our final goodbye. My heart broke as I watched Ingvold drive out of the yard with the sleigh bells ringing in the cold air. The snow was so white under the sparkling sun. It would have been a beautiful day to take a sleigh ride together. Ingvold's head hung low as I watched him disappear.

Thanksgiving came and went. It was not a very happy day, but Ingvold and I thanked God for our children and the time we were blessed to share with Peter and Amil. We knew that children were a gift from God, and they were only on loan to us for a very short time.

One evening when all the children were asleep, and Ingvold and I were talking about Amil, Ingvold turned to me with tears in his eyes.

"Belle, I don't know if I can get over Amil's death and go on. He was getting to be a real partner with the farming, and now I am all alone. He was so looking forward to helping with the field work next spring, and I was happy he would be able to help. He was so good at herding the cattle and sheep with Lucky working at his side. He was a natural when it came to farming, and I loved that in him. I guess that is what is so hard: I just loved him so much, like he was my own son." He broke down and cried.

I took him in my arms and held him. "Ingvold, we have lost a son, and it is something we will never get over, but Amil would not want us to stop living," I said. "He would want us to keep farming and doing the things he loved so much. We will get through this together, Ingvold. We love each other and will hold each other up. We have to think about our other children and how much they need us now."

We held each other for a long time, trying to make sense of everything. We would need more help without Amil, but I knew that would work out somehow.

Christmas passed and soon spring was in the air again. Amil's burial at the little cemetery in Parker took place on a beautiful, warm spring day. As they lowered his casket into the ground, I thanked God I was his mother, and that he had given me so many memories to cherish the rest of my life. *Goodbye my son; some day we will see each other again. I will always remember the day you were born to Gus and me, our first child. Goodbye dear one.*

The spring was wet due to the heavy winter snowfall. We had lost cattle and sheep because we were unable to get feed to them. Ingvold could not get to the field when he wanted to, but he kept busy by rebuilding fence that had broken down over the winter. He missed Amil helping him with the milking, but I was able to help more now that Tommy was a year old. Mary was a great babysitter, and she watched both John and Tom. She was happy to have two students to teach now, and she excelled at teaching.

I cherished my alone time with Ingvold as we milked the cows or worked in the field. We talked about how we wanted our children to have a Christian education, and we wished there was a church close for us to attend. "Belle," Ingvold said one day, "I think I'll send for some Bible lessons for the kids. We can teach them."

"I wish I could help, but I can't read English," I said. "I guess it will be up to you to teach the lessons. I will help as much as I can. It may help me learn English better too," I said.

So, Ingvold sent for the Bible lessons. When they came in the mail, he set aside every Sunday morning for Bible class. The children loved learning more about the Bible, and Ingvold was a natural teacher. He could make the lessons come alive, and sometimes I got more out of the lessons than the kids. Mary and John loved to sing the songs that came with the lessons, and Tommy tried to sing too. Those were wonderful days, and I will remember them all my life. The Lord had brought happiness to our family again, just as He had promised. He was with us when we cried and when we laughed.

SUMMER AND FALL 1887

HAT SUMMER I WAS able to help Ingvold quite a bit. We hired Ole's son, Thomas, to help us also. He was a year younger than Amil, but he could help stack hay. Ingvold and I kept up with the milking, and even Mary helped a little. Ingvold warned her many times never to walk behind an animal.

"I know, Papa, I will be careful, but I want to help with what I can" Mary said. "I am big enough now to do some of the chores that Amil did. I can take hay to the cows, and I love taking care of the little lambs we had this spring," she said.

"Mary had a little lamb; his fleece was white as snow, and everywhere that Mary went the lamb was sure to go," Ingvold teased. "You do have a way with those little ones."

I reminded her that she was also a big help when she watched John and Tom as they played nearby. "Run now and see what they are up to," I said. John was good at keeping an eye on Tom, who had turned one in March and was walking.

Soon Mary had them herded into the barn. "They just want to run all over, so I thought we could pen them up someplace to make it easier to keep track of them," Mary said with exasperation. "They just won't listen to me, Mama!"

"They won't follow you like your little sheep?" Ingvold asked. "Maybe we need to get some sheep bells for them. At least then we could hear where they are. What about that, Mama? Wouldn't that be a great idea? Well, the milking is done now, so let's all go in the house and get cleaned up. I need to get out to the field and get more hay done. We will need a lot for the winter."

At that, we took the milk buckets into the house and I separated it. We were having blackberry cobbler for supper, and the cream would taste wonderful on top of it. I had discovered some wild blackberries down the road, and Mary and John picked them.

After I separated the cream, I churned some butter. I kept the milk, cream, and butter in the root cellar. We sold some of it along with eggs at the town market and were able to get needed supplies from our profits.

When I wasn't in the field with Ingvold, I kept busy sewing with wool from our spring shearing, and Mary helped wind the yarn into balls. I was teaching her to knit, and she was getting quite good at it. John and Tom played with Amil's blocks for hours.

That summer we had a lot of fun together, riding to grandpa and grandma's Sletten's house and visiting with my Mom and brothers when they came to see us. It was a great reunion. I was happy they met Amil previously when they visited after my mom and sister Karin came to America. Mom was living with my brother Nils now, and Karin had married a man from Hartington, Nebraska. Mom said she was very happy. My other sister, Kerstin, and her family were still in Sweden, but their two oldest boys had come to America, and they were hoping to come in the next few years. She and I had been quite close, and I missed her terribly.

That fall we put up haystacks and moved the cattle and sheep into the barnyard for the winter. I always felt sorry for the animals that could no longer graze out in the pastures. They seemed content enough as we fed them hay, but they always kicked up their heels when we led them to the pasture.

Spring! I was already longing for it, and winter had not even started.

John's birthday was a special one. He was turning five and we promised him the new colt that would be born soon. He was so excited that he could hardly contain himself.

"Papa, you mean I can have my own horse in the spring?" he said when Ingvold told him. "Can I work the cattle like Amil and Lucky did? I think I'm old enough. I'll be almost six by then."

"Hold your horses, son," Ingvold cautioned. "Your little colt won't be ready for riding until I have worked with him and made sure he is ready. It may take a year before you can ride him and even then, I will need to lead him as you ride. Maybe by next spring, when you are six, I can start leading him with you."

"I can wait," John said. "I'm teaching Tommy to ride my stick horsey, and he and I ride all over. Maybe someday he and I will ride together on *real* horses. That will be fun! I used to love riding my horse with my brothers too. We had a lot of adventures together. Like the time—"

"OK, that's enough. No more tall tales this morning," I interrupted. "We have work to do. Mary and John, you pick the eggs, and Papa needs to get to the field. We also have to dig potatoes and clean up the garden. We can talk more about horses after supper."

November came quickly, and for Thanksgiving we went to Grandpa and Grandma Sletten's. All the family was there. It was a happy time since Ingvold's younger brother, Martin, and his wife, Augusta, were expecting their first child any day. I promised I would help with the birth if the weather permitted because the first delivery is often the hardest.

Three days later, Martin came riding up to our place and summoned me to come quick. "Augusta's in labor, and the baby's coming soon!" he reported.

I instructed Mary to get something for the boys to eat and keep them in the house until I returned. Ingvold headed out the door to hitch up the horses. I was ready to go with the supplies I needed. Rushing out of the house I said, "Ingvold, you stay here with the kids, I can drive over."

When I got to Martin's place, I went to the bedroom where Augusta was, and I saw that the birth was not going to be soon. Augusta was in a state of panic. "I can't do this Belle, it hurts too much. Please make it stop!" she cried.

I tried to calm her down. "Babies are born every day, and there is no stopping it, Augusta. You have to stay calm. The baby will come sooner if you relax and let nature take its course. I will help you through it, and soon you will have a new baby in the house."

I could hear Martin pacing back and forth in the living room. I always thought it was funny how big, strong men were scared of childbirth. Nevertheless, I was blessed that all my children had come so easy and fast. I was thankful for that.

About noon I went to the kitchen to see how Martin was doing. He was scrounging up something for lunch. I told him the baby was still a few hours away and grabbed a little food for Augusta. "You need to have a little something to eat to keep your strength up," I coached her. "You will need all the energy you can get soon. I think the baby is going to come before supper by the looks of things."

"Oh, thank God," she replied. "I don't think I could take much more of this. The pains started last night. I never dreamed it would take this long," she said, as she felt another strong contraction pass.

"OK, now breathe through the pain, and concentrate on breathing in and out slowly. You can get through this," I encouraged her.

When the time came, I instructed her to pull back on her legs and push as hard as she could. I could tell it wasn't going to go quite as smoothly as my deliveries, but it was not the first time I had delivered a baby. Even though I always had a knot in my stomach, I was always able to keep calm and do what needed to be done. I recalled delivering stillborn babies and how awful the experience was for the parents. I prayed silently, *Lord, please keep this baby safe, and help me to do what is needed to take care of it and Augusta.*

At four o'clock, a pink baby girl was born. It cried heartily, which I liked, and kicked and flailed away. Augusta was shocked when she saw her baby. I think mothers get so distracted by labor pains that they forget a baby is being born. I cut the cord and cleaned the baby off, then placed her in Augusta's arms. Her eyes were wide and in awe of what just happened.

"She is so tiny and beautiful," Augusta said, as she checked her child's fingers and toes. "Martin may be disappointed that it's not a boy. He was hoping for a boy to help him farm."

"Well, it would be many years before the child could help," I said. "I think he will love his little girl just as much. I'll go get him so he can see his new daughter."

When I entered the other room, Martin just stared at me. He had heard the baby cry and now all was quiet. "Belle, is everything OK?" Martin asked. "I heard a baby crying and then it stopped. How is Augusta doing?"

"You have a fine baby girl, Martin. She looks to be about six pounds and has a good set of lungs. Would you like to go in and meet her?"

I didn't have to ask again as he was out of the chair and into the bedroom before I could say more.

When everything with baby and Mama was OK, I said goodbye to Martin and Augusta and their new baby girl, Matilda. As I rode back to our home and our family, I thought, *I hope we have more babies. They are such a blessing.*

20

NOVEMBER 1887 TO JANUARY 1888

THE WEATHER WAS MILD for November, and we were enjoying the warm temperatures and sunshine because we knew winter was just around the corner. Ingvold was able to get another stack of hay up by the barn and move the cattle and sheep into the farm yard.

We were enjoying a cup of coffee one morning when suddenly we saw Martin riding into our yard pell-mell. "What could be wrong now?" Ingvold asked as he put his coat on and headed out the door.

Martin was breathless and could barely get his words out. "Belle, you have to come! Something is wrong with Matilda! She isn't breathing. Come quick!" Ingvold quickly hitched up the team and we raced to Martin's house.

When we entered the house, Augusta was seated in the rocker holding little Matilda in her arms and crying uncontrollably. "Matilda, Matilda," she said through sobs, "please wake up!"

I took one look at the baby and knew it was no use. She was gone, and nothing I could do would bring her back. I knew and felt Augusta's profound pain all too well. We sat in silence as Martin and Augusta held each other and Matilda for a long time. Then I softly asked to take the baby in the other room where I cleaned her up and wrapped her in a new blanket.

I heard Ingvold saying, "Martin, there are plots at the Norwegian cemetery where Mom and Dad are going to be buried and where little Christian is. That's just down the road, so you will be close and can visit her grave often. That will be comforting to you both. We should go now and arrange the burial before the ground freezes again."

I brought little Matilda out and let Martin hold her one more time; then he and Ingvold left to arrange the burial. I placed little Matilda into Augusta's arms and recalled how joyful she was when Matilda was born. Now her joy was replaced by unspeakable sadness and sorrow. With tears running down her face, she kissed little Matilda tenderly and held her close. No words would help at this point. I just let her grieve as she held her little girl for the last time.

Ingvold met with our family members to inform them of Matilda's passing. That afternoon he made a small casket for Matilda, and I lined it with a pretty pink blanket I had been keeping for our next girl. I figured I could make more blankets easily enough.

The next morning, we all gathered at the old cemetery where a small grave had been dug. Martin carried the small casket and placed it into the grave. Augusta knelt next to the grave weeping.

Nothing could console her. Martin took her arm and led her back to the buggy. We left before the dirt was placed over Matilda's casket. A beautiful life cut too short.

The twelfth of January dawned bright and unseasonably warm. The children wanted to go out to play, so I let them. They had their jackets on, but it was warm enough to play without hats and mittens. We had finished milking the cows and were bringing hay to the cattle when suddenly the wind shifted, and the temperature dropped.

"Wow must be a storm coming. I haven't seen temperatures drop that fast before," said Ingvold. "I think we are in for a doozy. I think I'll string the rope between the house and barn before things get crazy around here."

I had just finished shutting the barn door and getting the children into the house when I heard ice hitting the windows. I thought the windows might break because the ice was so heavy. Soon I couldn't see out the window to the barn. *Ingvold! Did he get the rope strung before the storm hit?* I opened the door and tried to call his name, but I could only hear the wind howling at a high pitch. I shut the door and prayed. Suddenly the door burst open with a gust of wind, and there was Ingvold looking like a frozen snowman.

"Ingvold, I was so scared that you couldn't find your way to the house. This storm came on so suddenly," I said as I helped him take off his coat.

"I know, I haven't seen anything like this in all my born days! I am worried about the kids at school," he said. "I hope they all had sense enough to stay put and not try to make it home. I'm happy that Mary is not in school yet, or she may have been trapped there. Who knows how long this could keep up."

As the afternoon wore on, the storm only intensified. When it was time to milk, Ingvold told me to stay inside with the kids. "No use both of us risking our life out there. I can do it OK." With that, he was out the door with a gust of wind. The children and I fixed supper and kept the cook stove going. It was hard to keep it lit because the wood burned twice as fast as usual. The children would need to sleep downstairs by the fire as it was too cold upstairs. They were excited about that, and Mary and John got to work bringing the mattresses and bed clothes down. Two hours later Ingvold came through the door, red-faced and covered with snow.

"Ingvold, come sit by the fire and have some hot coffee. How are the animals doing?" I asked.

"Well," he said, as he warmed his hands by the fire, "they are hunkered down, but I worry that their faces might freeze over and they won't be able to breathe. There's nothing I can do about that. We will just have to wait until the storm stops to assess the damage. The milkers are warm and content in the barn, and I brought the sheep into the barn before the storm hit. We have a good supply of hay in there, so I don't think we'll run out. I brought a small pail of milk for us, but I was unable to bring all of it. I'm sorry, but I had to dump it. The cats were having a hay day!"

"How's Lucky?" John asked. "Is he safe in the barn too?"

"He's keeping the cats warm," said Ingvold. "Now let's pray that everyone else is safe and warm in their homes, and that the school children were able to make it home before the storm. If not, we pray they are safe at the school and can keep the fire going," Ingvold said, as we bowed our heads.

"Let's eat!" John said at the conclusion of the prayer. "I'm hungry!"

The next day, the storm raged on while Ingvold made the trip to the barn to milk the cows and feed the animals. The snow drifted up so high that we couldn't see out of our windows. Ingvold had to scoop a path every day to the barn, being careful to stay close to the rope line. Every time he left to go to the barn, I prayed that he would find his way back to our family.

On the third day, I stood on a chair and saw the storm had subsided and the sun was out. I went to the barn with Ingvold that morning and helped him scoop a path through the snow. When we got to the barn, the cows were mooing, waiting to be milked. We milked and fed the animals and then we headed out to check on the cattle in the yard. What we saw was shocking.

The cattle were all standing in a circle with their heads together. The snow had drifted over them and only their frozen faces and closed eyes were showing. We heard no sounds or signs of life. Only when the snow melted in the spring would we be able to do anything about them. For now, they were frozen in time.

Just then we heard a faint mooing and looked around. There, standing up next to the barn was a cow, covered with snow. We made our way over to it, freed it from its icy encasement, and slowly led it to the barn. Inside we warmed it with our mittened hands and gave it some water and feed. When we left, it was munching happily. It was the only cow out of twenty to survive.

When we got to the house, the kids wanted to know all about it, and of course they wanted to know about Lucky.

Ingvold smiled. "Lucky was so happy to get out of that barn that he plunged head long into a drift and disappeared. But soon we saw his head again and he leapt into the snow. We think he was playing in the snow. He loved it."

Later that day, some men came to our house and asked if Ingvold could help them search for some of the school children who didn't make it home. They were going to try to check the school first. Ingvold dressed warmly and left with them. I had a hard time concentrating that afternoon as one of the children was Ole's son Thomas, and I feared they might be looking for him. He had been such a great help for us the previous summer, and we had grown close to him.

About the time the sun was setting, the men dropped Ingvold off and went on their way. I tried to read Ingvold's face as he walked up to the house.

"How are the children?" I asked before he even shut the door. "How about Thomas?"

"Thomas stayed home from school that day because he hadn't been feeling well. So, we can be thankful he is just fine," Ingvold said. "The others were all safe and sound in the school house, thanks to the wise teacher. Some of the kids wanted to try to get home, but she prevented them from leaving.

I tell you it is rough out there. The snow is so high, and we had a hard time scooping it to get through with the team. We were able to deliver all the children to their homes, and you can imagine how the parents felt when they saw us pull into their yard with their children in tow. I'm sure there is loss of life around here, but we will have to wait until the snow melts to search for people that may be missing."

That night we knelt by our bed and thanked God that He had kept us safe and returned all the school children to their homes and families.

21

SUMMER 1888

Spring brought a lot of sadness as the melting snow revealed the frozen bodies of both people and animals that had been killed and buried by the terrible blizzard. One teacher was found huddled together with her pupils in a snow drift. Many funerals were held in the county. Those who didn't experience loss of human life were thankful. In all, we lost about twenty cows. Though the roads were a mess from melting snow, people endured the mud to visit their neighbors.

Soon, the land was dry enough to plant, and the wild flowers were blooming. I loved spring; it was my favorite season. The fields were full of wild roses and Queen Ann's Lace, one of my favorite flowers. The land was bustling with new life, including our new calves and little lambs. Mary and John loved to bottle-feed the orphaned ones. One little lamb followed John all over the farm. John named him 'Blacky,' as he was the only black sheep born that spring.

John's colt was born, and John named him Dakota. He would go out to the fenced area where Dakota was corralled and feed him sugar cubes. He loved when Dakota would come to the fence and eat the cubes out of his hand, then toss his head and run to the other side of the corral to his mother. Soon, Dakota would be turned out to a pasture where he could really kick up his heels. John watched intently as Ingvold gently led Dakota around the coral. Dakota seemed to like being led.

"I think he will be easy to train," Ingvold said one day. "Maybe by fall you will be able to sit on him a little, John. By next summer, you will be riding him all over the place."

"I can't wait Papa, but isn't he big enough for me to sit on now?" John asked.

"No John, we have to wait until he gets used to the bridle first and then slowly train him with a blanket on his back before anyone rides him. It will be soon enough."

Throughout the winter I had knitted and sewed new clothing for the kids, as well as some small things for a baby we hoped to have. Each time I opened the drawer where the little things were kept, I longed for a baby to fill them. Imagine my joy when summer arrived and we found out I would be having a baby in January. We were filled with new hope again.

Thomas, Ole's son, helped us in the field again throughout the summer, and John, who would be six in November, milked the easy-milking cows and helped Mary with the chores. They were good workers and took turns watching three-year-old Tommy. Eight-year-old Mary now had two students to teach and she relished every minute of it. Having learned to read a little, she was excited to start school in the fall and continue learning.

"Mama, when will school start?" she asked one day. "I can't wait to learn how to read and write. Then I can read books and write letters to my Auntie Caroline and cousins. I can really teach Johnny and Tommy school then. I'll make sure they will be ready for school when it comes time for them to go," she said in a grown-up tone.

"That's great, Mary, I know you will do well in school, and someday you may be a teacher," I said. "School will start in a couple of months. We are so proud of you and will always remember how you taught the boys. Now let's get the dinner on the table. Papa will be home soon, and he will be looking for his meal."

When Ingvold came into the yard that day, John ran to tell him that Dakota came to him when he called. "He knows I am his owner," John said proudly.

"Well, I guess he does know you're his owner if he comes when you call," Ingvold said. "He is learning his name and getting to know you pretty well. By next spring he will be ready for you to ride while I lead him, and by the fall you can ride him yourself. Now let's go see what Mama has cooked up for us."

The garden was coming along nicely, and the children helped weed it and carry the fertilizer from the barn. Ingvold had purchased a few cows and hoped to have new calves to replace the ones we lost by the following spring.

Tommy was learning to talk, and when Ingvold came into the house he would say, "Ride Papa." Then he would sit on one of Ingvold's boots and cling to his leg as Ingvold walked him around the house. Tommy loved that. It reminded me of when Ingvold did the same for little Peter and Amil when we first met him.

"Now, horsey, Papa!" Tommy yelled with glee. Then Ingvold would get down on his hands and knees and give Tommy a ride around the kitchen.

"OK, Tommy, horsey is tired now. Better let him out to the pasture," Ingvold would say.

The children were growing like weeds. I had to make all new clothes for Mary before she started school. She loved trying on the dresses I made for her, and she would prance around the room for Johnny and Tommy. They were not interested, but they acted like they were judges at the fair and clapped for her vigorously.

In September, Mary was walking to school every day, swinging her dinner pail and looking very mature. Nevertheless, I was sad seeing her off to school; the house was so quiet without her singing, and I missed her help with the house work. The boys missed their sister too and often waited by the window for her to return from school every day.

"Mama, Mama, here comes Mary! Can I run and meet her?" Johnny asked.

"Yes, you can, but wait at the end of the driveway for her," I said.

He was out the door in a flash and waited for Mary to get to the yard. They walked to the house while Mary told him all about her day.

"Mary, tell us all about your day at school. Did you meet new friends, and do you like your teacher?" I asked as we sat down at the table. She was so excited and relayed everything that happened that day, including an accident in which a boy hit a ball into a girl's face. "She was OK, but kind of shook up about it. The teacher said she would have a shiner for sure," Mary said.

When Ingvold came in and said, "Time to milk," everyone headed to the barn. With four of us milking, it didn't take long to finish. After all the livestock were fed, we went into the house. Of course, Mary had to repeat everything she had told me so Ingvold could hear all about it. Mary hardly took time to eat as she shared nearly every moment of her day.

After the dishes were done, we did our Bible study and headed to bed. I was growing increasingly tired, which was a side effect of pregnancy I knew all too well. I didn't care though; I cherished each day and loved being pregnant.

Fall was beautiful, and I loved looking over the valley and seeing the beautifully colored trees down by the creek. Next to spring, fall was my favorite time of year.

We were well prepared for the winter. The garden was harvested, the produce was stored in the fruit cellar, the cattle and sheep were brought up to the farm yard and bedded down, and even the haying was done. This allowed Ingvold to spend more time with the family, and we made the most of our time together.

The snow started falling in November around Johnny's birthday. Mary was home from school until March or April because the school officials didn't want to risk exposing the children to another terrible winter. Mary was not happy about staying home with the boys, but I kept her busy sewing and baking bread and cookies. She also learned how to wash clothes with the wash board. She didn't like doing that so much, but she was always willing to help.

The kids loved sitting next to me with their hands on my tummy, waiting for the baby to kick. When it did, they would laugh and John would say, "The baby kicks like a boy!"

Thanksgiving and Christmas passed uneventfully with lots of family gathering and good cheer, and soon it was 1889.

1889

ON THE MORNING OF January 8, 1889, I awakened to the excitement of contractions. I was almost sure we would have a new family member by the end of the day. I got up and started the coffee, and Ingvold helped with breakfast. We let the children sleep longer since Mary didn't have to get ready for school. It was a great time for us to just sit and talk about things. I said, "I think the baby may arrive today. I have had contractions since about four in the morning."

"Do you want me to get someone to help you?" Ingvold asked. "I know you usually like to just handle it yourself, but I could ride over to Ole's and see if Caroline could come and stay until the baby is here."

"No, I prefer to do it myself. I can't concentrate when someone else is fussing around the room. I don't expect any problems. I'll be fine," I replied.

A few minutes later the children were tumbling down the stairs saying, "We're hungry, Mama, what's for breakfast?"

"Papa made his special pancakes today, thank you, Papa," I prompted them.

"Oh, boy," Johnny said, "I'm hungry for a lot of pancakes!"

"Pancakes, pancakes," little Tommy said.

As Ingvold dished up the pancakes he said, "Today you may have a new brother or sister, so I want you all to help Mama around the house. John and I will take care of the milking today."

"OK, Papa, you and I can handle the cows, and Mary can stay inside to watch Tommy and help Mama. That's a girl's job," John said in a grown-up voice.

After breakfast John and Ingvold headed outside while Mary and I cleaned the dishes. Tommy happily played with the wood blocks on the rug, and my contractions continued. Later that morning when Ingvold and John came inside, I was sure the baby was going to arrive soon because my contractions were about six minutes apart and regular.

Later that day while Ingvold and John were outside pitching more hay into the barn for the cattle, Tommy napped and the house was quiet. My contractions were now only about two minutes apart, but something wasn't right. Unlike my other deliveries, the pains were very intense, and I felt like my back was going to break.

I grabbed the bed post and held on to get through the contractions. *Was I losing it? Could there be something wrong that I couldn't handle?* By four o'clock the pain was excruciating, and I was losing control and scared.

When I reached down to probe for the baby's head, I was terrified by what I felt. It was not a baby's head, that was for sure. I was certain I was having a breech baby. I screamed in agony, and Mary came running to the bedroom. When she saw my predicament, her eyes grew wide with fear, and she held her hands over her ears to shut out my screams.

"Mary, run fast to get Papa! I need his help!" I screamed.

I could feel the next contraction coming on, and I didn't think I could endure another one. But I had no choice. I prayed Mary would bring Ingvold soon. I know he had helped animals with breech births and prayed he could help. It isn't easy to deliver a breech baby, and many times the baby doesn't make it. Sometimes even the mother dies. I had seen it all before.

A minute later Ingvold was at my side. I told him the baby was upside-down in my birth canal and said, "Ingvold, you have to stay calm to carefully maneuver the baby and try to get the feet out first. Then you will have to get the head out, which is the biggest part of the baby. You will need to work fast—or the baby will die and I might too!"

Another contraction hit like a freight train and made me scream again. Ingvold took hold of the baby's bottom and tried to reach up and find the legs. One came down without too much problem, but the other one was stuck. It was excruciating to have him maneuvering the baby while I was having contractions. I begged him to stop, but I knew he couldn't if the baby and I were to be saved.

Suddenly the other leg came out, and the rest of the body followed. With one last push, the head emerged, and out came our little daughter. But she wasn't breathing and looked blue and lifeless. Ingvold quickly held her upside down, gave her a good slap on her bottom, and sighed with relief when she started to cry. That was the most beautiful sound I ever heard. I was bleeding badly; but after massaging my abdomen, my uterus contracted and the after birth came out easily.

Ingvold held the baby and looked like he had just been through the worst experience ever. His face was pale, and he was sweating profusely.

"Belle, I don't ever want to do that again," he said, as he cradled our new little daughter in his arms. The good news is, she doesn't seem the worse for wear, considering everything she has gone through. Will you cut the cord? My hands are shaking."

"She is happy her papa was here to help her mama and so am I," I said as I sunk deeper into the bed, totally exhausted. Ingvold put the baby on my chest, and I cut her cord. Then I held her close and prayed to God, *Thank you God for being here to help me.*

"Ingvold, go and get the children so they can meet their new sister, Ellen." I said.

Soon, the children were tramping down the stairs and at the door of the bedroom. Mary still looked very scared and didn't want to come close to me. "Mary, it's OK, sometimes mamas experience more pain in order to get the baby here. I am sorry that you had to see and hear that."

"Mama, I don't ever want to have a baby! I don't want to have that terrible pain," she said.

"Mary, I'm sure you will have lots of babies, and you will forget all about the pain it took to bring them into the world," I said. "Now come and say hello to your little sister, Ellen. She will grow up to be your best friend."

I was overjoyed to have all my children gathered around the bed looking at little Ellen with awe. Mary decided she would like to hold her, so Ingvold let her sit on the bed and cradle her little sister in her arms. She rocked her back and forth and said, "It's OK, Ellen, don't cry. I will always take care of you, and we will be best friends forever."

Before we knew it, spring had arrived and the farm work was back in full swing. We loved having Ellen with our family, and she was dear to everyone. She was a good baby and she loved to sit on Papa's lap as he sang his "Trot, Trot, Trot" song. She giggled and clapped her hands as she tried to sit upright on his lap. The more she giggled, the more the horsey would trot.

Ingvold was very busy on the farm, but we had Ole's son helping again. Ingvold helped Ole the previous fall, and the crops were good. With Ellen tied to my apron, I took care of the milking with Mary and John. Ellen loved the cows and would try to see what was going on all the time. When she was strong enough to sit up, she sat on a blanket and played with corn cobs or just watched us work and sucked her thumb.

Ingvold thought I should do something to make her stop sucking her thumb. "She should not suck her thumb, Mama; it will make her teeth crooked," he said as he pulled the thumb out of her mouth.

"Oh, Ingvold, don't worry. When a baby sucks their thumb, it shows intelligence. She will be a thinker. Besides, it keeps her occupied and helps me get more done."

Ellen was a very smart baby. Not that she was any more intelligent than our other children, but she seemed to be thinking all the time. She was walking by the time she was eight months old. She always stood by the window, sucking her thumb and observing. I don't know what she was seeing, but I could sense the little wheels were turning in her head. Maybe she was thinking about going out into the big world by herself and what she would accomplish. From the very start, when she decided she wanted something, she went after it.

Of course, Mary tried to school her with the boys, but she was restless and couldn't sit for any length of time. Still, she loved her big sister and would follow her all over the house. Besides Mama and Papa, one of her first words was "Maye," for Mary.

One fall day as we were out milking the cows, I noticed Ellen wasn't on her blanket and was nowhere to be seen. "Mary," I said, "go find your sister and bring her back. She can't be far because I just saw her sitting there. She is so fast!"

A few minutes later Mary returned with Ellen in tow and said, "Guess where she was? I found her sitting by a lamb—one of the ones that we bottle-fed this spring. She was just sitting next to the fence, and the lamb was lying next to her. She was petting the lamb through the fence. She was so cute, Mama."

"Well, we all better keep a closer eye on her now that she is mobile. We don't want anything to happen to our little Ellen," I said.

In the fall we harvested our crops and brought in the garden produce as usual. I was happy that the garden was doing so well. We had planted some trees Ingvold found down by the river, and I hoped that someday they would grow tall so the children could play under them.

I longed for the trees of Sweden. Where we lived in Dakota there were very few trees, but I liked that I could see for miles and miles. The sunsets were beautiful with all the radiant colors across the sky. And the stars! We loved to sit outside and just watch the stars on a clear night.

John's birthday was getting closer, and he was excited to be turning seven. Papa said he could ride his pony around with Papa leading it the following summer, and that was all he talked about. He was growing so fast and would be starting school the next fall.

Ingvold got wood for our stove. Between the wood and the haystacks we made, we were able to keep the house warm through another frigid winter.

1889

THAT SPRING, INGVOLD WAS true to his word and let Johnny ride Dakota while he led him. John was a natural and sat so straight and tall on the horse. Dakota took to having him on his back just fine and walked slowly so John wouldn't tumble off.

"Papa, I think Dakota is the smartest horse that ever lived," John said one day. "He just seems to know where we should go, like maybe he doesn't need to be led anymore."

"Well, Johnny, it's been awhile since he has been ridden," said Ingvold. "We have worked with him this winter, so we need to make sure he still remembers what we taught him. I will lead him first while you sit on him, then you can reign him and see if he obeys. He may not like it at first and might try to buck you off his back, but I think in a few weeks you can ride him by yourself," Ingvold said.

At supper that night Johnny piped up, "Mama, guess what, Papa said I can ride Dakota myself."

"Ingvold, do you think John is ready to ride by himself?" I asked, "I worry about him handling Dakota. I'm concerned that Dakota is still a little too young and rambunctious."

"Oh, snicklefritz! I was riding a horse myself by John's age and did fine," Ingvold said. "I will make sure both of them are ready to venture out by themselves. We have a couple more months to work on this, but I think by next summer he will be able to ride without much problem. Next fall John will start school, and he and Mary can ride Dakota to school every day."

Mary jumped in. "Papa! Maybe I should have a horse too."

"No, Mary, I don't think you are strong enough to handle a horse," Ingvold said. "I will teach you to drive the team when you get older. Women like to drive the buggy so they can do their shopping. I know Mama goes to town to shop and to catch up on the latest gossip," Ingvold teased as he gave me a wink.

"We don't gossip, Ingvold, but there is always a new baby or something to talk about. It gets pretty lonely out here with only you and the kids to talk to," I retorted.

"How about the cows? You like to sing to them," Ingvold teased.

One day Johnny piped up at breakfast. "Papa, I think today is the day we should see if Dakota will ride with just me leading him."

"Well, son, I think it is a grand day to try that. Let's go out to the barn and get him saddled up," Ingvold said. "He's done quite well with you on his back and being led, but the real test is having you in the saddle alone. We don't need any buckin' broncos around here," Ingvold said.

"Oh, please, no," I interrupted. "Please be careful, Ingvold. I don't want to make a trip to town for broken bones."

By fall, John was riding Dakota all around the yard and Ingvold even let him ride over to Martin's place to get some practice.

School started in August, and John and Mary rode Dakota to the schoolhouse. John kept Dakota in the school stable, as many children rode their horses to school.

That night when they returned home, John announced that everything was just fine with the horse and they experienced no problems. "He just followed my lead and didn't give me any trouble. I think he liked being at school too," John said.

"I'm sure he did," Ingvold said with a smile. "Horses are natural students. That is the best place for them, so they can learn all about being a horse and what to do when they grow up."

"Papa, did you know that Dakota Territory will be divided between North Dakota and South Dakota this year? I learned that in school today," Mary said in an official tone.

"Well, yes I had heard that. I knew it was in the works and hoped it would happen. We'll be one of the United States now," Ingvold told her. "Now we better get the milking done so we can eat."

"I'm hungry as a bear," John said imitating his father. "Going to school makes me hungry. Let's get this milking done fast so we can have some of that pie I spied on the counter."

November came and Mary and John were out of school until March or so. It was far from quiet around the house with all the kids underfoot. Much to John's chagrin, Mary kept up with her school work, but he was good at reading, and Ingvold had him read Bible verses during Sunday school each week.

"I like reading the Bible, Papa. I think it says some important things besides all the boring stuff," John said one day.

"Yes, the Bible is important, even the boring stuff," Ingvold replied. "If we live by what the Bible says we will be happier for it. Do you want to learn to read your Mother's Swedish Bible?"

"Oh, no, Papa. I could never learn to read Swedish. I can say some things but learning to read it is hard. It's just a bunch of mumble jumble as far as I can see."

"Well," Ingvold said, "remember, that no matter what language it's in, it still says the same thing. God helped people write it in different languages so everyone on the earth could know about Him. Isn't that wonderful?"

"Yes," John said, "and I believe it is the most important book around. We read it every day at school too. And we always say a prayer before our lunch."

On November first of that year, John complained of aching and feeling tired. We knew something wasn't right because he didn't want to work or eat. We let him stay in the house while we did the milking as he was just too ill to go out with us.

About three weeks later, his temperature increased, and he was unable to keep anything down. I put him to bed, and he stayed there for the next week. I thought he just needed to rest, and I tried to get him to take fluids. I became deeply concerned when he stayed in bed a few more days and grew weaker and weaker.

"Ingvold, I don't think he is getting better," I said. "Now he is coughing a lot, and his temperature is still high. I'm afraid he may have developed pneumonia. I think we should get the doctor to come and see what more we could do."

That morning John was listless and still coughing, and I had a hard time getting him to wake up. Ingvold rode into town and fetched the doctor. The doctor came back with Ingvold, examined John, then motioned us to come out into the hallway to talk.

"Ingvold, I am afraid there is not much that can be done. He sounds like he has pneumonia, and once that happens, it is unlikely he will survive. I am so sorry to give you this news. About all you can do is keep him comfortable. It is just a matter of time now. You should prepare for the worst."

"No!" I cried, "There must be something that can be done for him. I am not willing to just sit by and watch him die!"

"Belle, don't get upset now. Let's ask the Lord to make him well," Ingvold said "Lord, we have had a lot of losses and have lost two children. We are asking that you spare John and bring him back to health so he can be with our family. He means so much to us, and we just can't think about the possibility of losing him. But I know things happen according to Your will, so we trust that whatever happens is in Your hands. Amen."

We showed the doctor to the door and joined the children in the kitchen, where they had been anxiously waiting, to tell them the news.

"Is he going to get better, Papa?" Mary asked

"Kids, the doctor said Johnny may not live because he is so sick," Ingvold said softly. "We need to begin accepting that he may die. Of course, we need to keep praying God will heal him, but sometimes God doesn't answer the way we want. We must trust God and accept whatever happens. God will be with us no matter what. Remember that."

That night after we got the kids in bed, Ingvold and I went in to check on Johnny one more time. I was preparing to sit at his bedside all night so he wouldn't be alone. Ingvold was going to get some sleep and would join me about midnight. Johnny seemed to be coughing less and was sleeping quietly. I touched his arm and said. "John, how do you feel tonight? You look better."

He opened his eyes and said, "Mama, I am a little hungry; could I have something to eat?" he said weakly. "I thought I heard the doctor say I was going to die. Is that what he said? Well, when I heard that, I just said to myself, I will not die! When you came in here and woke me up, I was already feeling so much better. I thought maybe I was in heaven."

"Oh, Johnny, of course you can have something to eat!" I said, trying to hold back tears of joy. "I will get you some nice cool water and milk toast. Does that sound good? Papa will stay here with you while I fix your supper."

With that, I went into the kitchen and continued to pray, *Thank you, God, for making Johnny better. I know that it may not be in the clear yet, but I am thankful there is at least a chance he will come out of this.* Then I lovingly fixed him the milk toast and brought it up to him.

Ingvold was sitting by his bed holding his hand and telling him all about how he had been sick when he was small and how the Lord helped him get better. "Johnny, I know you will grow up and be a strong man of God someday," he said, his voice filled with new hope.

24

1890

B Y THE BEGINNING OF 1890, John had almost fully recovered. Mary took it upon herself to help him regain his strength by walking with him around the house. He was very weak from spending so much time in bed that he had to learn to walk again. Day by day he grew stronger, and he could soon walk by himself and go out with us to watch the milking. It was a miracle.

"Papa, I am so happy that I am on the mend, I don't think I could take another day of sitting around the house being taught by Mary," John said. "She is a good teacher I guess, but I missed going out and seeing Dakota and Lucky. I think they missed me too as they both came running to greet me this morning when we came out to milk. Lucky could hardly stop licking me, and Dakota nuzzled his nose under my arm, asking me to pet him—or maybe he was looking for that sugar cube I had in my pocket!"

"I am sure they missed you terribly," I said. "I don't know if you remember this, but when you were so sick, and we didn't know if you would come out of it, I consented to letting Papa bring Lucky into the house to lay by you a while. He seemed so lost without you around, and I think he felt better knowing you hadn't left him."

"I didn't have to twist her arm too much," Papa said. "Mama really has a soft heart for Lucky, but she doesn't want to admit it. I think she would have him in the house more, but he really is happier being outside with the animals. Besides, the cats would miss him because he is their bed warmer."

Spring was beautiful and brought with it more birds than I had seen in a while. I loved hearing them sing in the morning. Our little trees were getting bigger, and our farm yard looked neat and well kept. How I loved the farm we had built. We made so many good memories there, and the Lord had been good to us.

More calves and lambs were being born every day, and Johnny and Mary kept busy caring for them. Tommy was now five and loved to tag along with them and try to help. He was a natural farmer and was soon carrying armloads of hay to the animals. He loved the chickens and had taken over the chicken chores. They loved him too and came running anytime he came into their yard. We sold our excess eggs and the butter I had churned to the market in town. It felt good to be helping with the expenses.

When planting time came, Mary and John were a big help. Ingvold taught nine-year-old Mary to stack hay into shocks while John rode Dakota to the field. All the extra help allowed me to spend more time with Tommy and Ellen. Tommy wanted to go with his siblings, but I convinced him that it would be better to stay home with Mama and Sissy, help with things around the house, and keep an eye on the chickens.

Tommy loved the cats, and he and Ellen would play for hours with them. Sometimes the cats let Ellen catch them, but she spent most of the time chasing them around the yard.

One day Tommy and Ellen came running into the house out of breath and announced, "We have kitties, Mama! I can count, and Minnie had six kitties and Blacky had seven. Minnie won't pay any mind to one of the kitties, but she is giving the other ones a lot of attention!"

"Well, let's just go out and see what those mama kitties are doing," I said. In the barn, Tommy climbed to the loft, and Ellen and I followed. "Here they are, Mama! Minnie is over there in the corner," Tommy said.

After checking on Blacky, we made our way over to Minnie and her litter. There they were. They looked to be about a day old and so very small. But one kitty was lying by itself and didn't look like it would live too long. "Tommy, sometimes if a kitty is not too strong the mama will leave it alone, and not feed it like the others," I said. "How about if we take it in the house and see if we can feed it. But it may not live. We have to accept that maybe it is too little, and no matter what we would do it might die anyway."

"Mama, I want to feed it, but how can we do that?" asked Tommy

"Let's go in the house and see what we can find," I said, as I gently picked up the kitten and we headed to the house.

When we got inside, I let Ellen cuddle the kitten and keep it warm while I fixed some warm milk and put it in an eye dropper.

Tommy gently put the dropper to the kitten's mouth, and it actually started sucking.

"Look, Mama! The kitty is drinking. He's hungry!" Tommy said jubilantly.

Tommy named the kitty Tippy and dutifully checked on him. All black with cute white accents, he was an irresistible little creature. Ellen made a little bed by the stove, and by the end of the day when Ingvold and the children came in, Tippy's belly was full, and he was quite content.

"What's this?" Ingvold asked when he saw the little bed by the stove. "Are we running a nursery here now? Looks like this cat may not make it. But I have been known to be wrong a couple of times. Tommy, what did you name the cat?"

"I call him Tippy because he has a white tip on the end of his tail. Look Papa!" he said, as he gently picked up the kitten and showed it to Ingvold and the other children. "Mama said if he eats real good his eyes will open. Mama, I think it's time to feed Tippy again."

"I think it's time to feed *our family*," Ingvold laughed. "Looks like Mama was able to get some other things done besides rescuing a cat because I smell something wonderful coming from the oven."

Soon we were all around the big table and talking about the day between bites. Mary and Johnny had a lot of stories to tell about their day in the field. Of course, the rescued kitty was the highlight of Tommy' day.

As I listened to the children talk, I noticed Tommy had fallen asleep on the table. "It was a busy day for Tommy, and he missed his nap," I said.

Ingvold carried him up to his bed, tucked him in, and came back down to finish his meal. "The little guy really worked hard today nurturing the cat," he said. "I guess we'll have to keep it up at night, so I will take the first half and Mama the second. Maybe in a few days we can bring him to his mama and see if she will accept him."

After feeding the kitten another day, I suggested taking Tippy out to the barn again. "It's really better that kitties have milk from their mamas, not from cows, and he needs his mama to teach him how to hunt and find food," I explained.

"But Mama, I want to take care of Tippy," Tommy protested.

"Tommy, it's better for Tippy to be with his mother, just like it's better for you to be with yours. After lunch let's take him out to the barn and see what happens," I said.

After the kitchen was cleaned up, Tommy and Ellen followed me out to the barn. Minnie was nursing her kittens. I gently put Tippy next to his siblings and encouraged him to nurse. Right away he latched on and happily began nursing.

"See, Tommy, now he can get milk from his mama and get to know his brothers and sisters," I said. "They will play all day when they get older. You can come and check on Tippy every day and make sure he's doing okay with his family." Tommy seemed okay with that so we moved on to Blacky's family. The babies were all sleeping in a ball, and Blacky was nowhere to be found.

"Mama, where did Blacky go? Why did she leave her kitties alone?" Tommy asked.

"Well, Tommy, mama kitties have to hunt for food so they have milk for their babies," I said. "She will return before they wake up. She is probably hunting for a nice, fat mouse to eat."

"Will babies eat a mouse?" Ellen asked.

"No, not yet, but Mama has to eat," I replied.

Back in the house we got things ready for Ingvold's lunch. The children loved to bring Papa lunch so they could see what he, John, and Mary were doing out in the field. It was a beautiful day for a walk, and Ellen stopped and picked wildflowers along the way.

John came running first, followed by Ingvold and Mary. I was so proud to see Mary helping Ingvold. She thought of him as her father, and Ingvold loved her as his own daughter.

When Tommy and Ellen saw their father coming, they ran to meet him. Ingvold lifted Ellen high in the air and she squealed and laughed. Tommy just wanted to be near him, and Ingvold lifted him up but struggled to put him above his head.

"Tommy," Ingvold grunted, as he put him back down, "you are getting so big! Soon you will be out here helping in the field."

Tommy puffed his chest out and said, "I will be a good farmer, you just wait and see."

Summer was soon upon us, and the crops were looking good; we had just enough rain at the right time for them to really flourish. My garden was also abundant. I was picking produce daily, and we were enjoying fresh vegetables with our meals. Tommy and Ellen helped me hoe and pull weeds. Ellen loved to pick the beans off the vines, and Tommy used the hoe with skill. He was careful not to chop out the plants.

One day Tommy yelled, "Mama, there is a snake in our garden! I can get it with the hoe."

"No, Tommy, we need to let it be as it will eat things that will hurt our garden. Just shoo it away and let it be," I said. But it was too late because he was already chasing it across the yard with his hoe. When he came back, he was clearly proud he had defended his Mama and Ellen like a man should.

By late summer, I was pretty sure that I was pregnant again because I barely had enough strength to clean up the garden and finish storing the produce. It had been two years since Ellen was born, and I was excited about adding a new member to our family. As I reflected on Ellen's difficult birth, I shuddered in fear and wondered, *what if this baby is a breach baby like Ellen?* Then I reminded myself I had six totally normal deliveries in the past, so everything would probably be fine.

In October I broke the news to Ingvold one evening while we were enjoying the sunset. "Ingvold, do you feel like someone is missing from our family?" I asked.

"Well, I miss Amil and little Peter terribly, but I am satisfied with our family now. Why do you ask?"

"Well, we'll have another baby coming in March or April. I've been feeling like our family just wasn't complete, and when I realized I was expecting, I felt so happy and excited."

Ingvold took me in his arms, kissed me, and said. "I told you I'll be happy as a lark with a bunch of kids. Whatever you want, I am more than willing to help," he said, with a smile on his face and a twinkle in his eye.

Then we relaxed and looked up at the beautiful stars God had planted in the sky. I said softly, "We are so blessed, and God is so good." Ingvold shared my gratitude.

1891

After a frigid but mostly uneventful winter, our farm was starting to show signs of spring. Green shoots of grass and flowers poked out from the thawing ground, and only a few small snow banks remained around the buildings.

I was feeling excited about our soon-to-be-born baby and wondered if it would be a boy or a girl. Of course, Ingvold wanted another boy, but I hoped for a girl so Ellen would have a playmate. She had turned two in January and was a very busy little girl. I thought it would be good for her to have a sister her age to play with and keep her occupied.

With Ellen and a new baby, we would have an even busier house; but Mary was now ten, and she was such a big help in many ways. Just as she helped with Ellen, I was sure she would help with the new baby. I hoped and prayed labor would be easier and that Mary could observe a less traumatic childbirth.

On April 3, I had contractions most of the day, and by 9 p.m. I knew the baby would be arriving soon. I was glad Ingvold would be there to help if I needed him. Unlike my other deliveries, I wanted him by my side to support me. Initially, he was a little nervous due to my last pregnancy, but after some assurances he was excited and ready to jump in and help.

We tucked the children in and decided to take a little nap before the 'main event,' as Ingvold called it. About midnight I woke Ingvold and said, "Honey, I think the baby will be here soon, can you make some coffee for us and wash up before the baby comes?"

Ingvold sat up groggily and looked at me as though I was in a dream. "Are you sure? You don't look like a lady about to have a baby. I will make some coffee and eat a cookie. I'll just wait in the kitchen until you need me."

"A cup of coffee and a cookie sounds wonderful. I think I will join you and move around a little; that will help things along."

As Ingvold left the room I got out of bed and looked out the window. It was so still and quiet outside. Nothing was stirring, and the farm was aglow with the light of a full moon. I felt so peaceful and calm, and Ingvold was doing well also. As I was standing in front of the window, suddenly my water broke, and I knew the birth was going to happen soon.

I walked to the kitchen, where Ingvold was happily munching on his cookie and sipping coffee, and said, "Ingvold, I think it is time now. Put down that cookie and follow me. My water broke and soon the baby will be here. I can tell it's coming head first, so everything will be OK. We will soon meet our new family member."

As soon as I was on the bed, I could tell the baby's head was right there, ready to exit the birth canal. Ingvold sat on the bed, held my hand, told me that everything would be fine and dandy, and said I was the strongest woman he had ever known.

Then little Samuel was born, —a big baby, probably about eight pounds. He was crying and kicking like he did before he was born. Ingvold gently picked him up, wiped him off with the towel, and helped me cut the cord. Then he wrapped him in the blanket I made for him and took him out to the kitchen to stay warm by the fire.

After I had expelled the afterbirth and cleaned up, I went to the kitchen to find Ingvold sitting with Samuel in the rocker, singing to him. My heart was so full. Ingvold was such a good Papa, and I could not have loved him more than I did at that moment.

"Well, Mama, I did a pretty good job with this one, didn't I?" Ingvold said proudly.

"I guess I didn't have too much to do with it," I said jokingly. "How does he look? I didn't have time to even look him over yet."

"He is the spitting image of me, I think, but he has a little different look from the other kids. Maybe he looks a little bit more like Ellen," Ingvold said.

"Well, let his Mama take a good look at him," I said, as I took him into my arms. "Oh, yes, he does look like Ellen, but I see a little of John in him too." We had chosen the name Samuel for our new son. "Samuel, how about a little coffee?" I always gave the new baby a little coffee as it seemed to stimulate them. "I think Mama would like some too. Soon you will want something to eat."

The three of us went to the kitchen where Ingvold got me a cup of coffee and a cookie and set a little coffee aside to cool for Samuel. As we sat there together, we talked about all our children and how they came into the world. We were delighted that the other children would wake soon to find their new little brother.

I knew Mary would be so happy that this baby came peacefully. I was sorry she had to endure my last painful childbirth, but she was old enough to understand what had happened and how babies come into the world. I had hoped her statement about not wanting any children was just due to her traumatic experience and that someday she would have many children, as I had. Children are what make a house a home.

After I nursed Samuel and tucked him into his little cradle, Ingvold and I slept a couple of hours before it was time for the milking. We slept in each other's arms and savored the memories of the night. Spring was abounding, and new life was everywhere. It seemed only fitting that little Samuel would be born healthy and strong on that day.

When the sun came up, Ingvold woke Mary, Johnny, and Tommy to help with the milking. He told me to stay in the house. I was happy to stay tucked into our warm bed for a few more minutes before Sammy would wake and demand to be fed. Ingvold let the older kids come into the bedroom and take a peek at their new little brother before they headed out to milk. Mary was disappointed, of course, that the baby wasn't a girl; but she loved any baby and was excited to hold him when he was awake. John said "Yay, now the boys are ahead!"

When they all stomped out the door, I basked in the glory of being a new mama. Being the best mama I could be was so important to me. I wanted always to love all my children the same so that none felt that they were not loved as much as the others.

I must have dozed off because the next thing I knew little Ellen had come downstairs and was looking into the cradle with eyes wide with wonder. "Mama, baby," she said.

"Yes, you have a baby brother now," I said. I got up and took Sammy out of his bed and let Ellen sit in the chair and hold him. She loved him instantly and wanted to kiss and hug him.

"Now it's time for mama to feed Sammy. I will make you something in the kitchen so you can eat too. How about some oatmeal?" I offered.

"O'meal, O'meal" Ellen said—just like little Peter used to say. It brought back memories of when Ingvold first came into our lives and made oatmeal for my two boys. Now I was making oatmeal for our four children. Since I was now forty-one, I figured Sammy would probably be our last baby. I was content and felt our family was complete; but of course, I would accept whatever the Lord had planned for us. I was twenty-six when I had Amil. So much had happened since that day. My firstborn was a son, and now— maybe—my last born was a son also.

As I sat in the rocker nursing Sammy, Ingvold and the children came tumbling into the house. They all wanted to hold Sammy first.

"First we need to have breakfast," Ingvold interrupted. "Let Mama finish feeding Sammy; he is hungry too."

After breakfast, the children all took turns holding their little brother. John was first. He looked into his brother's little face and said, "Sammy, you and I will be great buds."

Next Mary took him, and she said she would teach him everything she had taught John and Tommy. "Maybe you will be a teacher someday too, so you will have to study hard."

Tommy was not so sure about holding him. "I'm afraid I'll drop him," he said.

After I assured him that he would not drop him, he relaxed and talked to him a little.

Such a sweet time it was: seeing our family welcome a new member and knowing how each one would play a big part in Sammy's life.

We sat there for a long time before Mary said, "Johnny! We have school! We better get going."

"I already saddled Dakota and he is ready to go," John announced. "We can tell our teacher about our new baby brother!"

1891 - 1895

THE YEARS PASSED QUICKLY, and the children grew by leaps and bounds. Ingvold's younger sister, Alena, was married, and Martin and his wife had a baby boy. Every year two or three new babies were welcomed into the extended Sletten family, and soon the neighborhood was exploding with children from Ingvold's family.

Family get-togethers were fun with all the children playing "anti-i-over" and the usual childhood games organized by John and the older boys. They had quite a baseball team too with Ole's sons, Thomas and Selmer—even Mary and Ole's daughter, Clara, joined in. But one thing bothered Ingvold and me. His brothers usually had alcohol at the gatherings, and at times there were fist fights between the men. Of course, the children witnessed these heated exchanges.

One day after a family gathering, Johnny asked, "Papa, why do your brothers always fight so much? It seems every time we get together, they are fighting, and someone leaves in a huff."

"Well, John, you see, they have taken a liking to alcohol, and whenever you mix alcohol with an argument, it usually turns into a fight," Ingvold said. "I know they frequent the bars in town, and I have tried to talk to them about it, but they just don't listen. I can tell it's really hurting their family life too."

"I have noticed that some of the women are drinking too—even your Mother," I said to Ingvold. "She seems louder than usual and tends to slur her speech. I thought maybe she had a stroke or something. I know your father is worried about her. He said because of her asthma, the doctor prescribed wine to help her breathing. He said it has helped, but I'm afraid that she is now addicted to it."

"Belle," Ingvold replied, "all we can do is pray for them and hope they will see what alcohol is doing to their families. It's heartbreaking to see that they care more about drinking than being a good example to their kids. Some of their boys are getting older, and some day they may take up drinking too. I've seen some bad outcomes involving young people and drinking. Why, just last week a drunk boy was killed when he crossed the railroad track in front of the train. He never knew what hit him."

"Well," said John, "I don't ever want to drink alcohol if that's what happens. Someday I'll be a teacher, and I'll teach my students all about the bad effects of alcohol. I don't want to see anyone I love go down that path."

"You remember that, Johnny," Ingvold said, "and the rest of you kids remember it too. The Bible says, 'alcohol is a mocker.' You *think* you are in control, but you aren't. Other people can see how alcohol affects a drinker, but the drinker can't see it at all."

The children were excited when school started in 1895. Mary, then 14, wanted to get her teaching certificate when she finished the eighth grade. Uncle Sam was their teacher, and everyone liked him. Many of their cousins attended school also and more would be starting in the next few years. Our four oldest children, Mary, Johnny, Tommy and Ellen, attended the country school just down the road from us. Sam was four and still at home, but he begged to go to school with the other kids. During the day the house was so quiet with all the children in school. I started to long for another baby, but I thought I was getting too old to have anymore. We had lost a baby girl when Sam was about two years old, and it was hard on Ingvold and me. We buried it in the little cemetery in Parker.

One day when the children came home from school Mary announced, "Mama, I can take the test and get my teaching certificate when I am fifteen; then I can teach while I take correspondence lessons so I can finish high school. If I pass the exam, I will be a certified teacher. Uncle Sam said that's what he did to get his teaching certificate. I know it won't be easy, but I think I can do it if I start studying right away."

"Well, well," Ingvold interrupted, "that sounds like a pretty big undertaking. Do you think you are ready to handle a school by yourself? Some of those big eighth grade boys can be a handful. You don't want to bite off more than you can chew."

"I can handle the boys. I've had experience handling Johnny and Tommy and I haven't backed down yet," Mary said boldly.

John replied, "Yes, she certainly can handle the boys. None of them dare cross her or she will box their ears. Why, just yesterday, a big boy told her she should play with the girls instead of playing baseball with the boys. She gave him an earful, and he backed down. Besides, she is just as good a player as many of the boys."

"Well, Mary, perhaps you will be ready to take on a school in the next year or so," I said. "I think it will be good for you to have a job, and teaching is one of the best. It can stay with you for years and years. I always wished that I had been a teacher, but because I never had the opportunity to go to school, it just would not have worked out. I concentrated on raising a family instead," I added.

"Well, Mama," said Mary, "that was good for you, but I want to do things and go places, and a family would just tie me down. Maybe someday I will get married, but not until I have done the things I want to. There is so much in the big world to see and do, and if I had a family, I couldn't do anything."

"Enough of that talk. We need to get the milking done. Our cows are impatiently waiting," Ingvold chimed in lightheartedly.

Soon, everyone was in the barn milking and feeding the animals. Sam loved to come out to watch the milking and play with the cats and old Lucky. Poor Lucky; he was getting old and having a hard time getting around. Ingvold said that he was looking for another puppy so Lucky could train him to herd the cattle and sheep. So far, he hadn't found the right one. Lucky had been a very loyal dog, but we didn't think he would live another year.

Summer was fast approaching, and one day Ingvold came home with a puppy. Sam claimed it right away. The puppy took a liking to him also. The other children told Sam he could name the dog. Sam thought a long time before announcing that the puppy's name would be "Chester." The children were excited. None of us knew where he came up with that name.

"Well," said Ingvold, "Chester it is."

Old Lucky was a great teacher, and it wasn't long before Chester was running the livestock like a pro. He tended to get a little close at times, but he was fast and could dart around the dangerous hooves.

That fall old Lucky died and we buried him in the yard. The children made a tombstone and a cross for his grave. Then we said goodbye, and there were a few tears shed, including mine.

By August I knew I had some news to share with Ingvold. I was waiting for the right time to tell him—maybe some time when we were alone, and the children were at school. One morning after the children were gone and only Sammy was home, I said, "Ingvold, I have some news for you."

"You do? Is it good news?"

"I think it's good news," I said. "We're going to have a baby. It will probably arrive sometime in late January or early February."

When he didn't react, I said, "Aren't you happy that we are having another child, Ingvold? I thought I was past child bearing age, but here I am, forty-five and pregnant."

"Belle, I worry about your health," he said solemnly. "Having a baby at your age could be hard on you. But then again, I know how strong you are, and I'll be happy to have another baby in the house. You know I love babies."

"True, we don't know if this pregnancy will take, but we will trust the Lord to give us another baby if He sees fit. Soon the older children will be leaving home and be on their own. I just don't know how it will be without children here."

Ingvold leaned in and gave me a kiss. "Belle, I love you, so I just don't know what I would do if something happened to you. Please take care of yourself. I don't want you to do any of the milking or farm work. Just take care of Sammy and leave everything else to me and the older children. We can handle it just fine."

Just then Sammy came running into the kitchen. He had a basket of eggs he'd picked. "Mama, look what I got today!"

"That is a good day's picking," Ingvold said. "If those hens keep laying like that, we'll have an egg empire on this farm!"

1897

IN THE 1897 ELECTION, William McKinley won by a landslide. He was very popular with the people. He had been in the Civil War and obtained the rank of General. Ingvold thought a lot of him and said, "If we have a boy, I want to name him McKinley. That's a great name. What do you think, Belle?"

"Well, I don't know about that; it would be a hard name to spell, and what if something happens to the president?" I replied. "I like Anthony for a boy and Anne for a girl. Those are nice, sensible names. Maybe we should wait until the baby is here, and then we can decide by what he or she looks like. We can't name a girl McKinley!"

The sixteenth of February was a cold and blustery day, and the children were home because it looked like a storm was coming. We were all finding different things to pass the time. Mary was working on her studies for the teacher's exam; Ingvold and the older boys were out working with the cattle and checking on the horses; and Ellen and Sam were busy playing with the kitten that I, against my better judgment, let them bring in out of the cold.

"Mama," said Ellen, "look at Pinky, isn't he cute? He knows how to jump and get the yarn we drag across the floor. He loves to chase it around."

"Well, I'm glad he likes to play, but remember he is staying inside for only a little while, and then he is going back out with the other cats. He probably misses his mama, brothers, and sisters," I said.

"I know, Mama," said Ellen. "He just looked so cold and shivery out in the barn. He is the runt of the litter and not as big as the rest of the cats. He likes sleeping in his little bed by the stove."

"Kitty likes to stay warm by the stove," Sammy piped up. "The barn is too cold for him."

"Like I said, he can stay a little while, but then he needs to go back to the barn. His Mama is probably looking for him to give him his supper."

I had been having contractions since early morning and was preparing the children for their new brother or sister.

"Oh, Mama," Mary said. "I hope you don't scream like you did with Ellen; that was terrible."

"Mama, did you scream when I was born?" Ellen asked.

I thought it best not to tell the whole terrifying story, but Ellen wanted to know what Mary meant. "Well, Ellen, some babies, like you, don't come into the world the way they were meant to, so it is a little harder to have the baby." I said. "You remember the little calf that was born with its back legs first? Well, Papa had to help that cow so she could have the calf. If it had come out like most calves do, front feet first, the mama would have been able to give birth all by herself. That is how you were born Ellen: you should have come head first, but you didn't, so Papa had to help deliver you. But he did a great job. and you were born none the worse for wear."

That seemed to satisfy her, and she went back to playing with the kitty. Soon, Ingvold and the boys were coming through the door, wondering where supper was.

"Can a guy get a meal here?" Ingvold teased. "We are hungry as horses, and now that we have all the animals fed, we need some supper."

Then Ellen and Sammy came running into the room and wanted Papa to lift them up. "I don't know if I can lift both of you because you are getting so big now," Ingvold grunted. Sammy was little enough to sit on his feet as he walked around the kitchen.

"Mama said she is going to have the baby tonight. She said that the baby better come the way it is supposed to, head first, not like I did." Ellen announced.

"Is that right," Ingvold said. "Well, we better get our supper done as long as Mama is still up and about. We don't want to miss the main event of the day."

We all sat down to the table, and it was wonderful to know a new child would be joining us soon. After prayer, we dug in and shared the day's events with each other.

"Papa, Mama said we have to take Pinky back to the barn after supper. I don't like to have him out there in the barn. It's too cold," Ellen said.

"Ellen, kitties like to be in the barn. They can snuggle up to each other and their Mama and stay warm. They really don't mind it at all," Ingvold told her. "After supper we'll take Pinky out to her family; they are looking for her I am sure."

After supper, Pinky went back to the barn, and after worship all the children were tucked into bed. Tommy and Johnny stopped before they headed to their room. "Papa, we have decided that we are too old to still sleep with our cob doll, so we buried it in the yard," John said. "We hated to think about it being out there in the dark and cold, but we are too old for dolls."

"And we decided that we are too old to be called Johnny and Tommy; we want to be called John and Tom from now on. That sounds more grown up," Tommy said.

"Well, Mama, what do you think? Are they old enough to be called John and Tom?" Ingvold asked. "They certainly do help me out just like men."

"I think that will be okay. It will take some getting used to, so you may hear us call you Johnny and Tommy occasionally," I replied. "When you go back to school, we'll ask the teacher to call you John and Tom."

When they were upstairs and in bed, Ingvold and I laughed. "They are sure growing up, aren't they?" I said. "It seems like just yesterday they were asking to play horsey with you, Ingvold."

"Time has a way of passing by quickly," Ingvold said. "Soon we'll have another baby, and I think our family will be complete. I hope that everything will go okay this time; I am not ready to be a doctor again. Maybe we should get some sleep before the *main event*," he said with a grin.

"I don't think it will be long, but we should be able to get a couple of hours of sleep," I said. "Things seem to be progressing fine. If it were my first baby, I would be worried; but I have had enough babies to know when something isn't right. Good night Ingvold, I love you."

He kissed me goodnight and put out the lamp.

Sure enough, about two hours later I knew the baby was coming. The delivery was easy, and we had a fine baby boy. He cried heartily and right away Ingvold said, "See, he has a good set of lungs; maybe he will be president someday. With that voice he can give speeches."

"He does have a good set of lungs, and I am happy for that," I said. He was about the size of Sam and looked a lot like John. We talked about a name. "I like Anthony for sure, but what do you think, Ingvold?"

"I think Anthony McKinley Sletten is a substantial name. I can see it now," Ingvold said. "Introducing the president of the United States: Anthony McKinley Sletten. The crowds will roar and throw their hats in the air."

"Ingvold, let's get him at least walking and talking before we start making him the president," I said. "Now go get a little leftover coffee so I can give him some, then we can get some more sleep."

The morning came too soon, and as the children came down the steps, they heard Anthony crying. They all came into the bedroom, stood around the bed, and looked in awe at their little brother.

"Oh, Mama, another boy!" Mary said. "Don't we have enough boys?"

"Well, Mary, we have to accept what the good Lord gives us and love him just the same," I said. "He will need you to take care of him and watch out for him. You will learn to love him, and some day you won't want to be apart from him. Now, out to the kitchen with all of you; Papa is making pancakes to celebrate this special day!"

1897

MARY TURNED SIXTEEN IN May and received her teaching certificate. She and John planned on getting a higher education so they could receive teaching degrees. Tom also had an interest in teaching.

One day Mary came running into the kitchen saying, "Mama, I just got my first teaching assignment! This November I will be teaching a class!"

I was so happy and proud of her. "That's amazing! Congratulations! Are you scared?"

She blushed a little. "Well, I'm a little scared, but I think I can handle whatever comes my way. I won't let those big boys push me around. I'll make sure they toe the line. I've learned that when it comes to bad behavior you have to "nip it in the bud" or you will have problems the rest of the year. Uncle Sam has taught me well. He has helped John too, and I know someday we will both be teachers."

Not long after that, more good news arrived. "Now I have some great news for you," I said to Mary. "I received a letter from the family you wanted to board with this fall, and they are happy to have you stay with them. They are a good Christian family, and I know you will be in good hands. I will miss you terribly, but hopefully you can come home for Christmas," I said as I took hold of her hand. "Please tell me you will write often."

"Oh, I am so happy to hear that!" she exclaimed. "Mama, don't worry, I am a good letter writer and I will write you every week and tell you how things are going. I will probably write to John and Papa too, so you should get plenty of news from me. I will miss Ellen so much; even though she is much younger than me, she has a special place in my heart since we are the only girls in the family."

"Mary," Ellen said, "I am sad that we didn't get to go to school together, but maybe when I get grown up, we will have many happy times together. I'm glad that I have John and Tom with me in school at least for a year or two. They are good at sticking up for me when I get picked on. Then in a year or so, Sam will be in school and then little Anthony. I don't know if he will ever be ready for school."

"Well, you will have to teach him here at home like I did with you younger kids. I think that helped you be ready to start school," Mary said.

"Mary," I chimed in, "you sure did help with teaching from the time you were little. I remember when you had John and Tom seated at the table and you would make them write the ABC's over and over. They didn't like it, but they were well prepared for school.

I even learned a lot listening to you, so you even taught me some English!"

"Mama," Mary said, as she put her arm around my shoulders, "I was glad to help you, and you were able to read a little English, but I still like to hear you speak Swedish. It is such a pretty language." I kissed her on the cheek and told her how proud I was of her.

That fall Mary was off to her teaching job, and John, Tom, and Ellen attended the little school house. The days were quiet again with only Sam and Anthony at home. Anthony was now two years old and Sam was six. Sam helped quite a bit with the chickens and bringing hay to the animals. Anthony was busy getting into everything, but he was a pleaser and always minded me. He followed Ingvold all over the farm like a little puppy, and Ingvold doted on him too. I guess you could say he was a little spoiled. He was our last baby, and we had big dreams for him. Maybe he would be the president, but I would be just as happy if he wanted to be a farmer or a teacher like his older siblings.

One day Ingvold came into the house with John and Tom. He had a serious look on his face, and I knew something bad had happened. "Mama, it seems that Tom has gotten in with the wrong crowd at school. John says that he was caught behind the school house smoking with the older boys. "Tom," he turned and said, "what do you think we should do to make you understand that smoking is a terrible habit?"

Tom hung his head and looked like he was about to cry. "Papa and Mama, I am so sorry that I did it. I know that I need to make the right choices and think for myself. I promise I will never do that again—or do anything that will hurt you."

"Papa," John interrupted, "some of the older boys are not only smoking, but some have brought alcohol to school, and during recess they go in the outhouse and drink. I don't know if the teacher has noticed it, but I am sure it's only a matter of time before they get sent home. I'll make sure that Tom toes the line from now on. I'll keep an eye on him because I don't want him to go down that road."

"Thank you, John, but you will not always be with Tom," Ingvold said. Then, turning to Tom he said, "Son, in a few years you'll be out of grade school, and you'll need to stand up to the boys and not be influenced by them. I think you need to do some extra chores around here. Hopefully that will teach you a lesson, so the next time you are tempted you will remember that every choice has consequences. You'll start by cleaning out the chicken coop and the barn. Let's get started."

With his head hanging low, Tom followed Ingvold out to the barn while John and I looked on. The boys hated cleaning the barn and the chicken coop, but I thought it was fair punishment for Tom's lapse in judgment. I certainly didn't want him to repeat his mistake again.

John felt bad for Tom and said, "Mama, that is a hard lesson for a twelve-year-old, but I know Tom has to learn to think for himself and not just follow the crowd. I think I'll try to help him some 'cause I feel like I should have noticed what was going on. I'm worried about the drinking because many of the boys' parents don't see anything wrong with it. But I see how it has affected our family, and even grandma Sletten. It's so sad." I was thankful John was so conscientious and wise.

Later that night John gave his brother a good talking to.

"Tom, we need to stick together and not get involved with what the other boys are doing. "We need to be a good example for the younger students. They look up to us, and we can show them that there is a better way. Bad habits turn into addictions, and addiction can control your life. You be sure to tell me if they are trying to get you to do things that you know are wrong. Will you promise me?"

"I promise," Tom said, "I have learned my lesson, and I'll tell you if the big boys try to get me to do things like that again. I just didn't want to be teased by them; they can be so mean, and I wanted to be liked. John, do you think things are getting out of control with the boys at school? I worry about the younger kids, and if they will be influenced."

"We can only do what we know is right," John said. "Mama and Papa have taught us right from wrong, and we need to follow their instruction. I know that they only want what is best for us, and they are not trying to keep us from anything that would be good for us. We'll stick together from now on, OK?"

"You bet, John. You and I are a team, and together we can resist whatever may come our way. None of that old smoking and drinking will get us!"

1900

MARY CAME HOME THAT spring all excited about where her teaching career was taking her. "I've been asked to teach in the city of Hartington, Nebraska," she said, as we were eating her 'welcome home' meal. "They will pay my way to Wayne Normal School, so I can get my teaching degree. I can hardly pass up an opportunity like that."

"That sounds like a great job, and it's wonderful to get your degree at the same time. Will you go to school in the summer?" I asked.

"Yes," she continued excitedly. "I'll teach the school year, and then in the summers I'll attend Wayne Normal School for two years. When I graduate with a teaching degree, I can go most anywhere to teach. I'll stay in Hartington for two years, so I can repay the schol-arship. I want to better myself and gain a higher degree. Someday

I want to teach high school and maybe even be the principle of a school."

"But Mary," Ingvold kidded, "I thought you would come home and help with the milking and putting up hay every summer? What will we do without you here?"

"I'm afraid this may be my last summer at home, so you'd better get as much work out of me as you can," Mary said.

"That's not fair," Tom said, "how come she gets to get out of all the summer work, and we have to work like slaves around here? Next year John will be off to teach school, and I'll have to do most of the work."

"Wait a minute," Ingvold jumped in. "I happen to know that you will not be the only one working around this farm. Ellen is thirteen, and Sam will be eight and going to school with you in the fall. He can help with the milking and in the field this summer. We all work together in this family. I want you to remember that, Tom."

"I know, Pa", Tom said, "I am just a little jealous of Mary and John because they get to go to school and don't have to be on the farm anymore. Someday I hope I can go to school and be a teacher too. Not that I don't like working on the farm, but I just get tired of it day after day. I know that you and Ma have given up so much to build this farm for our family. I'm sorry for grumbling. I want you both to know that I do appreciate all you have sacrificed for us."

Tom was a hard worker and usually never complained. Nevertheless, I understood how he was feeling as his older sister and brother entered a new and exciting phase in their lives. Tom was the one in our family who always tried to make the best of things. He was quite a joker, and he and Ingvold would go back and forth trying to see who could top the other with a joke.

Meanwhile, Ingvold and I had been discussing the possibility of making a move to Hartington, Nebraska, where my brothers, Magnus and Nils, lived. My sister, Kerstin, and her husband, Anders, along with their daughter, Kristina, and son, August, had just immigrated and were living near Hartington. Their two older sons had immigrated a few years before. I was excited about being able to live close to my sister and her family. My other sister, Karin, also lived there with her husband, Charles.

There was a church there too, so we could get the children in a Sunday School with other children. For many years I had longed for a church we could attend together. It seemed like a better place for our family, especially given our concern about the increasing number of bad influences in our community.

We made a trip to Hartington in early August to take Mary for her teaching job. After we got her settled in the home where she would be staying, we went to see my brother, Magnus. It was a great family reunion, and I was so glad to see my sisters. I learned that Kirstin and her husband would be moving to Sioux City soon. That made me sad as it had been so long since we last spent time together.

Magnus told us about a farm not too far from him that was going up for sale sometime in the next year. He took us over to look at the place before we left for home. It was a good farm with a nice house and barn. It had a grove of trees, a small orchard, and even a little creek that ran through the property.

When we got home several days later, we were excited about the Hartington place we had seen and talked about the possibility of moving there. It would be a big move, but we would be close to Mary, and John could teach there and attend Wayne Normal

School. In a couple of years, Tom would also be able to attend and fulfill his dream of being a teacher. We talked long into the night and decided to move in the spring when the children were out of school.

A few days later we sent a letter to the owner of the farm in Hartington. In it we stated our desire to buy the farm in the spring, after we had sold our farm, and move in during the summer. We also included a cash down payment so they would not sell it to anyone else. The next week the owner approved our offer, and the deal was finalized.

We didn't say anything to the children at first because we knew it would be hard for them to leave their school friends and their cousins. In the meantime, we started making plans and strategizing on how to move our livestock.

One day in late November about six o'clock, Ingvold and Tom came riding into the yard pell-mell leading John's horse, with John slumped over his saddle. I was struck with terror. *What now!* I thought, as I ran out to meet them.

John's right hand was bloody, and he was moaning in pain. "What happened?" I asked, as soon as they came to a stop.

"John was picking up corn on the ground and throwing it into the wagon when one of the horses lurched forward and a wheel ran over his hand. With the ground being frozen, it crushed it pretty bad. Let's get him into the house."

We all led John into the house where I washed his hand and saw the damage. "It looks like it only crushed the end of one of his fingers," I said, with a sigh of relief. "The rest of his hand is not damaged as far as I can see. He will lose his nail for sure, but I don't think he should have any lasting effects from this. John, we will need to keep it clean, so it doesn't get infected. I think you have done the last of your corn picking this year. You need to keep your hand elevated, and hopefully you will be OK to start teaching in a month when school starts."

"I'm not too upset about not being able to pick corn," John groaned, "but I don't want to miss any school. This is my first year of teaching, and I hope this hand injury won't cause me problems with my writing. So, do I get out of milking too?"

"Wait a minute," Ingvold interrupted, "who said anything about not milking. Your left hand is perfectly fine, so I think you can do something with that. Right, Ma?

"Let's give him tonight off and see how he is in the morning," I said.

The next day John's finger was very swollen and looked worse. I kept cool cloths on it, and he kept it elevated to prevent more swelling. He got a few more days off from milking, but eventually he was able to help.

Some weeks later, his finger festered, and a piece of bone came out. He was left with a rubbery tip on one of his fingers, but it healed up nicely. A month later, John was teaching Tom, Ellen, and Sam in our little home school. John taught them well, but his real goal was to be a pastor.

We were thrilled when he talked to us about his plans. "Ma and Pa, I really want to study to be a pastor. I want to help people to know about God and how much he loves them. This is something that I have been thinking about for a long time. I can teach while I go to school."

"Well, John," Ingvold said, "we are happy that you want to be a pastor. We were waiting to tell all the children about our plans next spring, but since you are the oldest now, we will tell you. We have put money down on a lovely farm near Hartington Nebraska and plan to move there next spring after we sell this place. There is a school in Nebraska called Wayne Normal School, and they offer teaching and ministry degrees. It will be close to us, so you can come home often. What do you think about that?"

"I think it's a dandy idea," John said, "I just can't believe you are willing to sell this place that you both have worked so hard to establish. I mean, we have lived here all our lives, and it will seem strange to leave it. But I like the idea, and I know we will make new friends there, and it will turn out to be a great move."

"And it is close to a church," I added. "As you know, we have longed for a church to attend. Some of the influences in the area we are living now are not the best for you children, and we think this will be a good move for all of us. It will be hard to leave this place since we have so many memories here, but we will make even more memories in our new place. And we will have apple trees, and I will make all the apple pies you want."

"Apple trees too? Let's get going!" John said.

After we told the rest of the children, we made plans in earnest so that we would be ready to have a farm sale in the early spring. Ingvold and I knew in our hearts that this was going to be a fresh, new start for our family.

30

SPRING 1901

As soon as the snow melted, we packed the items we would take with us, prepared other items for the farm sale.

I packed a few special keepsakes for the move. Along with some furniture. The first was a mantel clock Gus and I received as a wedding present back when we lived in the sod house. It still keeps time and chimes on the hour. I carefully wrapped it in a blanket and placed it in a small chest Gus had brought from Sweden and given to me.

The second keepsake I packed was Gus's precious Bible, which I read daily. It had been his sister's, who died at a young age back in Sweden, and her name was written in the front. Gus had inherited the Bible after his mother passed. It was written in Swedish and always made me feel close to home. I planned to place it in a prominent place in our new home along with the clock.

I also wanted to bring my spinning wheel, but Ingvold said I should leave it. "You will be too busy making apple pies and working on other things," he said with a smile. "Furthermore, the sheep will be too expensive to transport, so I think we should sell them. Our new place has a nice chicken coop, so we can always buy more chickens when we get there."

The farm sale was set for March 15, and we prayed for good weather. Thankfully, the spring had been mild, and the yard was dry enough so people could get into it without getting stuck.

I worried about people tracking mud into the house. "Ingvold, I think we should make people take off their shoes before they come into the house. I don't want to have all that mud on our floors. I want the house to look its best for prospective buyers. What do you think?"

"Belle," he said teasingly, "if we make everyone take off their shoes, we will have a really bad smell in the house for sure. How about if we put a wooden pallet in front of the door so people can scrape some of the mud off. Who knows, maybe the sun will be out, and the yard will be dry. I really hope we have a large crowd. I think having plenty of coffee on hand with some of your great cookies will make for a great sale."

"Some of the neighbor ladies said they would bring cookies and pies," I said. "It will be hard to say goodbye to our house and belongings. I hate to see the sheep go too. The kids always look forward to lambing each spring, and they are attached to more than one of the bottle lambs. But I know it would be too difficult to get them to Nebraska."

Just then little Anthony ran up and said, "Lamb, Mama." Then he pointed his finger out the window and tugged on my skirt.

"OK, Anthony," Ingvold said, as he hoisted him up on his shoulders, and out the door they went.

Anthony loved the new lambs and calves and wanted to pet them and watch them play in the yard. He liked to feed them with small pieces of hay, saying, "Food! Food!" He imitated their sounds and clapped his hands together when one would come over and talk to him—at least he thought they were talking to him. He also loved being outside with Papa and would ride high on his shoulders. Both Ingvold and I doted on him terribly, but he was our last baby, and we loved spoiling him. He was growing up as fast as all the children. Mary had been teaching for two years, and John had taught at our little school for a year. The kids loved him, and he certainly loved all the children. I knew he would make a wonderful teacher or pastor, whichever he decided to do.

The day of the sale dawned bright and sunny, and the turnout was unbelievable. The women of the community gathered in the house, made coffee, arranged food, and took it out in the yard for people to enjoy. Many children came, Tom started a game of softball, and the older children joined in. It was quite an event for everyone. I realized how much we would miss all our friends and family. They would always have a special place in our hearts.

Later that evening, after everyone departed, we loaded up the rest of the household items. In the morning, Ellen, Sam, Anthony and I would board a train for our new home in Nebraska, and Ingvold and the older children would herd the cattle and bring our household goods. Mary volunteered to drive the wagon while the boys herded the cattle some seventy miles to Hartington, Nebraska. They would be crossing the James River and the Missouri River at

Yankton. I was worried about that, but Ingvold assured me there was a good bridge that many people had used to cross the river.

On the last night in our house, we put some blankets on the floor and slept on them. It wasn't very comfortable, but we were so excited about the next day that we slept very little anyway. I was so proud of Ingvold and our children for all their work and dedication.

As I drifted off to sleep, with Ingvold by my side and Anthony snuggled in between us. I prayed, *thank you, God, for being with us in our lives so far, and please guide us in our new home. Amen.*

31

1901

INGVOLD WANTED TO GET an early start with the cattle, we were all up before sunrise on moving day. Ingvold's brother, Martin, and his wife would be driving me and the younger children to the train depot in Canton, which was about thirty miles east. From there we would take the train to Yankton, where my brother, Magnus, would meet us. I figured we would be to Magnus's place by nightfall.

It would be a long day with the children being restless and hungry, but I had packed sandwiches and fruit for our lunch. Ellen was a good help with Sam and Anthony; she knew how to keep them interested by reading them books, which she loved. She had quite a collection of books Mary had given her, and she guarded them jealously.

After breakfast, Ingvold had the wagon packed and the team hitched up. Mary was stationed in the driver's seat and looking official. The cattle were gathered in the yard, and John and Tom were mounted and ready to ride. Tom would be guiding the group and leading the head cow, and John and Ingvold would follow on the sides. Bringing up the rear would be Chester, our dog, who would keep any cows from straying. Mary would follow behind the group.

Ingvold had mapped their route and gone over the plan with everyone until they knew it by heart. The drive would take them four days—that is if they didn't run into any problems. In a nutshell, it would be a fairly straight shot to Yankton, then the river crossing. Ingvold planned to stop short of the river to stay the night, then head out the next morning and get to our new place before dark.

The excitement was high as they anticipated the long drive ahead. This was a great adventure for all of them, but especially for our cowboys, John and Tom. Even the horses showed their readiness by pawing the ground and nodding their heads, as if to say, "Come on, let's get going!'

Finally, Ingvold gave Tom the signal to start. Tom raised his hand, and with an official shout of "HO!" they were on their way. I watched them until they went over the hill to the west. It was a very sad day, but at the same time it was a very exciting day. Soon, Martin drove up with his buggy, and we piled in for our trip to the train station. As we pulled out of the yard I took one last look back at the farm and the house we had established. I had a hard time holding back the tears as it disappeared from sight.

We arrived in Canton and boarded the train with several other passengers. It was the first train trip the children had ever taken, and they were excited to say the least. Ellen made sure she hung on to Anthony's hand, and Sam stayed close by my side. The train pulled out of the depot and we were on our way.

The train made several stops, and it was fun to see the different towns and people along the way. At noon we ate the sandwiches I had packed and enjoyed them as we traveled along. Still, the "clackety-clack" sound of the train reminded me of my sad trip away from Sweden long ago. My heart had been heavy then, and I was so young and scared. Since then it seemed I had lived many lifetimes. I hoped the move to Nebraska would be the sweetest new beginning of all and the last time I had to move.

After lunch, Anthony curled up beside me and fell asleep while Ellen and Sam looked through the window and pointed to various things along the way.

"Mama, I saw a buffalo!" Sam said excitedly.

"No, you didn't," Ellen replied. "That was just a clump of grass by the side of the track. We have seen some really high hills, and I see a bridge coming up soon."

"Well, maybe it was a bear then," Sam insisted.

"There aren't any bears or buffalo around here, Sam," Ellen said. "It was just a clump of grass!"

"That would be the bridge over the James River," I said "It's a small river usually, but sometimes it can get quite high. We should be getting close to Yankton. It won't be long now before we see uncle Magnus and his buggy. Wake up, Anthony, we are almost there. You want to see uncle Magnus, don't you?"

Anthony sat up, rubbed his eyes, and said, "I'm hungry, Mama."

"Here's a cracker for you to munch on until we get to Uncle Magnus's house for supper," I said.

Soon, we were pulling into the train station in Yankton. There were a lot of people milling around the platform; some there to greet someone, others to continue down the line. When we stepped off the train, I spotted Magnus and his wife waiting for us. Magnus helped us gather our belongings and loaded us into his buggy, then we were off to our new home.

The pontoon bridge at Yankton was the only way to get to Hartington, and the ride over it was interesting to say the least. Each section of the bridge was held up by a pontoon and tied together. Our horse and buggy made it across easily, but I worried about Ingvold and the children on the bridge with our cattle. What if the horses lurched and drove the wagon right over the side with Mary in it? My mind raced with anxious thoughts. I put my trust in God and prayed He would get my family home safely.

1901

THE FIRST NIGHT IN Magnus's house I didn't get much sleep because I couldn't stop thinking about Ingvold and the children. I wondered where they were, what they had encountered, and what lay ahead. I had no idea what they were experiencing. Here is Ingvold's account of their journey, as told to me later:

After we disappeared over the hill to the west, the drive went well. We stopped about every five miles to let the horses and cattle graze a little. Two little calves stayed close to their mamas to nurse.

"Pa," Tom said, "this is really exciting, isn't it? Just think, this is just like when you and Grandpa Sletten came across the prairie to Dakota."

"Well," Ingvold said, "except we didn't have all the trails left by others, so we had to make our own trails and watch for landmarks. This time we are following the trails of others who have gone before us, so it's much easier."

"It sure is," Tom said, as he chewed a blade of grass. "I'm glad we have good weather. I think I could do this forever."

"Yup, the sky is blue as far as I can see," Ingvold said. "We should have a pretty good four-day drive, but we can't stay long at these little stops; we need to get to our camping spot for the night."

Soon, we were back on the trail again. Tom was doing a great job of leading the lead cow, and the others were following behind, mooing as they went. Chester kept a close eye on the lagging cattle and nipped at their heels to keep them moving along. Mary was bringing up the rear, singing as she jostled along.

"Oh, give me a home, where the buffalo roam,
Where the deer and the antelope play.
Where scarcely is heard, a discouraging word,
And the sky is not cloudy all day."

The first night we found a good place to make camp where there was a clump of trees for firewood. We staked the horses and gathered the cattle in a group by a small creek so they had plenty of water and grass. Mary fixed us supper and got beds ready under the wagon for us "men," as she called us. She was just like a little mother. I knew she would be a great mother someday after she became a teacher.

This was the first time the children had camped outside for the night. It was very exciting for them. They all lay on the grass, looked up to the sky, and wondered at all the stars and the big, bright moon that night.

"Pa, why do you think people talk about a man in the moon?" Mary asked.

"I think I can see his face," John joined in, with a twinkle in his eye.

"How would anyone ever get all the way up to the moon, John?" Tom said. "There is no way to get there. You would have to fly and that would be a long way to fly. I heard that to get off the earth you must defy gravity. It isn't that easy. It's like if you tried to throw a ball up in the air far enough that it didn't come down. It's just impossible."

Ingvold chimed in, "Well, I remember when people said that there was no way to go all the way across the ocean to America, but we did it. You just never know. Now we have trains, and I have heard that soon everyone will have a motor car, so they won't have to use horses anymore. They are called Horseless Carriages."

"I heard that too, Pa," John said, "they say in the next ten years motor cars will be all over the roads. The next thing will be cars that can fly. And who knows, maybe someday man will fly to the moon!"

"OK, boys," Ingvold said, "we need to get some sleep. Morning will be here before we can say Jack Sprat. Good night, sleep tight, and don't let the gophers bite."

"They wouldn't bite me 'cause I will be up in the wagon," Mary said as she snuggled under the quilt.

When the men awoke, they smelled coffee that Mary had already started. Mary was banging pans around as she fixed breakfast. The cattle were mooing to their calves, and the horses were snorting as if they knew they were about to start out again. Somehow food tasted so much better out in nature.

"Everything is wonderful," John told Mary. "You can cook for me anytime."

After breakfast, we packed and were on the trail again.

We got an early start and were blessed with good weather, but by evening we heard thunder and lightning. When the wind picked up, we made sure the horses were tethered good and tight. Sometimes horses would spook with the thunder.

"We better hunker down tonight and hope this storm blows over fast. John and Tom, make sure everything is in the wagon and we all better take cover before the downpour," I instructed.

It wasn't long before the rain was pounding us. We could see out from the wagon just enough to make out the shape of the cattle all bunched up in a circle. The horses were whinnying and snorting because they wanted to run, but they were tied securely to the wagon.

"It's OK, Dakota," John called out from the wagon, trying to calm him. The rain subsided about midnight, and we all fell asleep wherever we could find a dry spot. At least we were dry, and it would be morning soon.

The next day was bright and sunny, but the roads were muddy, and it was hard to make much progress. John took over as the lead and let Tom have a rest. John was a little more experienced at riding, and he was good at scouting the landscape to find the best place to get around the little creeks that had formed from the rain.

By noon we had only made it about five miles. The cows were full of mud and the horses too. We all sat down under a big cottonwood tree and had lunch. "We have only gone about five miles so far," John said. "At this rate it will take us a week to get to Hartington. Ma will be beside herself if she doesn't see us coming in three or four days."

"We can only go as fast as the cows will go," I said. "I don't want to push them too much or they won't be worth much when we get there. They can lose a lot of weight on a drive like this. I told Ma to not look for us until she sees the whites of our eyes. But I know she will fret every day until we show up."

"Well, Mary announced, "we better get going then and see if we can make it a little farther this afternoon. We may have to go past supper time and wait to eat when we stop."

Then we loaded up and hit the trail again, the sun help things dry somewhat, and the cattle moved a little faster.

"Pa," Tom asked, "would it be okay if I rode ahead a little? I see a great big hill up ahead and want to see what I can see from there."

"I suppose that would be OK," I said, "but be careful and keep us in your sights. We don't want to lose you out there."

"I will," Tom answered. And he was off like a flash of lightning.

A half hour later Tom was back, and he was so excited he could hardly talk.

"Pa, there's a great big bunch of trees down in the valley. I have never seen so many trees. I wonder what it is."

"That's probably the James River" I said. "It goes through this part of the country, and you always find a lot of trees wherever there is water. Maybe we can get there by nightfall. It would be a great place to make camp. Tom, you make a good scout."

That night we made camp by the James River, and I was deeply concerned about how high it had risen with all the rain. "It will be a bugger to get across this here river tomorrow," I said. "Maybe we can scout out another place where crossing would be easier."

The next morning, me and the boys went in search of a better place to cross. Thankfully, we found a place where it wasn't as wide and hopefully not as deep. About 9 a.m. we loaded up and headed out.

I gave the children clear instructions. "I will ride across first and check the depth," I said. "If I think it's OK, I'll drive the wagon across with my horse tied to it, then I'll come back, and we will drive the cattle across. Once we are across, I don't think it is much farther to Yankton. Hopefully we can camp there tonight. Tomorrow I think we can make it to Hartington."

"OK," John said bravely, "let's get this done!"

I carefully rode my horse across the river, and it was only up to my saddle. "OK," I said, "when I get back to our side, I'll take the wagon across first and then come back for you boys and the cattle. Chester will have to swim."

I drove the wagon across with Mary on the seat beside me. It was going smoothly when suddenly one wheel sank down and water started flowing into the wagon.

"John, come help guide the team across so we can get out of the hole!" I yelled. "You will have to grab on to the harness and pull hard to get them going again."

John bolted into the water, grabbed the horses' harnesses, and encouraged them along. With Dakota pulling for all he was worth; we were soon out of the hole and on the other side of the river.

"Wow," John said, "I didn't think they were going to move, but I'm glad they did. I hope it will go smoother with the cattle!"

John and I crossed the river again and started herding the cattle across. They took to the water as if they had done it before. The little calves swam along next to their mothers, and soon they were all on the opposite bank, mooing like crazy. After they grazed, we were on our way to Yankton. As the sun began to set we saw the city of Yankton in the distance. I decided we should camp rather than make the rest of the distance in the dark.

We hit the hay and were on the trail again as the sun came up. We reached Yankton about 8 a.m. that morning. I looked over the bridge system and strategized how we would cross. A few kind men weighed in also.

We decided we would take the wagon across first. I would drive the team with my horse tied on the back, then I would ride back and help move the cattle across in two groups at a time so the bridge would not be overloaded. Tom would lead one group over with me following behind, then I would do the same with John and another group.

Thankfully the plan worked, and everyone got across safely.

"I was holding my breath a couple of times," Mary said. "At one point I thought the whole bunch of cattle, along with the calves, were going over the edge of the bridge! But they all followed each other and made it just fine. I'm glad I had Chester in the wagon with me. He wanted to jump off and be with the cattle, but I held him tight."

I got the team back on the trail, and we made great progress. About 1 p.m. we stopped for lunch and were all glad to have time to stretch our legs and fill our stomachs.

"Pa, it was fun to see the town of Yankton across the river. It really is close to the river isn't it?" Tom said.

"Yes, it is," I said. "I guess they didn't learn when most of the town was wiped out due to flooding on the Missouri. The flooding also wiped out most of Vermillion. Hopefully that won't happen again. But you never know. I guess it shows that it's hard to tame the 'Mighty Mo,' as some call the river."

Then we were startled by the sound of Mary clanking a pan to tell us it was time for dinner.

We made pretty good time as the cattle were getting used to the routine. They happily walked along, following each other, chewing their cuds. The little calves jumped and romped in the grass, but when they got too far away from Mama, she would moo to call them back, and they would come running.

Later that afternoon Mary yelled, "Pa, somethings wrong with the wagon! Come see."

As I rode up, I could see the axle needed grease because it was squealing like crazy.

"Pa, I can't take this if I have to listen to it all the way to Hartington.!" Mary yelled.

Fortunately, I had packed some axle grease.

As I greased the axle, the cattle grazed, and everything was going fine—until I heard a familiar sound that startled me. *A rattlesnake!*

Mary heard it too and yelled, "Papa, jump in the wagon, it is right behind you!"

"You don't have to tell me twice," I said as I swung up into the wagon. I got my gun and shot the snake. "That old snake was out to get me, and I was afraid it would scare the horses and they would run. That was a close call!"

Mary was shaking like a leaf and started to cry. "Papa, I thought you were going to get bit and that would be the end of you. I heard that anyone who gets a rattlesnake bite usually doesn't live."

I gave her a big hug and said, "It will take more than an itty-bitty rattlesnake to get me, you remember that."

Soon, we were on our way, and I rode up to tell John and Tom what the holdup had been. They were surprised that we had come across a rattlesnake this early in the spring. Then again, it had been warmer the last few days, so I guess the snake was probably out for the warmth.

The sun was just dipping behind the horizon when we arrived at the new farm. We got the cattle into the cattle yard and the horses bedded down in the new barn. John was glad that the cows were still nursing their calves, so he didn't have to do any milking.

Belle was waiting on the porch waving her handkerchief as we drove through. She ran to the barn, with Ellen following behind, to see how the trip had gone.

"Well," she started, "how did it go? Did you have a hard time getting over that bridge at Yankton? Did you have trouble finding your way to Nebraska?"

"Wait a minute, Belle," I said, as I grabbed her and held her close. "You know we are all very capable of whatever we come across. You don't have to worry about us. Now, we are hungry as bears and dead tired. We'll tell you all about our trip tomorrow, after we all get a little sleep."

We walked hand in hand to the house, thankful to God for our reunion. We had done it, and now our new life would begin.

33

SUMMER 1901

THE SPRING WAS BUSY as a beehive around the new farm as Ingvold and the boys planted the crops, and the younger children and I took care of the milking and hens. Mary was off at summer school at Wayne Normal School in Wayne, Nebraska, and she would be teaching again in the fall in Hartington. John decided to stay on the farm and help Ingvold for a couple of years until Tom was old enough to attend Wayne Normal. Ingvold convinced him that he might have to fall back on farming if teaching jobs were not available, so the experience he would gain would help when he was on his own.

By late summer the farm was really shaping up. The apple trees were full of apples, and John asked every day when they would be ready to make apple pie. "Well, soon I'll be depending on you to pick those apples, and then you can have all the apple pie you want,"

I said. "We'll dry a lot of them, and they will keep all winter, so I can make fresh pies."

The kitchen in the new house was much more modern and spacious. It even had a pump at the sink, so we didn't need to make trips to the well outside. I loved the trees around the place too. They provided much needed shade in mid-summer. I had a huge garden, which Ellen and Sam helped with. Anthony wanted to help, but he usually pulled up things that shouldn't be pulled. Sometimes Ellen would take him with her out to the chicken coop to pick eggs, but he really didn't like that job.

One afternoon Ellen went to the hen house to pick eggs, so she brought Anthony with her. Then I heard a ruckus outside, followed by screaming and crying. When I looked out the window, there was Anthony running as fast as he could from a pursuing hen. I opened the screen door and he came running in crying. "Chicken got me!" Chicken got me!"

"You don't have to be afraid of the chickens, they won't hurt you Anthony," I reassured him, as I took him on my lap and dried his tears with my apron.

"I hate the chickens, Mama," he sobbed.

"Well, you don't have to go to the chicken house anymore. Ellen and Sam can take care of those duties," I said reassuringly. "You just stay with Mama and help her. Let me get you a cracker, and then you run can along and play in the yard."

I loved attending Spring Valley church; it was only a short ride from our place, and John and Tom, always polished and handsome, rode their horses there every Sunday. John had another reason for staying on the farm for a couple of years: he had his eye on a young lady, Nellie Bixby, who attended Spring Valley. She was quite a few years younger than him, and she didn't notice him, but I could tell that he was keen on her. Mary noticed it too and teased him about it mercilessly before she left for school.

She had said, "John, you need to get your head out of the clouds and concentrate on school. Nellie is way too young for you, and you have a lot of time to find a girl. I plan on getting my education and teaching for many years before I think about marriage. Besides, I don't want any children because I know they would just tie me down. I am also afraid of the pain I would have to go through during and after child birth. Children are for others, not me."

"Mary," I said, "you shouldn't talk like that. You know you love children and are so good with them in school. I think you would make a wonderful mother."

Of course, Tom did his share of teasing too. "John and Nellie sitting in a tree, k-i-s-s-i-n-g," he chided his brother one night at the dinner table.

"Tom, enough of that," Ingvold said. "We mustn't tease about such things. I know John will make the right decision when the time comes, but right now he needs to concentrate on farming if we are going to make a go of it. I agree with Ma: he has a lot of time before he needs to worry about getting married."

"Thanks, Pa," John said with a red face. "Marriage is the farthest thing from my mind now. In a couple of years, I'll be attending school in Wayne, and I'm sure there will be a lot of girls there that interest me. But I want to have a good job before I get married, so my wife doesn't have to work."

One fall day, John came running into the house after he had been in town picking up some supplies. "Ma, Pa, did you hear?" he said breathlessly. "President McKinley was shot and killed. They are talking about it all over town. Can you imagine anyone wanting to kill the President of the United States?"

"Oh, no," I cried, "that's terrible! Who would want to harm him? He was so loved by everyone—at least I thought so."

"There are a lot of nutcases out there," Ingvold said. "Some say he was just too friendly and always wanted to shake everyone's hand. It's a shame because I felt he was doing a lot of good for the country."

"What will happen now?" Tom asked. "What will we do without a president?"

"That is why we have a vice-president. If something happens to the president, the vice-president becomes the president," John said. "We can't be without a president even for a day. I guess they swore in Theodore Roosevelt the same day McKinley was killed."

"Well, it sure is a sad day when we have to worry about someone trying to kill the president," I said sadly. "Now, John, you better get your books out and study for that teacher's exam you want to take."

Life on the new farm was great, and I loved being so close to my family. My brother, Peter, had moved to a farm out west, and my mother had moved with him. He was the one who could take care of her the best since my sister, Karin, had married some time before. Karin and my mother had immigrated to America together, but now Karin was married, so my mother moved with Peter, who was the youngest among us.

My brothers, Magnus and Nils, and my sister, Karin, were also close. My other sister, Kirsten, had come to America in 1900, and lived for a short time in Hartington before we moved there, but she and her husband moved to Minnesota to be close to her children. I missed her terribly and hadn't seen her since I left Sweden.

"I hate that we live so far away from Peter, my mother, and Kirsten," I complained to Ingvold. "It's just about impossible to travel that far. The trains are so expensive, and we can't leave the farm and milking for even one day."

"I know it's hard, but once the children are all grown, I think we can make some trips here and there," he said, as he kissed me on the cheek.

I just couldn't see it, but I hoped his prediction would come true someday. I would like to see where Kirsten lived in Minnesota. We wrote letters back and forth, but I just wanted to see her and her children.

My brother, Peter, had his share of heartache, much like I had. His first wife, Ingeborg, died of pneumonia. They had four children together, and the baby, Fredrick, was only about a year old when his mother died. It was a very hard time for Peter. I had grown close to Ingeborg when I stayed with them and helped with the older children. She died about the same time Gus died.

About a year or so later, Peter married again to Karin Jernberg, and they moved to a farm near the town of Edgerton in the western part of South Dakota. Karin had a son, Carle Eric, born out of wedlock, before she emigrated from Sweden with her parents. Her family settled in Clay County where Peter lived, and she was hired to help take care of his children after his wife, Ingeborg, died.

They were married in 1884, before they moved to Edgerton, Peter and Karin had a son named Peter August. In 1886, daughter Bertha was born, followed by another baby girl in 1888 named Esther. They were a happy little family, but in 1890, both little girls came down with Diphtheria. Little Bertha died first; Esther died five months later. The word "Diphtheria" sent waves of terror through me. It was a terrible disease and took so many babies and young children back then. I am thankful it would eventually be defeated.

Later in September, Mary was off to teach at Hartington again, and John was at home studying for the teacher's exam. Tom, Ellen, and Sam went to the Waucapona school, which was closest, and little Anthony would be four in February.

Those early years in Hartington close to my extended family were very happy ones for us. I was content to hear all about the children's school adventures as we milked together out in the barn every evening. Life was so much easier as the children grew and took over some of the farm duties. I took care of my garden and the chickens and helped with the milking.

With all the changes, I felt like we were entering into a new phase of our life. Our children would be marrying and having families, and it made me happy to dream about who they would marry. Yes, God had been good to us, and He gave us strength through the hard times; but now I believed the hard times were over, and life would be only happy times from now on.

1903

By 1903, we were settled into a routine in our home in Nebraska. John, Tom, Sam, and Ingvold were managing the farming and had a good herd of cattle plus about ten milking cows. Tom had taken the teachers exam and was excited to start school in the fall with John at Wayne Normal School. He had passed the teachers exam, so they accepted him even though he was only seventeen. He would turn eighteen before the end of the school year.

"Just think, Ma," Tom said, "in a couple of years I'll be able to teach anywhere. I would love to teach in a two-room country school where I can teach the upper grades. I think my experience going to country schools will help me understand what the children need. I feel like I can relate to the older students and know I can keep them interested. Now schools are going most of the year and only closed over Thanksgiving and Christmas. I would still be able to help on the farm in the summers, but I still hope to take over our farm someday—that is when you and Pa are ready to retire and move to town where you can spend your 'golden years' in luxury."

"Tom," I replied, "we are a long way from retiring from the farm but would be happy if you stayed and helped for a few years. Anthony will be in school in a couple of years and can help with some of the work around here. Right now, he is only interested in playing outside most of the time."

Ingvold had made quite a little farm yard for Anthony out in the front yard. He made little barns, a house, and other buildings so he could play farm. Anthony set up little sticks for fences around his farm. He played out there for hours, which made it easier for me to get housework done.

One spring afternoon Anthony came running in the house saying, "Mama, I need some cows for my farm. It's not a real farm without cows!"

Ingvold and I were having coffee, and Ingvold said, "How about if I give you one of the new calves that are being born now to have for your very own? You can feed him and take care of him. You can even name him if you want."

"Oh, Papa, that will be great. I can't wait, but I want a black one!" Anthony said.

"OK," Ingvold said. "The next black calf is yours. I have a couple of mamas that are about ready to calve, so we will see if they have a black one. If they don't, would you be happy with another one?"

"Well, I really want a black one, but I guess any color will be OK," he said as he ran out the door to continue "farming."

Sure enough, in a couple of days one of our cows gave birth to a pretty little black calf with a white face. Ingvold took Anthony out so he could see it being born, and when Anthony saw it was black, he jumped up and down excitedly saying, "My calf, my calf!"

"Well," Ingvold said, "it isn't totally black, but do you want it anyway?"

"Yes, yes," Anthony said, "I already know what I'm going to name him. *Mudpie!*"

"He sure does look like a Mudpie," Ingvold said. "Now you need to make sure he gets over to his Mama so she can feed him. If you make sure he gets fed, he will grow strong and healthy."

Anthony went over to the calf and gently tried to get him to move towards his Mama, but he didn't want to budge. "Come on, Mudpie, you have to meet your Mama because she has something special for you," he said to the calf.

Finally, little Mudpie and its mama drew close to each other. "Look Papa, he knows where his meals come from," Anthony said.

The summer was busy with farm work. My garden was looking beautiful, and little Mudpie grew right along with Anthony.

Before I knew it, John and Tom were ready to go off to Wayne for school. Mary had one more year there, so they would all be together, which they were excited about. Tom had turned eighteen and was so excited to start his higher education. He was a good student and often helped Ellen and Sam with their school work.

"Mama," Ellen said one day. "I will miss John and Tom terribly. I wish I was old enough to go to school there too."

"Ellen," I replied, "you will be old enough soon. Right now, you need to concentrate on your school work. You won't have Tom to help you this year."

"I think I'll be OK," she said. "Tom has taught me so much. Besides, they will all be home for Thanksgiving and Christmas, so if I have any problems, they can help me."

In September, John, Tom, and Mary all boarded the train in Hartington to travel to Wayne, which was about a two-hour trip. They all looked so grown up. I had to cry a little as the train pulled out of the station. I wondered what adventures they would have at school and how they would fit in with the other students. Three of our children were gone from home and three were still with us. We were half done raising our children, even though I still felt like we were raising all of them until they were on their own. I was comforted to know they would be home for a break in November.

We couldn't take the younger children with us to the station as we just didn't have room in the buggy with all their belongings. Ingvold and I rode along, deep in our own thoughts.

"Belle," Ingvold said, breaking the silence, "we have been blessed with all our children. They have all grown up to be wonderful adults, and now they are going to school to learn how to be productive people in society. I can't help but wonder what Amil and little Peter would have turned out to be." His voice cracked as he spoke.

"Ingvold," I said, "I was just thinking the same thing. It seems like that was so long ago, and I just can't imagine what they would be like now. John and Mary remember Amil and talk about him often. I'm happy they haven't let their memories of him fade."

When we got home that evening, Ellen had a wonderful supper prepared for us. She was quite a housekeeper and cook for being only fourteen.

"Ellen," Ingvold said, "this is wonderful. You've made my favorite meal and apple pie too."

"Mama taught me how to make pies this fall, and I am getting pretty good at them. Sam kept Anthony busy outside so I could concentrate on the meal. I hope you like it."

"I will love it, I know," Ingvold said. "I will expect many more apple pies, young lady," he said endearingly.

The fall term flew by and soon it was time to go to the train station and pick up the older children. I was so excited to see them as it had been three months since they were home. Thankfully we had a train station near us, and it was not too far for them to come home for winter break.

That Thanksgiving our house was buzzing with conversation about what was going on at Wayne, and Christmas was extra special. We went to the Christmas Eve church service and had all our children in one pew. Ingvold and I were so proud of them, and our celebration at home the next day was amazing! Anthony didn't want to wait until after lunch to open presents, so we let him open one before we ate. I couldn't help thinking about the first Christmas Ingvold and I had together. Christmas was much simpler at that point, but I don't know if we are any happier when we had less. God had blessed us with a wonderful family and healthy children, and we couldn't ask for anything more.

When we all sat down for dinner, John wanted to say the prayer. He prayed, "God, I want to thank you for giving us some wonderful parents, who have taught us to love You. We are so blessed with everything we have and want to thank you for giving us our daily needs. Be with us as we go back to school in January, and please watch over Ma, Pa, and the little kids. Amen."

35

SPRING 1905

Mary, John, and Tom were at Wayne again for the 1904-1905 school year, and soon Ellen, Sam, and Anthony were in school too. What a difference! Though it was quiet, and we didn't have as much help, Ingvold and I enjoyed our time together.

The older children didn't come home for Christmas that year because Mary decided to go home with a friend, and John and Tom stayed at Wayne to work. We had a quiet Christmas with just the younger children. They were growing so fast. Ellen was sixteen and couldn't wait to be old enough for high school.

Ellen would be the first of our children to attend a high school. There was a good one in Hartington, and Ellen could board with the same family Mary had boarded with. Fourteen-year-old Sam was doing well in school, but he just wanted to be a farmer. He didn't think he needed an eighth-grade education to do that. Anthony was in second grade. He was an energetic nine-year-old and loved to ride the horses and help Ingvold with the cattle.

We were just getting ready to leave for church one Sunday morning when someone rode into our yard. It was the man from the telegraph office in town. Fear struck my heart because when you received a telegraph, especially on a Sunday, it was always bad news. I wondered, *did my mother die? Maybe one of my brother's children had died.* I prayed it would not be some bad news from John and Tom at school. I was shaking by the time the man came into our house to give us the telegram.

I held Ingvold's hand tight as he read the news. It was from Wayne Normal School.

To whom it may concern,

We are sorry to inform you that your two sons, John and Thomas, have contracted the measles and are quite ill. Your daughter Mary is well. We have had quite an epidemic of measles throughout the school. Many are severely ill and need to be sent home. At this time, it is recommended that your son, Thomas, be moved home. John feels he can manage and stay here.

Mary has offered to accompany Thomas home on the train and will be leaving here tomorrow, Monday. You can expect them to arrive in Hartington Monday around noon. We are extremely saddened to have to inform you of this matter and will pray that all the students return to health and be back with us next fall.

Sincerely, Mr. O.T. Johnson, Principal of Wayne Normal School

We were speechless.

Measles!

I was beside myself. Measles had killed many, and now two of my children had contracted it.

"Ingvold, what should we do?" I cried. "If Tom comes home, he could infect the younger children. And what about Mary? She could be infected also."

Ingvold replied, "We'll have to send Ellen, Sam, and Anthony to stay with your brother, Nils, until Tom is no longer contagious. We will stop to see the doctor in the morning before we pick up Tom and Mary to see what he recommends. If John feels he is getting better, perhaps Tom will recover as well. Let's go on to church to get our mind off things and ask the church to pray for Tom and John. Belle, don't worry, things will be okay. John and Tom are strong young men, and I feel they will fight this off."

We loaded up in the buggy and headed to church. Ellen, Sam, and Anthony teased each other as usual. Ellen would say, "Sam, don't sit on my dress!" Then Sam would say, "Then keep your dress away from me." Anthony was hungry. "Mama, I'm hungry; did you bring crackers for church?"

"Tony [that's what he insisted we call him now], you are too old to have crackers in church. You should have eaten more breakfast like Sam," I replied.

Ingvold raised his voice, something I rarely heard him do. "Children, please be quiet and think about what you will learn today in church. We all need to settle down and pray for your older brothers and sister. Tomorrow, Tom and Mary will be coming home because Tom is very ill. He is so ill that we are going to ask your Uncle Nils and Auntie Anna if you can stay with them for a week or so while Tom gets better. Would you like that?"

"What is wrong with Tom?" Ellen asked.

"He has the measles and so does John, but John is not as sick as Tom, so he is staying at school. Mary is coming with Tom because he is so ill," Ingvold explained. "I want you children to remember what we have taught you, and don't act like a bunch of little hooligans at your uncle's house. We'll take you there later today after we get your things together."

"Will we still have to go to school?" Sam asked hopefully.

"Yes", I said, "you will still go to school. Uncle Nils will take you."

When we pulled up to the church, I felt peaceful. We were greeted warmly by everyone as we entered. We talked to the pastor about John and Tom and asked him to pray for them.

After church, Ingvold talked with Nils and Anna and asked about having the children stay with them for a while until Tom was no longer contagious. "I don't think it will be more than a week or so, but we will talk to the doctor tomorrow and see what he recommends before we pick the kids up at the train station."

"Oh, yah," said Anna in her Swedish accent. "Vee love to have them."

We were blessed to have a great family and a plan. The next thing would be to see what the doctor said about Tom. I knew people who got the measles, especially when they were older, could suffer lasting health problems and some had even died.

The next morning, Ingvold and I headed for town and the doctor's' home to find out what to expect.

"Come in," said Dr. King, as he motioned for us to have a chair. "What can I do for you this morning?"

Doctor King was a kind old country doctor, but he was very wise, and we felt so comfortable about him taking care of all our children.

Ingvold said, "Well, our son, Thomas, is coming home today from Wayne because he has contracted the measles. Mary is coming with Tom because he is so ill. We want to know what to expect and when he will no longer be contagious."

The doctor replied in a soft tone, "Measles, well, that is a very serious disease, and there is no medication to ease it. Much will depend on how well Tom can fight off the disease. It will weaken his system, and he will be vulnerable to other things, like pneumonia. If that happens, we will do what we can to help him. Measles can be lethal."

"You mean he could die?" I asked with alarm.

"It's very possible, Belle. If his organs fail, he could die," Dr. King told us. "We'll hope he can fight it off with no residual effects—many do. But you need to understand it may not turn out well for Tom. Take him home and keep the other children away from him. It will be two weeks until he is no longer contagious."

Ingvold replied, "We have arranged for them to stay with Belle's brother Nils. Is there anything else we can do?"

"I'll come out and take a look at him tomorrow," said Dr. King. "And I'll give you something now that will help him rest and be more comfortable. Make sure he drinks plenty of water and eats healthy food. He may not have much of an appetite, but he needs to eat to get his strength up. This will be a long battle for him and you. You need to get rest as well or you could end up with the disease too."

"What about Mary? She has been exposed. Should we worry about her also?" I asked.

"Well, if she has been exposed and has not become sick, she may be immune, in which case you should not have to worry."

As we left the doctor's office, we held each other and then headed to the train station to wait for Mary and Tom.

The train pulled into the station right before noon. We watched for Mary, thinking she would try to find us first to help Tom off the train. Then we saw her waving from the train and went closer to see if she needed help.

"Mary," Ingvold asked, "Should I come on the train to help Tom off?"

'Yes, he is very weak, and it was all I could do to get him on board this morning. Be prepared; he is very ill and has lost a lot of weight."

When I saw Ingvold coming off the train holding Tom up, I almost fainted. He was gaunt and had a grayish color. "*No Lord, please, I can't deal with seeing Tom this way. Please give me the strength!*" I prayed.

We bundled Tom into the buggy and set out for home. He didn't say much on the way, but when we pulled into the yard, he whispered, "Where are the younger children?"

"They are staying with Uncle Nils and Auntie Anna for a while until you feel better. Let's get you into the house and to bed. It has been a long trip for you," Ingvold said.

After we got him in bed, I gave him a few glasses of water and a bowl of chicken soup. As he slowly ate, I told him how much we loved him and promised we would do everything in our power to help him recover.

"The doctor is coming tomorrow to see you, and I know he will have good news for us. He gave us this medicine to help you sleep, so I think you should take it and get a good night's rest.

To my surprise and delight he said, "Oh, Ma, I'm not worried. I'm too ornery to let some little measles get me. This soup is wonderful. I have missed your good cooking, Ma."

Then he was fast asleep and looked slightly better. I knew he had a long road ahead, but my hope was renewed.

The next day Dr. King came out to our place and checked on Tom. "Well," he said, "he has lost quite a bit of weight, and we need to fatten him up. Make sure he has many small meals during the day. Lots of pie and cake, which will put some fat on him. That will help him fight off this thing. If all goes well, I think you can bring the other children home in about a week." Looking at Tom he said, "Drink plenty of water, and try to exercise as much as you can to build up your muscles."

I was even more hopeful after the doctor left. I started baking for Tom right away. It always made me happy when my family enjoyed what I cooked.

When a week had passed, Ingvold went to pick up the younger children. They were so happy to see Tom. Ellen ran to him and gave him a big hug and kiss. "I have missed you, Tom, even though I still have Sam to tease me," she said.

John was recovering well, and Tom was getting stronger by the day, but the doctor said Tom's kidneys were not healing as quickly as the rest of his body. Nevertheless, I remained hopeful because Tom could go outside and walk a little—although he didn't have the stamina to walk too far. He and Sam and Tony played checkers for hours until Ingvold said they had to do the chores. Ingvold even told Tom that he didn't have to do anything this summer, which made Tom happy, even though he loved working on the farm.

John was staying in Wayne to finish some class work that he missed when he was sick, so he and Mary wouldn't be home until July.

Tom faithfully wrote his siblings and kept them up to date on our family news.

The following are letters that Tom wrote to his brother John in Wayne, Nebraska. Spelling and grammar are mostly as originally written.

Hartington, 4/24, 1905

Dear Bro. John,

Yes, I was going to be awful prompt in answering.

I got home so I would get more time. I guess I have too much time now, for I sleep nearly all the time. They tell me it is good to sleep late in the morning and I believe that is so I can sleep sometime not too late.

As to how I am feeling I must say I am still able to walk and do chores with a little more ease, although walking is about the same. I eat like a pig, so it is not much of a wonder it is a difficult task for me to walk. It's a shame, says nature, to waste so much energy and accomplish nothing.

I tried Ellen's gold pen, but it feels a little too heavy.

Must say all the folks are feeling well. Tony is as usual, something like a parrot, lives mostly on crackers. Edd has been home helping Pa haul manure. They made things ripe too. Pa is going to commence plough tomorrow I think, if it does not rain.

The farmers are waiting for rain, it has been misting all day, but not much water has come.

I notice the wheat is coming nice, so is the grass, although it is slow, which is to be expected since the weather has been so coldish.

We have at present about 60 little pigs, all look like pigs except two look rather shackey in the back extremities.

Pa sold 3 loads of hogs yesterday. Martin & Thompson helped him. He got 4.80. He is putting in posts for the hog pasture now.

Did you have any rain down there yesterday? Well I hope you got good grades in your exams and suppose you are getting ready for another try this time. In two more weeks, your folks will be home. Am glad of it too. Does Mary intend to finish before coming home or can she finish this term? She said she had worked hard at Actual Business.

Hoping to see you soon. I will not write anymore. Yes had a dance across the creek last Saturday evening.

Good Bye

Your Bro. Thos.

Hartington, 5/28,1905

Dear Bro John,

I suppose you think it is about time for me to answer your letter and I don't doubt your thoughts. Quite a letter I got the last. I really wondered how you could pick up so much news, and by the way some statements ran. You

must have been a little spunky. I hope you felt better after
you had the letter written.

The reason I did not answer sooner was because I was
waiting for a letter from Mary and finally got one. Yesterday and see by her letter that everything down there is
well. I also got a letter from Prof. Yesterday, he seems to
be satisfied with everything.

It must be nice to go to school now the weather is quite
cool although it is summer, and everything looks so beautiful. Still it can't be much nicer than it is for me to sit under
shade trees all day reading magazines etc.

I am about the same. I suppose I shall have to lay around all
summer. I am getting fleshier so that is a little improvement
although fat don' help me much. I was up and seen Dr.
King last week, he said he could cure me but it would take
a long time and Pa says I do not have to do anything this
summer so I would consider it foolish to kick the bucket
when so tempting a proposition is set before me. Although
if I get well there is no danger of me laying around.

Edd & I were down fishing yesterday but didn't get more
than 2 fish so were not paid for our time.

It is useless for me to say I suppose you are through with
your orations, for you aught to be fit this time, it must have
been tiresome to the ear to listen to so many orations and
especially the girls'. It makes a fellow feel like he had eaten
too many green apples to listen to some of these for fear
they will break down at any moment.

I can imagine Miss McLaughlin felt good when she got the
prize and a little more of the scientifics. This got Henry Clay's
head alright. Ha ha and Tom got an extra dose of Clay in his.

Can you manage all your studies? You got quite a fervor. I have not got enough grades yet, I will have to write to him. I am thinking although if I do get them I will not much.

Got quite a rake? on my geometry math book, didn't I? I wonder if she looked in it what an elegant teacher she certainly was. I hope she will get an education someday; it would do her such a lot of good. Does she stand much of a show of getting math yet?

How does Halla get along with Miss Neptune now?

You spoke of a cripple fellow back, which one do you mean. Was it Archer or that fat fellow?

Have you got your guns yet?

I had one I'd hunt gophers. I was snaring them the other day. I can snare yet. I got four but didn't kill more than one, the rest got away. It was too bad Pa didn't get to send your money before he did, but he was too busy. Have you heard from Olaf sine I go home? I gave him a scolding. He is getting along fine in town. He earns about $5 every day, that is beside expenses so you see things go well with him he works pretty hard tho. But my, he enjoys it he has built very nice out buildings already.

We seen a funeral procession go by here today. Charley Rosenhach's baby died, he is married to Grace Bottolfecn's sister you know.

I guess Grace's baby is not feeling very well either. If it should die Grace would get crazy or nearly so, for she is so close hearted to it.

I guess Waucapona school will be out Friday. I think they will have a picnic dinner don't you wish you were here thou? We were over to the Lutheran church Sunday.

My back nearly cracked of on account we had to sit on benches as they hadn't got their seats yet. While the doings were going on, I forgot I was in America. The best part was the story telling before and after the church. Edd wants to go fishing every Sunday. I have to laugh at him.

Well I could write a whole lot more but will quit for this time as it is robbing me of my valuable time and will detain you from your studies and lead to total destruction on the coming morning.

Love your Bro

Thomas

Tom let me read the letters before he sent them to John. I had to laugh at his letter. He was growing stronger all the time, and by June he seemed more interested in what John was doing at school than what was happening at home. Mary and John would be home in July and in the fall, John would be teaching at a school of his own. He planned to stay with Ingvold's parents as they were getting on in age, and he felt he could help them.

The day that John and Mary came home, Tom was so excited to see them and find out what was going on at Wayne. They talked non-stop, and Tom seemed to tolerate it pretty well. He still had to get a lot of rest, so he spent some time in bed. But then he suddenly seemed to be sleeping more and more.

The doctor came out and said Tom's kidneys weren't working well. "This isn't a good sign," the doctor said. "If his kidneys fail, there isn't anything more I or anyone can do for him. I can tell you, that it will be a peaceful death if it comes to that. He will just sleep away without much pain."

I was shocked and couldn't take it in. I had so hoped that Tom was getting better and that he would be back in school the next year. I had no idea how I would manage if Tom died. The doctor told us that we should tell Tom his prognosis so he could prepare. Ingvold and I looked at each other in shock. The doctor said Tom may only have a week or two to live.

After the doctor left and Tom was sleeping, we told the children what the doctor said. It was the hardest thing that I have ever done. It brought back memories of when I had to tell the children that Amil and John may not live.

John was the first to speak. "I know that Tom is ready to see his Savior if that is what happens. We have to be strong and believe that he is in God's hands now. We have done all we can humanly do for him, and now it is up to God. We must accept whatever happens and believe that God knows what is best. I want to be the one who tells Tom."

John went quietly into Tom's room and sat by his bed until he woke up.

"John boy, what are you doing sitting there watching me sleep?" Tom asked.

"I just wanted to talk to you when you woke up. How are you feeling?"

"I wouldn't lie to you; I am so sleepy I don't know if I can keep my eyelids open without a toothpick."

"Well, Tom, I have something to tell you," John said. "You have to be brave and trust God to do what He thinks is right. The doctor told us that your kidneys are not working and that's not good. He said that you will be sleeping more and more, and it may come to the point where you don't know we are here. I want you to know that I will always be by your side, Tom. Remember, we are buddies forever."

"Do you mean that I am going to die?" He said with a whisper. "If that is what's going to happen, I will be sad, but I will be OK with it. I will be brave and trust that God will be with me and will take care of you and Ma. I worry about Ma. She has had a lot of loss in her life. I don't know what she will do if I die, but we have to trust God, that is for sure. If we don't have Him, what do we have?"

"That's right, Tom, what do we have if we don't have God. Now you go back to sleep and I will talk to you again soon."

The next time we all went in to see Tom, he was harder to wake up when we called his name.

"Tom," I said, as I took his hand in mine. "It's Ma, can you hear me?"

"Sure Ma, I can hear you. Where's Pa?"

"He's right here beside you."

Tom reached out his hand and took Ingvold's hand and said, "Pa, you have taught me so much in my life. How can I ever thank you? Because of you and Ma I am ready to die. Don't be sad because I've had a wonderful life, and I'm ready to see Jesus. Please promise me that you won't hate God for taking me. He always does what is best."

After he said that he slipped back into a coma, and we all wept. John said we should leave the room so Tom wouldn't hear us crying. You know that the hearing is the last thing that goes. We all said our goodbyes and left the room—except for John. "I told him I would stay by him till the end, Ma. He knew it would be hard for you."

Two hours later, Tom breathed his last. All of us were in shock, and Tony couldn't understand why we couldn't see Tom anymore.

"Mama, why can't we see Tom anymore? Will he have to be buried too?"

"Yes," Ingvold said, "he will be buried in the little cemetery near where he was raised in Parker where little Peter and Amil are. The funeral home will be here soon and take him, so we need to get things ready. You have to be brave, Tony; you have to remember Tom as he used to be and remember all your good times with him."

Everything would be so different for all of us now. I didn't know if I could face life after Tom's passing, but I had to try for the other children's sake. I had to be thankful for all the Lord had given us, and the strength that we would need in the coming days.

FALL 1905

Tom's funeral was a sad day for many—not just for the family, but for the community, as many had grown to love that fun-loving friendly boy. The funeral was held in the Spring Valley Church, and it was totally full, standing room only. Many people were out on the lawn to pay their respects.

That day, I felt totally abandoned by God. I was so numb that I barely said two words to anyone. It was like a black cloud covered everything, even though it was a sunny day. All I could see was my son laying there in the casket. It just wasn't real.

It brought back the terrible memories of my other children who died, and it was more than I could take. *How can this be real? I* asked myself. Tom was so alive and loved by everyone. He had so much promise, and I felt he would have been a great man. *Lord, I hate you!* I said to myself. *How can you say you love us and yet allow something like this to happen? I have served you all my life, and now you have taken another of my children from me.*

Suddenly the funeral was over, and Tom's body was being carried to the funeral hearse, which would take him to the train station in Yankton. From there he would be taken to Parker, South Dakota, where he spent most of his childhood. His body was going to be buried in the little cemetery where his two half-brothers, Peter and Amil, were laid to rest. Ingvold, Ellen, Mary, John and I went on the train with his body. The younger children stayed with my brother, Nils, until we returned home the next day.

It was a long and trying day. It was hard for me to see my first husband, Peter's grave and our two little boys, little Peter and Amil resting next to him. Now Thomas was being lowered into the ground and covered with dirt. It was like someone else was watching, not me. My heart broke, and Ingvold and the children all cried.

Why can't I cry? I wondered. I was just numb.

We stayed with Ingvold's brother, Martin, after the burial. It was good to see Ingvold's family, and we went past our old place, which brought back more memories of Thomas. I remembered how grown up and important he looked the day we all left the farm. He was in charge of leading the trail ride, and I could tell he was so excited about the whole adventure. That seemed like a lifetime ago, even though it had only been four years.

John had learned while we were there, that a teaching position was available in the little school he had graduated from. He secured that position and would return to teach in the fall. Ingvold's mother was not doing well; we were glad we could see her, perhaps for the last time.

The next day we all went back home to Hartington. When I walked into the house, it seemed so quiet. Tom was the life in the house. He was always so cheerful and ready to please. When I went to his room, all my repressed emotions overtook me, and I fell on his bed and wept. I called out to God, but I didn't believe he heard me. Suddenly Ingvold was by my side, taking me in his arms. We cried together. "Ingvold," I sobbed, "How can God do this to us? I don't understand why God allowed Tom to die just when he was about to start a new life."

"I don't know, Belle," Ingvold said, tears streaming down his face, "there are a lot of things we can't understand, but we have to go on. The other children need us, and we can do nothing else for Tom. Now we must dry our tears and go on, no matter how hard it is."

"But, Ingvold," I cried, "I don't know if I can go on. I don't think I can forgive God for letting this happen. I don't ever want to talk to God again, I am so angry!"

"Belle, God understands our feelings, and He doesn't hold it against us when we cry out in anger," Ingvold said. "He is still there even if we turn from Him. This is how God is. He never gives up on us, and we have to remember that God is the one who will give us strength to get through this."

"Oh, Ingvold," I sobbed, "You are such a good man. I am so lucky to have you in my life. You have been like a rock when I had nothing to hang on to. I love you so much."

"We better go be with the children because they are hurting too. We will all get through this if we rely on each other for strength," Ingvold said, as we left Tom's room.

The summer passed quickly, and I gradually regained my faith in God. I realized that He would always be with us even though we couldn't understand why things happened as they did. I came to understand that He wants us to cry out to Him when we can't do it alone.

In September, Mary headed back to Wayne, and John traveled to Turner County to teach school there. Now it was Ellen, Sam, and Tony at home, and they were off to school together.

I kept busy harvesting my garden and helping Ingvold and the children with the milking. Being in the barn listening to the cows all munching on hay while we milked them was soothing. Ingvold was always so fun to be around, and now Tony was helping too. He and Sam were more serious boys. They made a good pair even though they were five years apart. Ellen enjoyed helping with the garden and was a good cook like Mary had been. We had many good talks together as we fixed meals for our family.

"Ma," Ellen said one day. "I love being in the kitchen with you, making pies and meals for the family. I've been trying to decide what I want to do when I get out of school this year. I don't know if I'm cut out to go to normal school like Mary. I haven't thought about what I want to do for a profession. I really just want to be a wife and mother. I would like to go to high school if possible. I know it would mean boarding with someone in town, and that would leave you without my help here."

"Ellen, your Pa and I are not getting any younger, and I can see that farming is harder for Pa now," I said. "We haven't told any of the children, but we have talked about selling the farm and buying a place with some good farm land for Sam and John. However, John seems set on teaching or being a pastor, and it will be a few years before Sam could take over a farm. It has been hard for your Pa and me living here where Tom died. The memory is just too painful.

Maybe you should try to take the teachers exam this year, then you could teach. There is always a need for teachers."

"That would be a good idea until we figure out what you and Pa want to do," Ellen said. "I have a lot of friends here and would hate to leave them, but it would be a new start for our family. Maybe we will move someplace in town, so Pa doesn't have to farm. Then I could go to high school," Ellen said excitedly.

Shortly after John started teaching, he sent word that Ingvold's mother had passed away. John had been there when she died and wondered if it was due to her asthma. "She just couldn't get her breath," John had said. Ingvold was comforted to know that John had been with her, and that he would make the arrangements for her to buried in the Norwegian cemetery. Ingvold's dad planned to move in with his brother, Ole.

In November, I received the sad news that my Ma had passed away. She was living with my brother, Peter. She had been quite well but took to her bed about a week before she passed. I cried over not being able to see her one more time, but we had sent letters back and forth. I would never forget how she encouraged me to go to America and be with my brothers, even though she would be alone with my sisters, Karin and Kirsten. She was a special person, and I had already begun to miss her terribly.

John and Mary came home for Christmas that year, and we had a wonderful time catching up on all the happenings of their lives. For the first time, Ingvold and I told the children what we were planning.

Ingvold said, "Kids, your Ma and I have decided to sell the farm and move to Canton, South Dakota. I am not able to keep up with all the farm work, especially since Sam and Tony are not old enough to help. I have been having some back problems, and the doctor feels it best if I give up farming. We have heard about a Canton home Nils Dahl will be selling next spring. We hope to sell or rent out this place and buy Mr. Dahl's home. I know it will be a change for all of us, but we feel it's a good move for our family."

"Will we move into the town of Canton?" Ellen asked.

"Yes, it's a nice big home in Canton, and you and Tony will be able to start school there next fall," I said.

Tony piped up, "Town school! That will be great, even though I'll miss all my friends here. I don't think I will miss milking the cows though."

"No more cows to milk," I said, "I will miss them some—but not the smell. It will be nice to have a house that is far away from the cattle yard and the smell. We'll miss the little church here too, but there is a nice Methodist church in Canton we can attend."

"Well, it's settled then," Ingvold said. "Mary and John will be out on their own, but our home will always be open to them."

"I plan on staying with you for a while next summer before I get my next teaching assignment," Mary said.

Our next move would bring a totally different kind of life for us, but Ingvold and I looked forward to it. It would be easier for us not to have a farm to manage, even though Ingvold would miss the work he had done all his life. Nevertheless, we were so blessed and grateful to be on our life journey together, and I was hoping it would be the last time we moved.

37

1906

BY THE SPRING OF 1906, all arrangements had been made for our family to move from the farm in Cedar County, Nebraska, to Canton, South Dakota, a little town about thirty miles east of Parker, South Dakota. Ingvold had arranged to rent out the Nebraska farm until the next year, at which point he planned to sell it and buy another farm in South Dakota. He had dreams of our sons, John, Sam, and Anthony, having farms in the area and raising their families near each other.

The children were excited about the move and helped with packing. This time all of us would be taking the train to Canton with our belongings. Mary and John would move with us; however, John had to finish up the school year in Turner County. In the fall he and Mary would return to Wayne, Nebraska, to finish their education.

Ellen, Sam, and Tony were excited about attending public school. "Just think," Ellen said one day as we were packing, "Sam and Tony will not be with me in class anymore. I will just be with kids my own age. That will be so fun. I will have friends who live in town, and I can spend time with them. Oh my, Ma, I will need new clothes if I am going to town school."

"We'll have plenty of time to sew new clothes for all of you. I'm sure they have a very nice mercantile there where we can find as much material as we could ever want."

"Mary said that women are wearing beautiful hats now and very stylish dresses," Ellen continued. "Not to school, but when they go to parties and things. Do you think they wear them to church?"

"Well, we will have to talk to Mary about that," I said. "She has certainly been around and probably knows what is best. Now let's get this packing done. We are leaving in two days."

Just then Ingvold and the boys came in from the barn, hungry for dinner. "Where's our dinner?" Tony asked. "We've been working to get the barn cleaned up so the people who rent the place won't have to do it right away. I'm going to leave my little farm village Pa made so if there are kids, they can play with it."

"That's nice of you Tony," Ingvold said. "I thought you wanted to bring it with us since you aren't done playing with it."

"Oh, Pa, I had such fun times playing with it, but I am too big for it now," Tony said.

Ellen was seventeen, Sam was fifteen, and Tony was ten. Ellen would be finishing high school in a year or two and Sam would finish in about three years. The grade they were placed in would depend on their previous study marks. Tony would be placed in third or fourth grade. He was looking forward to school since he had developed into quite a book worm.

On a windy March day, we pulled out of our yard for the last time. It was a sad goodbye for all of us. We had only lived there about five years, but so much had happened in that house. Now we were headed to a new home and town. I was looking forward to living in town. No more cattle, no more field work, no more feeding men during harvest, no more fighting the elements when going out to milk the cows.

Overall, I was happy about the move and was glad that Ingvold would not have to work so hard. Both of us had developed some health problems, and we felt it was best to move. I was turning fifty-five and Ingvold was forty-three—not that old really, but life had taken its toll on us. We were ready to settle down and have an easier life. We would be close enough to walk to the Methodist church in Canton each week, and I was looking forward to that.

It was a long day on the train, and we finally pulled into Canton about 4 p.m. Ingvold had someone meet us at the train and help get our belongings to the new house. Though I hadn't seen the house, from what Ingvold had told me I knew I would love it.

When we pulled up in front our new home, I had such a happy feeling; it looked just as I had imagined. It was a large two-story home located on fifth street, the main street that went East to West through Canton, with a bay window on the east side. It had a large screened porch, a nice-sized yard with lilac bushes, and a perfect place to plant my garden. We could hardly wait to get inside.

The children ran from room to room and picked out their bedrooms. It was the first time they would each have their own room. Our bedroom was on the first floor, along with the living room, dining room, and kitchen. There were three bedrooms upstairs with nice big windows to let the sun in. I had always wanted a bay window where I could put geraniums in the winter. It reminded me of Sweden and the flowers we had there.

We were all excited to get our things into the house, and soon we were eating supper around the large table Ingvold had made back in Turner County. After living in a sod house, then a frame house, then a house with water in the kitchen, the new house seemed like a mansion.

When we were all settled in our own rooms, Ingvold and I talked about how blessed we had been. The Lord had certainly taken care of us throughout the years. "Ingvold," I said, "Tom would have loved this house. I only wish that things were different. I don't know when I will be able to get over his death. I just don't know."

"I feel the same way, Belle," Ingvold said lovingly. "I think he would be happy that we made the move and that we were all happily starting a new chapter in our life. I can imagine him saying. 'Pa and Ma, thank you for all you have given us; I know how much you sacrificed for us.' It means so much to know that our children have grown up to be such wonderful adults, even though we are not finished with Tony yet. He will have a very different experience than our other kids."

Then we drifted off to sleep, each with dreams floating around in our heads.

That summer was a wonderful time. Ellen and I planted flowers all around the yard, and Tony planted a tree that he was very proud of. Ingvold's father, Thora, came and stayed with us for a couple of weeks. Tony loved Thora's stories about life in Norway, his experiences in the Civil War, and the journey to South Dakota. Thora was very bright and alert even though he would be eighty soon. He was staying with each of his children in the area, but most of the time he stayed with Ingvold's brother, Ole, on his farm.

Tony spent much of his time reading everything he could get his hands on at the town library. He also bought things at the corner drugstore with the money he made from helping people around the neighborhood. He loved seeing all the bottles and concoctions in the drug store and always bought an ice cream soda.

That fall, Ellen, Sam, and Tony started school, and were placed right up there with the other children. Ellen made lots of friends, and the boys pursued sports. That Christmas Mary and John weren't home since they both had teaching jobs. John was teaching at a school near Hartington and was boarding at Chauncy Bixby's home. We had become good friends with them since they attended the same church we did. John had written about getting to know the Bixby's daughter, Nellie, quite well, and on most weekends, he made the trip to the school where she was teaching. He brought her home on Friday nights and then back to her boarding home on Sunday.

We had a wonderful Christmas with our other children. Ellen and Tony loved to sing and were in the choir at church and school. They took part in school and church Christmas programs. Sam was more interested in going into the farming business for himself.

Ingvold had plans to sell the farm in Nebraska the following year and buy land somewhere near Canton for Sam to farm. He planned to rent out the land until Sam turned eighteen.

I still had a lot of pain in my heart over the loss of Tom, and some days it was all I could do to get through the day without bursting into tears. But I was learning to cope with my grief more every day. It was exciting to see what the children were involved in; they were growing to be wonderful adults. I dreamt about what life held for all of us in the coming years.

1907 - 1911

I N THE SPRING OF 1907, Ingvold sold our farm in Nebraska for a good profit. He was interested in some farmland with a house about 12 miles southwest of Canton. He figured Sam could start farming when he turned eighteen and out of high school. Sam was excited when he first saw the land.

"Pa, this is just great! I will have plenty of land to farm and pasture land for cattle. I know I can make a go of it and have you paid back within ten years," Sam said.

"Ten years!" Ingvold exclaimed. "That would be nice, Sam, but it may take more time than that. I'll charge you interest just like a bank would. For now, I will rent the land out since there are always people who want to rent land. It will give me some income until you are eighteen and can take over the farming."

"I plan on saving every penny I make working for the livery here, and I'm learning a lot about taking care of horses. I can't thank you enough for doing this for me, Pa," Sam said.

"My pleasure, Sam," Ingvold said as he patted Sam on the back. "We've been able to help Mary and John with their schooling, so I feel it's only fair to help you do what you have your heart set on. You are growing into a very industrious man, and I know you will do well if you keep your head about you and don't get too far into debt."

John was now teaching at a school in St. Helena, Nebraska, and he and Nellie wrote to each other constantly. John also wrote us and kept us apprised of his experiences. He said his biggest challenge was keeping the eighth-grade boys out of the saloon at noon hour. "Can you imagine?" I said to Ingvold, as I read John's letter.

Ingvold replied, "He has his hands full for sure. I know he is convinced that alcohol is the plague of the country. I tend to agree with him. It seems nothing good happens when people are dependent on alcohol. That's what we have tried to instill in our children, but they all have free will to do what they want when they get of age."

John also wrote to us about his romance with Nellie. He hoped to see her soon and ask her to marry him at a big family party that was being held in her honor. He looked forward to meeting her many cousins, aunts and uncles. He planned to move in with Sam the upcoming summer and help with farming. He had attained his preacher's license, but wasn't sure if he wanted to preach or farm.

In one letter he said, "I could make a better livelihood with the farm. Being a pastor doesn't pay too well. I plan on having a large family, and I will need the income. Plus, I think a farm is the best place to raise a family."

The next two years passed quickly for us, but not quick enough for Sam. When he walked down the aisle at graduation in 1909, we were proud as peacocks. He was ready to start farming.

We helped him find some furniture for the house, and he had enough money saved to buy a team of horses, a plow, and some cattle. He planned to hire help for the fall harvest. Of course, Ingvold could not stay completely out of it, so I knew he would be spending a lot of time out there helping Sam. It was far enough away that he would spend a week at a time there.

Ellen had worked on the school newspaper in high school. She graduated a year before Sam and had expressed interest in working for the local paper called The Dakota Farmer Leader.

One afternoon Ellen came home all excited. "Ma, I got a job at the paper! I'm so happy, and I know I will do a good job at finding things to publish. It involves talking to people and finding out what's happening in their lives. Everyone wants to know what's going on in Canton and the surrounding area. I start next week, so I am going to start looking for things that can be published in the paper now. Do you have anything that I could report on?" she asked.

"Well," I said, "You can report that your Pa bought a farm and that your brother Sam will be farming there. I'm sure there are lots of things happening in the city. You may just have to dig a little."

"I have to go to the store to buy a nice tablet so I can keep notes and things. I think I will go now and get the right kind," she said, as she headed out the door.

In the fall of 1909, a new stockyard went in not far from our house on 5th Street. I complained to Ingvold about it. "Ingvold, I thought I would get away from the smell of cattle when we moved into town, but now we are close enough to the stockyard that the smell comes on the wind and I just hate it. I love this house, but I can't tolerate that smell every day. I know Ellen hates it too. Do you think we could look for another home in Canton that is far away from the stockyard? I hate to complain, but the smell is just unbearable and gives me a terrible headache."

"We can look and see what might be available," Ingvold said. "I have a nice place here to have a good garden, but I have seen a property about a mile west of the city that has a for-sale sign. It looks like it has quite a bit of land around it. I could have a very large truck garden next summer. I'll see who I need to talk to about it, and maybe we can look at it soon. Now that we are in town you shouldn't have to smell cows anymore, even though I know you love cows," Ingvold said with a chuckle.

We looked at the house and decided it would work for our family. It would be available in the spring, and we hoped our house on 5th Street would sell in time.

Thankfully, our house sold in April, and we moved into our new home in May. I was so happy I could go outside and work in the garden without smelling the cow yard. I wouldn't say it was my dream home, and I hated to leave that beautiful bay window in our house on 5th Street, but we were happy for the time being. We thought maybe when all the children were out of the house we could find someplace to truly retire.

In the summer of 1910, John moved to Sam's farm with him. He had asked Nellie to marry him, and of course she said yes. He was walking on air. He hoped they would be married the next year. For now, they would have to continue writing letters.

Sam was happy to have John to help him, and I was glad that Ingvold didn't have to spend as much time at Sam's farm. Ingvold had enough to do for the large garden at our new place, which would yield plenty of produce to sell locally in the summer and fall.

Tony was looking forward to starting high school the next year, and he was getting good grades. He loved chemistry and the sciences. He spent a lot of time in the drug store and had an interest in pharmacy. "I will need to take chemistry and anatomy if I am to pursue being a pharmacist," he said one day at the supper table.

Mary had recently started a teaching job in Canton and was home for supper. She said, "That's great, Tony. There's a good school in Brookings called the South Dakota State College of Agriculture and Mechanic Arts. I know they have a school of Pharmacy too. If you work hard and get good grades, I will help you to attend there when you graduate from high school."

Tony came over and gave her a big hug. "Mary, you are the best sister ever! I will do my best to get good grades and make everyone proud of me," he said.

The next spring was an exciting one for our family. On May 21, 1911, John married his sweetheart, Mary Ellen (Nellie) Bixby, at her home in Hartington, Nebraska. Tony hadn't been feeling well for several days and was home from school. I was worried that we wouldn't be able to go to the wedding.

Two days before the wedding, Tony broke out with the measles. I was in a panic and called the doctor to come see him. The doctor thought he had a mild case and didn't think Tony was very sick and told us to keep him in bed with a lot of rest. I would make sure he drank plenty of liquid and continued to take nourishment. I didn't think that would be too hard for him since he loved to eat. Because of Tony's illness, we had to miss the wedding, but Ellen went with John. She was happy to wear her newest hat.

John and Nellie arrived at Sam's farm a couple of days after their wedding. They had stayed in Hartington to see her family and wish them goodbye. Tony was doing much better, so we left him at home while we went out to the farm to see John and his new bride. Mary came with us since her teaching job had prevented her from attending the wedding.

John and Nellie made such a cute couple and were so in love. I had to cry a little when I saw them. I remembered the day John was born and everything we had faced when he was growing up. Now he was starting a home with his new wife, and I was overjoyed for him.

Life was really starting to change, and we knew we would probably be grandparents soon. I couldn't wait to be a grandma, but Ingvold wasn't so sure he wanted to be a grandpa.

1912 - 1915

On MARCH 7, 1912, John and Nellie welcomed a little girl they named Edith Belle. Of course, I thought she was named after me because everyone called me Belle; but Nellie's mother's name was Eliza Belle, so I assumed she was named after both of us. Ingvold was so proud as he held her for the first time. We had a hard time leaving after visiting for three days.

Nellie had problems with her pregnancy due to having the measles back when she was teaching school in Nebraska. The doctor was there when Edith was born, which was good, since Nellie had very high blood pressure. After the birth, the doctor advised John not to have any more children because he felt Nellie would not survive another birth.

"She has suffered some long-term effects from the measles that have damaged her kidneys and heart, causing high-blood pressure. She will have problems with her blood pressure for the rest of her life. She needs to take it easy, and we will have to watch her blood pressure closely," the doctor told John, as John walked him out to his buggy.

"I hope she lives to see little Edith grow up," John said with a heavy sigh. "I don't know what I would do without her. We were hoping to have a big family. Now Edith may have to grow up without any siblings. But the most important thing right now is that we have a healthy baby girl, and that Nellie came through the birth OK. I praise God for that."

John went back into the house with heavy steps and a breaking heart. He wondered how to tell Nellie that they could not have any more children. But when he walked into the bedroom and saw Nellie there holding little Edith in her arms and singing her a lullaby, his heart soared. *This was enough for now,* he thought. *We will be a happy family of three, and we will be thankful.*

Ingvold and I could hardly keep away from Sam's farm, and about every other week Ingvold thought of something else that he needed to help with. We would stay about four or five days, and I would help Nellie with the baby and the house work. It seemed every time we visited Edith was doing something new: sitting up, rolling over, and saying "Mama" or "Papa," depending on who you asked.

Ellen kept an eye on Tony when we were gone—not that he needed it because he spent most of his time reading. Ellen had, of course, heralded the birth of Edith in the Farmers Leader paper, and we had received many well wishes from family and friends.

We were beginning to feel part of the community. Both Ingvold and I were active in our church. I joined some women groups, Ingvold was a deacon and helped with church maintenance.

When we purchased the house on East 5th Street, we also bought an empty lot next to it where Ingvold had a huge garden. We sold the produce in town, and people really enjoyed having fresh vegetables. It turned out to be a family affair with the children helping in the garden and taking a wagon load to town where it was sold on a street corner. When we sold that home and bought the house west of Canton, we continued to have a large garden every year. It turned out to be a good business for us and gave Ingvold a chance to dig in the dirt—something farmers love to do.

Tony did well in high school and still had his sights set on being a pharmacist. He talked to the pharmacist at the corner drug store daily and found out that the college in Brookings was always looking for students who wanted to study Pharmacology. He read every book he could get his hands on about the human body and illnesses that could be helped with different medications.

"Ma," he said one day after school, "if there had been some of the medications we have today back when little Peter and Tom were sick, maybe they would still be alive. I know someday there will be a medication that will prevent many diseases. I want to be a part of that, to help people get well and live long, happy lives."

"That's wonderful, Tony," I said. "I am so proud of you, and Pa and I will support you in making that dream come true. Keep your grades up, and you will be a pharmacist before you know it."

Mary taught in Canton, and she and Ellen had a lot of fun going to different events at the opera house in town. They also loved to shop, and they would find nice clothing in the stores. Since they both were working, they could afford new store-bought clothes. Almost every week they came home and modeled their new outfits, complete with new hats. Some of the hats were quite outlandish, but they assured me everyone was wearing them. Ellen was getting to be a well-known reporter around town, and she also found new items to report on in nearby towns like Beresford and Parker. Mary was good at snooping out newsworthy tidbits too, and she always shared them with Ellen. They were quite a pair.

One day Ingvold told me about a newspaper article that Ellen wrote. "It's about my brother, Ed, and his son, Delmar." Ingvold said. "They were coming home from the field and thought they would cut across a neighbors' field. When they were about halfway across, a big, unhappy bull charged them out of nowhere. Ed tried to distract the bull so Delmar could get away. He fought that bull for about an hour before a neighbor heard their cries and came to the rescue with his shotgun. Can you imagine him with his short little legs trying to out run a bull! Well, I guess he got away with only some scrapes and bruises. I bet he learned his lesson: never take short cuts." He ended his story with a hearty laugh.

Ellen had begun to see a young man named Fred Yarbrough, and she was quite smitten with him. He had come from England to America in 1910, and his family came in 1914.

Fred and his family attended the Methodist Church with us; we thought they were a wonderful family, and we liked Fred a lot. When Fred came to town, he and Ellen would go to Chautauqua Park, which was a place for people to swim, fish, and picnic. Fred liked to fish, and Ellen like to swim, so it was a great place for them to bring their lunch and make a day of it. Fred had a farm north of Canton, and he totally swept Ellen off her feet. By the end of the year they were planning their wedding, which would be May 8, 1916.

The gardening became too much for me, and Ingvold was having more problems with his back, so we both thought it best to sell our home and move to a smaller place. In March of 1915, we moved to a small home at 209 Lincoln Street, which I knew would be our last. It was only a block from the Methodist church and just seemed to fit us. It was also close to downtown, so we could walk most anywhere we wanted. Tony was happy because it was practically across the street from the library. The best part was that it had a wonderful bay window that faced the south, where I could have my flowers.

That May, 1914, Tony graduated from high school with high honors. He earned the first-place ribbon in the science fair, and we were so proud of him. His project was based on fighting disease. That fall he took a teaching position at one of the country schools here in Lincoln County. He planned to go to the college in Brookings in 1916, after he took some time off to work and save money for school. He worked at the corner drug store that summer. It was a dream job for him, and it paid quite well.

Meanwhile, Edith grew like a weed, and whenever we pulled into the yard, she ran out with her arms opened and squealed, "Gramma! Grampa!" She was our little ray of sunshine. She loved to have Ingvold put her on his knee and sing the Norwegian trotting song.

John and Nellie started a Sunday school at the little church close to them. Edith loved Sunday school, where she played with all her friends. She would sing and clap her favorite song to us: "Jesus wuves me, iss I know."

John and Nellie had saved enough money to help buy a farm about two miles from Sam's farm. Ingvold purchased half of it, and John purchased the other half. They were excited to start their new life on a farm of their own. Nellie was so excited to think about how their things would fit into the house. She had been doing some gardening, and John helped her a lot. Edith loved being outside with Mama and Papa. Nellie was a very good seamstress and loved to make dresses for Edith. She was so cute in her little frilly dresses and matching bonnet.

I experienced more heart problems, and we had to call the doctor one night. He prescribed something called "nitro," which helped ease my chest pain. Tony said it was a great drug that allowed people to stay active. I only had to take it when I felt chest pain. I was glad for that since I hated taking medicine. I didn't want to get old, but I didn't have a choice. I prayed that God would give me a long life, and that I would get a chance to see all my children get married and have many grandchildren.

1916 - 1917

M AY 9, 1916, WAS a beautiful day with blue skies and spring flowers peeking up from the earth. It was Ellen's wedding day, and our house was abuzz with all the final preparations. Mary helped Ellen do her hair, and she also fixed my hair into what they call a 'coiffure.' I was told that it was the latest style for women. It looked nice on the girls, but I was not sure how it would look on a sixty-five-year-old woman.

Ingvold sat on the porch drinking his coffee and enjoying the morning. Tony was also there, and they were just trying to stay out of the way. "I don't want to get caught up in all that lady stuff," Tony said to Ingvold. "It is like a bunch of hens having a party!"

"Well, son, it is a special day for Ellen and your mother since this is the first church wedding she has had with any of her children. I am sure she will still have one when Sam and you get married, but it is different for a mother and daughter. The bride's family has the responsibility for the wedding, I guess."

"What is the groom's family responsible for?" Tony asked.

"I guess just to make sure the groom shows up," Ingvold said with a laugh.

I did some last-minute fitting on the dresses. Ellen's dress was beautiful, but she thought it needed to be a little more fitted around the waist. My, they wore those tight corsets and wanted them cinched as tight as possible to make their waist look small. I would faint dead away if I had to wear one of those.

The wedding was to start at two o'clock in the afternoon, and we were all ready to walk to the church an hour earlier to take pictures outside while the sun was best. Ingvold, Sam, and Tony looked handsome in their suits, and the girls all looked beautiful. My heart skipped a beat when I first saw Ellen in her beautiful dress and veil. The memory of her birth how I almost lost her came back to me. If it were not for Ingvold she may not have survived. But there she was all grown up and ready to get married and start a family of her own. She was the most beautiful bride I had ever seen.

Ingvold had to take a second look when she came down the staircase. "Wow, Ellen, you are beautiful. I always thought you were beautiful, but in that dress, you take my breath away! But you will always be my little girl," he said with tears in his eyes, as he took her arm and helped her down the last few steps. "I guess we better hoof it over to the church. We don't want to keep Fred waiting."

We made quite a procession walking the block to the wedding, all of us in our wedding finery. Ingvold gave me his arm as we walked, "Belle, we sure have made some handsome children haven't we," he said with a wink.

After the photo session, we all took our places in the church. Then the music started with the bridal march and Ingvold, looking so handsome, walked Ellen down the aisle. *Please Lord don't let me cry*, I prayed, but I could not help it. My heart was bursting with pride and joy.

Up at the altar, Fred looked star struck when he first saw Ellen. The look of love in his eyes said it all. In his eyes, she was the most beautiful woman in the whole world.

The ceremony was beautiful, and the decorations and flowers were perfect. Mary had overseen that, and she had done a beautiful job. Mary and a brother of Fred's were the attendants. I couldn't help wondering when Mary would be a bride.

After the ceremony we gathered outside the church by the stairs and waited for Ellen and Fred to emerge. Mary had prepared rice in little bags for us to throw, and everyone waited in anticipation. "Here they come!" someone shouted. Then there was a shower of rice as they ducked into Fred's buggy and headed out for their honeymoon. Ingvold stood by my side and whispered into my ear, "Ellen is beautiful, but she is no match for her mother."

We had supper at our home with a few relatives who were staying with us for the night. It was a fun time as we reminisced about times past and shared what all the different children were up to. It was a beautiful day, and that night as we snuggled in bed together, Ingvold and I talked about the events of the day and how perfect it had been.

That summer we had a small garden in our backyard next to lots of flowers that had been planted by the people who lived there before us. Roses, hollyhocks, irises, and tulips seemed to bloom everywhere in the yard. It was beautiful. Ingvold had a few vegetables planted and we even had an apple tree. Tony was excited about the apple tree because he knew there would be a lot of apple pies to follow.

One day he told Ingvold about a ski hill that would be ready that winter for people to snow ski. "It will be a great place to ski, just like in the mountains. They say the plan is to have tournaments there in the future. I think they may rent skis since most people don't own them here. I am up to try it. Just think, skiing in Canton, South Dakota."

"You wouldn't catch me on that slope," Ingvold said, "I need all my bones intact. I do have amazing flexibility though." Ingvold was known to be able to wrap his leg around his head and he could stand flat footed—without bending his knees—and put his palms flat on the ground. Many times he entertained the children with his amazing flexibility.

After another cold winter, we woke up one morning to read the horrible 1917 newspaper headline "United States Declares War!"

I was terrified that my sons might have to go to war. Both John and Sam had farms, and John had a family to support, but Tony was young and had no responsibilities. The Spanish Flu was also raging in the U.S. and was a threat to people of all ages. Tony planned to attend college that fall, so I prayed he could finish his schooling and avoid the draft.

"Well, Pa," Tony said one day after reading all the news about the war, "if I have to go, I will. I want to be part of those who go to defend our country. I wouldn't shy away from it even if it meant I couldn't complete my degree in Pharmacology."

"No, Tony," I responded. "They'll have plenty of boys that can go who are not going to school and are not married. Please tell me you wouldn't go. I can't stand the thought of you in a faraway country fighting in a war that we don't even care about."

"Ma, we have to care about it. It is defending our freedom and the freedom of other countries too. I will go if asked, that is all there is to it, and I will be proud of it."

"Tony," Ingvold said slowly, "we are proud of your choices you have made so far, and I know our buttons will pop with pride if you choose to go fight. We will pray that you will stay safe and return home to us when it is over. But let's not worry, unless it actually happens."

Tony loved to read, and he showed us a book he had been reading about a war battle, *Somme*. He was very intrigued by it. I had never learned to read, but Ingvold shared some of what was in the book, and I was terrified by what it said. "Ingvold, you can't be thinking that we should just let him go off to war, can you?"

"Belle, we don't have any choice in the matter; it's up to Tony. He is a grown man and can make that decision for himself. Now let's drop the subject for now and enjoy the summer that is coming."

About ten days later, on April 16, 1917, Ellen gave birth to a big baby boy who they named Victor. He was a nice baby, and Ellen said he was so good and slept well at night. Their farm was not too far from Canton, so we could drive out to see little Victor often.

In May we had to say goodbye to Ingvold's father, Thora. He had been staying with Ole on his farm and passed away there. The funeral was in Parker, and he was buried next to his wife Sarah in the Old Norwegian Cemetery east of Parker. At the cemetery, Ingvold and I walked over to where Christian was buried so long ago and remembered the hard winter everyone had that year. Caroline was unable to attend the funeral. I had hoped she could so we could catch up on our lives. We did correspond by letter, even though I had to have Ingvold write for me. We had corresponded like that for many years.

That spring, Ingvold and John bought the farm close to Sam's farm. John and Nellie were busy moving, and Ingvold and I stayed with them to help. The house needed a complete cleaning from top to bottom and Nellie was not up to it, so I took the lead. By the end of the day everything was in place, the beds were made, and I had fixed a nice supper for everyone. Sam and Tony were along to help with lifting. We stayed the night, and the next day Ingvold, John, Sam, and Tony helped bring John's cattle from the other farm. Tony was excited since he didn't have much opportunity to ride horses. Ingvold made sure he rode John's most docile horse.

Soon came the sound of mooing, and Nellie, Edith, and I went out on the south porch to watch the cattle being herded into the cow yard by the barn. The milk cows had to be milked before we could have our supper. Ingvold said, "I think me and the boys can take care of the milking, Ma."

Tony had a surprised look on his face. "What, you mean I have to milk a cow? It's been years since I milked a cow."

"Well," Ingvold responded, "it will all come back to you, my boy."

With that, the men were off to the barn to do the milking while Nellie and I took the apple pies out of the oven. Edith tagged along with the men since she loved to be in the barn. She had brought her favorite kitty along and helped find a place for the kitty to have her babies.

After the milking, everyone was back inside and hungry. "Something smells awful good coming from the kitchen," Ingvold said, rubbing his stomach, "and I smell apple pie too."

That fall Tony left for college in Brookings, South Dakota. He had his trunk all packed with needed supplies, and we took him to the train station. It was a sad goodbye for me because he was the last of our children to leave the nest. Life would be very quiet without Tony. He waved to us from the train window, and we both had tears in our eyes as we waved back. Our last child was on his own. Time had passed so quickly.

Back at home as we sat in our rockers on the porch, Ingvold and I reminisced about how our children had grown up so fast. "It seems like it was just yesterday that they were all home and under foot. I miss those days," I said, "but it is nice to have some quiet time now—until the grandchildren come, then it will be far from quiet." He took my hand, and we sat in silence for quite a while.

1917 - 1918

Tony was a good letter writer, and he sent letters to his brother John and his sisters regularly. He wrote to us also, but I felt he left things out so we wouldn't worry. I was still worried that he could be drafted for the war.

One day, John, Nellie, and Edith visited while they were in town to get a few supplies. They were excited because Nellie was expecting again, and the baby would be born the following July. I was a little afraid for Nellie because she had not been too well over the winter, and it had been five years since Edith was born. Despite their excitement, I could tell John was worried too. I prayed the birth would go smoothly and that everything would turn out OK.

Little Edith was five and could carry on quite a conversation. "Grandma, I know all my A, B, C's, and I can count to twenty," she beamed. "I have learned all the letters that are on the oven door. Mama is teaching me to read too. You want to hear me?"

Ingvold took her on his lap and listened intently while she repeated what she had learned. "That is wonderful, Edith," Ingvold said with pride. "You are the smartest little girl I know."

"I know, grandpa, I am smart and almost ready to start school," she said, while puffing out her chest. Then climbed down and played with the toys that grandma had in the corner.

Meanwhile, John brought out a letter he had received from Tony and read it to us:

Brookings S.D.

Nov. 17, 1917

Dear Bro John___

Your letter received a long time ago, so I must take the time to talk to you for a little while this afternoon.

It is Saturday afternoon and cloudy looking. Yesterday was a very fine day, it was the big day for us here, being Hobo Day. We had an enormous crowd. People from all over the state. I never saw as many cars in my life as yesterday.

In the morning we had our big hobo day parade. Most of the boys were dressed up as hobos but a lot of them dressed up in little costumes to represent different characters etc. We also had many mighty fine floats. Our Pharmacy society put on one of the first. We worked a long time on it to get it completed but it sure was fine when ready.

At noon all the hobos went to back doors for grub, and to talk about swell feeds. I was almost sick. In the afternoon we played football against North Dakota Agi. College and beat them 21-14. It was some battle. This gives us Championship of N.D. and of S.D.

Yes, I know Don Leavitt here, I knew him when he was at Canton, a mighty fine lad.

You must have had the whole dog-gone Sletten tribe visiting you that Sunday, I imagine it was real interesting.

Am glad your Sunday school won the banner for Lincoln County, it reflects on your good works and effort. Well I am getting along fine so far, have been usually lucky in getting good marks in Chemistry. I was a little afraid of advanced Chemistry when I came up, its a deep subject.

Am getting so I can study a little better then I did at first, however I often wish I was back in the store. In Feb. the second draft will be made and undoubtedly, I will have to go in the second bunch from Lake Co.

I don't feel worried about it but would like to finish my year here first. Am sure glad you and Sam are way down on the list. Well I must write to about five other neglected people on my letter list so will close, hoping this finds you all well and happy.

Bro Tony

Lots of love to Edith

It was so good to hear that Tony was having a good time, and we were proud to hear about him being in the Pharmacy Society. He always loved sports, even though he never played any in high school. We talked about what Tony said about the second draft wave. I prayed it would never happen. I hoped the war would be over before he had to go.

John was doing well with farming and had his family to support, so I didn't think that he would be drafted. Sam was farming, and the government said that farmers would be needed to keep food on our tables during war time. I almost wished Tony had also decided to farm.

"Well, I don't want him to go either," John said, "but we need men to defend our freedom, and if he goes, I will support him one-hundred percent! I am going to buy a war bond to support all our troops. He is a smart boy; I just wish he had learned to spell better," he said laughing.

We all laughed, and I felt much better. We had a little lunch, and then John and his family departed for their home. As they were driving away, Edith waved out the buggy and yelled, "Bye, Grandma, bye, Grandpa. See you later."

Ingvold called back, "See you later, sweet potater." We both waved until they were out of sight. Then we went back in the house and took a little nap because Edith had, as usual, worn us out.

By January 1, 1918, Tony had been drafted and was scheduled to ship out to France. He hoped he could finish his first year in college. He had been working at a pharmacy in Madison, South Dakota, and really liked it. He hoped to be in a medical unit because of his experience, but he told us he would be happy to be in any capacity on the front line. I could tell he desired that experience and found it exciting. I hated that he might not be with a medical unit, but as Ingvold pointed out, "It is his decision."

After completing his pharmacy degree, on April, 25, 1918, he shipped off to military training camp. He had come home for a couple of days before he left and brought his college things with him. As he packed up his duffle bag, I could hardly keep from crying. *How can this be happening? My little boy going off to war.* My heart was breaking.

We took him to the train station, just like we had the year he entered college, but this time he was going off to war instead of school. As the train pulled out, I wept uncontrollably. "Oh, Ingvold, will he come back? I just can't face the possibility of not seeing him again." We both walked to the buggy in silence. Ingvold was trying to hold back tears too.

A few weeks later, John came to town by himself to read us a letter he had received from Tony. Tony had made it to his training camp and had a lot to tell.

May 5, 1918, Camp Funston

Dear Bro John__

I am now located here at Detention Camp, we will be in quarantine here about 2 or 3 weeks. After that we go to Camp Funston proper and will be put where they want us. I put in an application for the medical dept. but don't know how or when they can transfer me. I have been appointed temporary Corporal in my company here so if I am allowed to keep it I will get a couple of dollars (about 4) more per mo.

I was vaccinated for small pox and injected for typhoid day before yesterday. Was quite sick the first day but am fine now, some of the fellows were very sick. We were all examined the same day by a bunch of Dr's. They went like clock work, each Dr. had his work.

I passed OK, a few were thrown out. We then received our suits, putting them on as we went.

Say there sure are a lot of buildings here and soldiers. Soldiers everywhere tents and barracks as far as you can see on each side. When you get on a hill back of our camp to look, Fort Riley is just a mile or so south of us. It is interesting to see the artillery and trucks and the like go past in the morning. The artillery have a lot of drill west of us a few meters we can here it booming all day.

We have mighty good grub for an army menu. We sleep 8 in a tent at present.

It's a nice life in some ways but pretty hard I'll tell you. The bed and grub is a long way from being like home. You work hard and long hours. Strong discipline you have to get out for duty unless you are real sick.

I was corporal of the Guards last night and today. I had charge of 8 men. I had to awake them and take them to there different parts and also go and get them again. We were on yesterday from 7 to 9 and from 1 to 3 at night. Today the same hours. We have been having some hot weather here and is trying to rain today. Between here and Kansas City it is much like S.D. but more sandy.

We went through part of Missouri coming down looked rather poor hilly and lots of chalk rocks and lots of small houses. We went through Omaha, Kansas City, Ft. Leavenworth and Topeka.

Well I must close now and go to work, my address is

Pvt. Anthony Sletten
70th Co. 164 Depot Brigade
Detention Camp #1
Camp Funston
Kansas

Love to all as ever Bro. Tony

Don't know if you can read this but am writing this in
my tent on a little box. Tell me if you can't and will do
better next time.

It was good to hear that Tony was well and seemed to be enjoying
the whole experience. I didn't like the part where he was injected
with typhoid! "I don't understand why they would do that to them,
Ingvold," I said. "What if they died from that?"

"It is to develop immunity, so they won't get it overseas," John
explained. "I see he has not improved his spelling any. It's just like
Tony to always find the best in any situation. He sees everything
as a big adventure."

"Well, this is one adventure I wish he wasn't on," I said, "But I
am learning to accept his decision and feel better about it. It helps
that he writes about how things aren't so bad. I don't think I could
handle it if he told about his hardships."

I didn't understand at the time that all his letters were censored,
which meant someone read all the letters, and if they included
anything that the officers felt shouldn't be sent to loved ones, they
had to take it out of the letter. I guess it was because they didn't
want the public to know what their plans were, but I think it was
to spare their loved one's heartache.

Early in May John came to town and told Ingvold and me that
Nellie was very ill. He was worried that she may lose the baby.

"Ma, can you come and help her, she is so sick she can't even
get out of bed. Edith has been so worried about her and just sits by
her bed all day. I stopped by the doctor's office and he will come as
soon as he can."

When we drove into the yard, Edith came out and yelled, "Grandma, Mama is sick!"

"I know honey; I am going to help her feel better now. Don't worry your little head about it anymore. Go help your Papa now and I will take care of your Mama."

As I entered the bedroom where Nellie lay, I was shocked by how ill she looked. She was writhing in pain and her legs were swollen to twice the usual size. I don't think she knew I was there. I knew she must be suffering from eclampsia as she had problems with her blood pressure. I knew that many women die from the condition and I prayed that she would hang on until the doctor arrived. I tried to make her comfortable by putting cool cloths on her forehead and rubbing her feet and legs. She did not respond to me but continued to call out in pain holding her head. I knew she must have a terrible headache.

It seemed like hours before the doctor came. He assessed the situation and took Nellie's blood pressure. "She should never have gotten pregnant," he said in a stern tone. "I'm afraid she may not make it through. She is probably about four or five months along; a long way from delivering this baby. I can give her something for her blood pressure and something to help her get rid of the excess fluid, hopefully that will help. When she is able to take fluids, I want her to take these pills. The only thing that will save her is to deliver this baby as soon as possible."

I objected by saying, "The baby will not live if she has it now: can't we wait and see if she improves with the blood pressure and fluid pills first?"

"We have to save the mother; you don't want John to lose his wife and Edith her mother, do you?"

Even though I knew he was right I just knew how much Nellie and John wanted this baby. I thought back to when I lost the baby between Sam and Anthony and remembered the sadness I felt when the baby was born lifeless. I loved the little baby that I carried for six months, but knew when I went into labor that it would not be born alive. Now Nellie will have to suffer this loss also.

John and Edith came in the house and looked in on Nellie and me. She was sleeping a little more comfortably and Edith came over to her and gave her a kiss and said, "Mama, I love you, Mama. Please wake up and play with me, Mama."

It was heartbreaking. We left the bedroom and let Nellie sleep while I fixed something for supper. I didn't mention what the doctor had said or about the pills he had left, even though I knew they were to induce a miscarriage.

About two hours later after Edith had been put to bed, I heard Nellie calling from the bedroom. We ran to her side and found that she looked much better and even wanted something to eat. Now I had the task of telling her about the pills the doctor had left.

"Nellie," I started as John listened, "the doctor feels that you cannot continue this pregnancy to term. He is afraid that your heart will not withstand the rest of the pregnancy and then labor and delivery. He said the only thing that will make this situation better is to deliver the baby as soon as possible."

"But, Ma," John said," the baby will not live if it's born now. We just can't lose this baby!"

"I know, John," I said." The doctor left these pills and asked me to have Nellie take them when she woke up. I know what these pills are for; they will induce labor and the baby will be born. He said that is the only way to save Nellie."

"Ma" Nellie said weakly, "I just can't take those pills, I would feel like I was killing my baby. I believe that God will help me keep this baby. I have dreamed of having another baby and never thought it would happen; now that it has, I know this baby will be born healthy and strong. I will do anything the doctor says, just not those pills."

John came over and sat on the bed and held Nellie as they cried together.

"I'll stay on for a while and help you with Edith and the house," I offered. "Your job is to take care of yourself and that baby."

I stayed with them until the crisis was over and Nellie seemed better and able to manage without me. As John drove me back home, he told me how much he loved Nellie and that he would do anything if it meant not losing her.

"I think you'll have Nellie for many more years and that new baby will be a blessing to both of you. I know Edith will love to have a baby sister or brother," I said reassuringly.

By the end of May we had another letter from Tony, and John brought it in and read it to us.

"It sounds like he is having quite an experience so far. He is seeing the world for sure," John said, as he began reading.

May 30, 1918

Camp Mills
Co.K 355 Inf.
89 Division
Hempstead L.I. N.Y.

Dear Bro John and all

I may possible be on the Atlantic when you get this. We expect to go across any time now although we may possibly be here some time yet.

We are being issued our overseas cloths now and are just about fitted out.

I hardly expected a month ago to be here now, they sure are putting us through in a hurry, of course we will be in training a long time before we see active service. I think I sure was glad to get away from Funston. I did not like it at all there but feel right at home here and am ready to go over anytime.

Have been fortunate in staying well so far, and the first month or so is the biggest show I think.

We had a fine trip we went through St. Lewis through Ill, Indiana, marched through the street of Indianapolis one evening it is some city. We also went through Ohio (Cleveland) Penn, Buffalo N.Y., Rochester N.Y. down along the Hudson river along the Caskile Mt. Landed in New Jersey took a boat into New York Harbor. Around the Statue of Liberty passed the great building on the shore and rode under Brooklyn Bridge and then landed at Long Island. It seemed to me sailing around in N.Y. Harbor it was beyond description.

I'll tell you John you can hardly realize the great preparations of war being carried on by U.S. until you have been in the camps. It is wonderful to see the endless movement of troops, supplies etc. and everything moving at a swift pace.

I got your letter today and was certainly glad to get it mail is so uncertain now with me. Am glad crops are good in good old S. Dak. I hope you will have a good bumper crop this year. I would like to get in on the watermelons believe me ha, ha. When you write don't forget to put 98th Division on the address so that it will be forwarded if we move.

The climate is damp and rainy but just opposite from dusty Kansas. Ha ha

I certainly saw some great scenery on the way here but give me S. Dak to live in every time. My Co. is composed of men from S. Dak. and Neb. We have some great talks, most of them are nice men. Not like New Mexico men and a few others. Well write when you can John and I will write whenever I get a chance. With all kinds of love to your Nellie and Edith.

As Ever

Bro Tony

"By gum," Ingvold said, "he has seen more of our U.S. in the last few weeks than I have seen in my whole life. I am a little envious of him. I have always wanted to see New York and the Statue of Liberty. Now he will see France too."

I didn't have much to say about the letter, but Ingvold and John talked a long time about what Tony was experiencing. They acted like he was on vacation. It was as if they didn't know we may never see him again. I could not see how it was so wonderful and

continued to hope the war would be over before Tony had to go.
But it was not to be.

1918

IT WAS JULY AND a hot one at that. Nellie was doing well, even with the terrible heat. Edith was so excited for the baby to arrive that she hardly left Nellie's side for fear she might miss seeing the baby.

Ingvold and I kept busy in our little garden and tried not to think about Tony over in France. Every day there were terrible war stories in the newspaper, and many men were losing their lives. A list was printed in the paper, and we knew many of the boys on it. Sad funerals took place when the bodies were brought back, but sometimes the bodies never came home and were instead buried in France as the terrible war raged on.

We hadn't heard from Tony since May, which caused me a lot of worry. Then one day John came to our house with a letter from Tony. It was dated July 7, 1918. I started shaking as John read the letter, thinking something bad had happened.

John said, "It sounds like he is still having an adventure over there." He began to read but was careful not to read the part about Tony taking out a life insurance policy. He knew it would be upsetting to Ingvold and me.

In France

July 7 '18

Dear Bro John and all

This is a beautiful bright Sunday morning in France. I can hardly realize we are so far from S.D. The climate here is mild we have not had any real hot days so far. The 4th was very cold. In the morning I went to a French church and in the afternoon, we had a few races stunts etc.

The French language seems rather hard to learn. I have learned a few common words but don't believe I could ever talk very much.

The people are a better looking race then I expected not small and dark as I supposed but many of them light complexion and good looking, of course it is hard to get used to their old fashioned ways, when a person has always lived in the states. We always heard a lot about the quite peaceful French villages and they sure are.

Say John, in case you ever want to write to the war Department or Insurance Bureau in regard to me give my identification tag no. which is 2846523 also my Co. (Co K. 355 inf at the present time).

I have taken $10,000. Gov. insurance. I made it out to Father, so if anything should happen look after it will you? I hate to write to the folks about it.

I hardly know what to write as most things that would be of interest will be censored.

There is one thing you seldom see in these countries and that is frame buildings. France is great on rock building, shingles of rock even. England is great for brick buildings.

A person sees a lot of fine roads, very few dirt roads. They are very narrow however and would hardly do in our country.

Must close now, hoping to be able to see you again before very long so that I can tell you all the interesting things. I am in good health.

I received letter from Mary and Mother the other day. It was written the 10th of June I believe.

As ever your loving Bro Tony

Address
Pvt Anthony Sletten
Co. K 355 Inf. A.E.F
via New York

"It doesn't sound like he is in the fighting yet," John said, as he folded the letter up and put it in his pocket so his father wouldn't ask to see it. "Well, I think we are ready for our new little family member to come," he said, changing the subject. "Nellie has been resting quite a lot, and Dr. Park has been out to see her several times. He said she is still having some high blood pressure, but that she should do well if the delivery is not too hard. Edith can hardly wait, and she asks every day if the baby is coming. Ma, do you think you can come home with me today and help with things around the house? I know Nellie would appreciate it."

"You don't have to ask me twice," I said, as I went upstairs to pack. I had made a few things for the new baby, and I carefully placed them in my suitcase.

"Ingvold, there is plenty to eat in the pantry. I just baked bread yesterday, so you can make sandwiches," I said. "And there are a lot of vegetables to harvest from the garden." Soon, we were on our way, and I was already thinking about what would be needed when we arrived.

When we pulled into the yard, Edith ran out to meet us. "Grandma, we are going to have a baby soon, Mama said!"

"You are?" I answered, "that will be wonderful for you to have a playmate."

We all went into the house, and I got to work sweeping, mopping, and washing windows. I stopped long enough to fix a nice supper for all of us. I wanted Nellie to sit and relax. Over the few days, I cleaned the milk house, baked bread, and fixed meals for the family. I had Edith help me with the garden work, and she was so happy to do so.

"Ma," Nellie said, "I can't thank you enough for all of this. I have tried to keep the house work up, but I just run out of steam. Edith is a big help but not quite big enough yet to take on too much."

"Don't you mind, Nellie, this is where I want to be right now. It gets my mind off Tony too."

"I miss Uncle Tony," Edith said. "He played with me and told me stories all the time. When is he coming home again, Mama?"

"We hope soon," Nellie said, but I knew she was worried about him too.

The busy days passed quickly while the rain came down in buckets. One morning John came out of the bedroom and announced

Nellie was in labor. He went to the phone, which was a new item in the house, and rang the doctor, but the phone was not working. The rain had evidently taken the line out.

"I'll ride to the neighbor's house," John said. "They are on a different line; hopefully their phone is working. The doctor will have a challenge getting out here with all this rain, and the roads will be terrible, but hopefully he will have enough time to make it."

He took off on his horse to ride to the neighbor's. Soon, he was back and informed us that the neighbor's phone was also out. "It's terrible out there; the roads are like a swamp," John announced as he entered the house. He was soaking wet, and I worried about him since he had the flu earlier in the spring and had been quite ill. Ingvold had to come out and help him put the crops in.

"I have to try to make it to our other neighbor's, who are on still another line. Ma, can you handle things here for a while?"

"I think I can manage," I said. "I'm the best person to be here if the doctor can't make it. I delivered all you children. I think I'm capable of delivering my own grandchild if need be."

After John left, I went into the bedroom to see how Nellie was doing. She was obviously close to delivery, and I reassured her that the doctor would be here soon, and that I would stay with her until he arrived. She was complaining of a terrible headache, which I knew was a complication of pregnancy. I was very worried about her at that point, but I had to stay calm.

After about an hour I knew the doctor was not going to make it before the baby made its appearance. "Nellie, you are going to have a beautiful baby soon; keep thinking about that and just get through one contraction at a time. It won't be long now," I said.

Nellie did a wonderful job birthing the baby, but I was worried about her as she was so lethargic afterward. I worried she could have a stroke from high blood pressure. "Nellie, you have a beautiful baby girl," I told her, but she didn't seem to comprehend what I was saying.

After I got the baby cleaned up, I took her out into the kitchen where Edith was sitting in her little rocking chair. She jumped up when I came into the room holding the little bundle.

"Grandma, is that my baby?" she asked, with eyes wide.

"Yes, it is," I replied, as I lowered the baby down for her to see. "You have a new baby sister. Are you happy about that?"

"Oh, a sister, can I hold her?" she asked.

"If you sit in the big chair, I will let you hold her for a little bit while I check on your Mama again," I said.

After Edith was seated in the big chair, I placed her little sister in her arms. She cuddled her carefully and sang a little song to her. I needed to get back to Nellie, but just as I was about to turn and go to the bedroom, John and the doctor came in the door. They were both wet to the bone. John saw Edith holding the baby and hurried over to her.

"Edith, who is this you have?" he said, his voice filled with joy.

"Papa, it's my little sister. Don't you know?"

"I didn't know she would come while I was gone," he said, "but I'm glad she has a big sister to take care of her." Then he went into the bedroom where the doctor was checking Nellie over.

The doctor was worried about Nellie, and he told John she would have to be watched closely for any signs of stroke. Then he went out and took the baby into his arms and said, "She is in fine shape, and I say she is about seven pounds and was born about one o'clock."

"Papa," Edith asked, "what are we going to name my little sister?"

John answered, "We have talked about naming her Mary Ellen, after her Mama. Do you like that name?"

"I guess so, but I kind of like Petunia, like the pretty flowers," she replied.

It was time for supper, and I busied myself getting things fixed. John was holding and rocking little Mary Ellen and gently patting her on the back. I told him I should give her a little coffee, as I always did that for newborn babies. He consented and then took little Mary Ellen in to meet her mother. Nellie was awake and feeling a little better. She was so happy to meet her little namesake.

About a week later, Ingvold came out to the farm with Mary. Mary had decided to stay with John and help until she had to start school in the fall. I was happy to be relieved of my duties because I was having mild chest pains, and I knew it was because of the stressful situation. Ingvold and I said goodbye to Edith and little Mary Ellen, and then we headed down the road to Canton. I was glad to get home and lie down.

We hadn't heard anything from Tony since July, and now it was September. Just when we were beginning to wonder when we would get another letter, John came into town with Nellie, Edith, and Mary Ellen and brought a short letter from Tony with him. John had sent Tony notice of Mary Ellen's birth and he had responded. Tony had also sent a letter to Edith.

As John read Tony's letter, I tried to read between the lines.

Sept 10, 1918

Dear Bro John

Just a word of congratulations. Am certainty glad that Nellie and little Mary Ellen are getting along fine and hope they will continue to. I will have a new neice to visit when I get home. I wish it were possible to make you a visit now.

I received 3 letters yesterday one from Mary, Ellen and Dad they were very interesting. According to their letters crops were unusually good. It certainly will be fine if you get a real corn crop again. Well I really haven't any news except that I have and am seeing real service in the trenches now. So far I have gotten along fine. I wish I could tell you a few of the interesting things.

With all kinds of good wishes to you all as ever,

Your Bro Tony

Pvt Anthony Sletten
Co. K 355 Inf
A.E.F.

Censored by E.T. Moore
Capt. 355 Inf.

Then he read the letter to Edith, which I thought was very sweet.

Sept 10 1918

Somewhere in France

My Dear Neice Edith

I have been thinking about you every day so will write you a letter this morning. How are you anyway? I am just fine.

I wrote a letter to Aunt Mary this morning and also received one from her yesterday. She says you were going to start school. I wish I were there to go with you. Who is your teacher and how do you like school? I'll bet you will make rings around those boys and girls out there. Ha ha.

Did you have any watermelons this year? Aunt Mary said you had some nice fried chicken when she was there. Better send me a piece.

It has been raining here every day lately. The soil is kind of a clay so you just ought to see me walk around with a bushel of mud on my big hob nailed shoes. Ha.

I wish you could be with me for a little while. I would show you the French soldiers in their spic and span blue suits and the American soldiers in our brown suits.

You should see the heavy tin hats (we call them that) we have to wear sometimes makes us look like China-men Ha ha. We also have some very neat little caps to wear.

Have you seen your little cousin Victor lately? Aunt Ellen writes me that he is learning to walk.

Say another thing I'll bet you would like to see over here is the little boys. They nearly all wear aprons to protect their clothes. I think you have seen them in pictures, great big aprons you know.

Some of the boys wear little blue uniforms like their dadies, they feel quite proud I think.

The little girls wear cloths much like ours do. Well Edith I must close now with lots of love to you and Mama and Papa from your Uncle Tony

Pvt Anthony Sletten
Co K 355 Inf. A.E.F.

Censored by F.T Moore
Capt. 355 Inf.

"Tony's spelling hasn't improved," John remarked," but he sure can paint a picture of things over there."

I wondered what Tony meant when he said had seen some real service in the trenches, and why didn't he know where he was in France. That worried me.

We enjoyed seeing Edith and little Mary Ellen, and they stayed for lunch. Nellie seemed to be doing well, and she looked like she had her color back. They left around two o'clock to get home to do the milking.

After they left, I repeated what Tony said, and Ingvold and I talked about it. That night I had a hard time sleeping because I was thinking about my Tony someplace in France in a trench fighting a war. I cried quietly so as not to wake Ingvold.

43

1918 - 1919

O N OCTOBER 19, 1918, Ellen and Fred had their second boy. They named him Harry. They were such a happy little family. I was still waiting for Mary to announce she had a beau, but she was only interested in teaching. She liked to travel and had taken a trip east the previous summer. She had also taken many summer school classes and was working towards her B.A. degree.

John and Nellie and the girls were doing well. Nellie was handling a family with two little girls just fine. Edith was a great help for her, running to get a diaper or a bottle when needed. John had come to terms that he would not have a boy to help him on the farm, but he was head over heels in love with those two little girls. The doctor had told them in no uncertain terms that Nellie shouldn't have any more children, as she wouldn't live through another pregnancy and birth. They seemed to accept that, and they were happy that Edith had a sister to grow up with.

We got a letter from Tony in October telling us that he had been gassed while in the trenches and was in a hospital. I was relieved that he was not seriously injured and that he would probably be sent home.

We waited to hear more from him, and finally John got a letter from him dated December 16. I wondered why he was still there; I had thought he would be on his way home by then.

As John began to read, I got a panicky feeling. *What news will we hear?* I wondered.

Dec. 16 1918

Dear Bro John

Well I guess I will spend this Christmas in France seems rather unusual. It doesn't look like Christmas over here yet no snow but rather warm and plenty of rain.

I suppose you read the letter I wrote home outlining roughly where I have been. However will tell briefly a few things I haven't been allowed to write before. But will wait until I get home to tell you all my interesting experiences.

As you know we sailed on June 4 and landed in Liver-pool on June 15. We came by way of northern coast of Ireland. We took a train across England to Normandy (near Southampton) were there a few days then sailed from Southampton and landed at La Havre. From there we took a train across northern France to a small town (village) near Neaucheakition where we trained nearly a month.

We left for the trenches the last week in July. On Sept 12 we went over the top at 5 o'clock in the morning. It was the St. Mihiel drive toward Metz that you know doubt read about. I was slightly gassed and very much exhausted so was taken to a field hospital. Was there about 2 weeks and then returned to my Co. Was back less than a week when I became sick so was sent to a base Hospital and have been here ever since as you have seen by my letters. Am a member of a casual Co. here now and expect to move soon. I don't know where. We may be kept here in France for awhile for work or may be sent home.

I'm felling fine and dandy hoping this finds you the same.

Loving Bro. Tony

Pvt. Anthony Sletten
Casual Det.
Base Hosp. #64

"He said he is fine and dandy, so that makes me feel better," I said. "It sounds like he might come home soon. What he described sounds terrible, but at least he was not shot. I feel like I can breathe now that I know he will be coming home. The war has been over now for almost a month, so I think all the troops will be coming back soon."

"Belle," Ingvold said, "It may be a couple of months before he can be sent home. I am sure there is a lot of rebuilding to be done over there, and our troops will help with that. He should be home before summer."

"Summer!" I said, "I was expecting him to be home by February."

"These things just don't move as fast as we think. It takes a lot of time to move all the troops back home," John said.

I busied myself for the next few weeks, cleaning Tony's room and making it nice for when he returned to us. It was the happiest I had been since Tony left the previous May.

We received a little post card from Tony wishing us a Merry Christmas, but he had no more news. He had also sent Edith a postcard saying Happy New Year, which was postmarked January 7.

One morning Ingvold and I were having our breakfast when there was a knock on the door. "I wonder who that could be at this time of the morning," I said. I went to the door, and when I looked out the glass I froze in my tracks. "No, no, no!" I cried and collapsed on the floor. Ingvold came running to see what was wrong.

There, standing on our porch, was an Army officer, and I knew why he was there. Ingvold let him in, He took off his hat and said. "I am sorry to have to inform you that your son, Anthony Sletten, has died in the hospital in France. He suffered damage to his kidneys when he was gassed, and that is what caused his death. He died on February seventh."

I couldn't take it and didn't want to believe it. "We just got a postcard that was postmarked January seventh. He was fine!" I cried. From then on, I couldn't be consoled.

When the officer left, Ingvold called the doctor. He came and gave me something to help me sleep. Ingvold and the doctor helped me to the cot in the dining room by the bay window. The sun was shining into the window, and my geraniums were blooming pink and red, but I couldn't see them. Everything was dark. I was still crying when I finally slipped into unconsciousness.

When I awoke, I looked around and saw all the familiar things in the room: the table and buffet, my geraniums in the window, and our children's pictures on the dining room wall. Then I saw Anthony's picture.

"Ingvold, Ingvold!" I cried. He came at once and sat by the bed and held my hand. "What is it, Belle?" he asked. "I'm here, don't worry." I could tell he had been crying too. His eyes were red, and he looked like he hadn't slept in days.

"Tell me it was a dream and that it isn't true about Tony," I sobbed.

"Belle, it is true. Anthony is gone. The officer said we would receive his belongings soon. He said he will be buried there as it is too hard to ship his body back with all the troops they are sending back."

"Don't talk about him being a 'body,' Ingvold. He is our son. I just can't have him buried way over the ocean in a strange country. Tell me you will do what has to be done to bring him back here."

"I will see what I can do, but it may take some time," said Ingvold. "The officer brought a letter from a Red Cross worker who was with Tony when he died. Do you want me to read it to you? It may give you some comfort to know that he was not alone when he died—that someone was there comforting him."

"I don't know if I can listen to it now, but I don't know if I can listen to it later either. I am having a hard time believing all this is true. Go ahead and read it now, it may make me feel comforted."

As Ingvold started to read the letter, his voice quivered, and he almost broke down a couple of times.

Le Mans, France Camp Hospital 52 February 11, 1919

Subject: Private Anthony M. Sletten, 2846523 Company A, 328 Machine Gun Bn.

Mr. I.T. Sletten,

Canton SD.

My dear Mr. Sletten:

I am the Home Communication Representative of the American Red Cross at Camp Hospital 52, here in Le Mans, and the link between our sick men and their families. Therefore, it is with the greatest sympathy and with a full realization of the privilege that is mine that I am writing to tell you something of the last days of your son's life; which were spent in this hospital. You will already have received the cable from the Government, telling you that he died at 9:30 a.m., February 1, from acute nephritis.

It was on January 30th, about 5:00 p.m. that on an impulse of the moment I went to Barracks 11 of this hospital. There I saw your son. He was very sick----vomiting as I entered. After a while I talked with him and he gave me your address, saying he would like to have me write to you. That was all. He was semi-unconscious all the time and could be roused for only a minute or two. I stroked back his hair and he smiled at me before he dropped off again.

Before I left the chief surgeons and physicians of the hospital had arrived and were in consultation over him. He had every care from the finest physicians and nurses, but he did not rally. His semi-unconscious condition deepened, and so he slept away without pain. I am sure that even this little news of him will help your aching heart.

I am enclosing a description of the funeral service as it is conducted here. The grave is registered with the American E. F., and will be cared for by them. If your son had any personal effects they will reach you in due course of time through the Personal Effects Bureau in Washington.

Sincerely,

Mary A. Rolfe
American Red Cross

By the time Ingvold had finished the letter, we were both sobbing. We held each other and cried. What could we do? Nothing, but grieve the loss of our dear Tony.

It wasn't until several days later that we read how our Tony was buried. It was hard to think of him over there being buried with hundreds of other men, but it was a comfort to hear how they honored those that had fallen.

An American Boy's Burial in France

Full Military Honors

It was nine o'clock on one of those soft gray days common in France, which remind us of April at home---that I went to the hospital with the purpose of going out with some of the boys on the journey to their last resting place. I climbed up on the seat of a big horse drawn ambulance with the American soldier driver and a Chaplain from a camp 14 miles away, who had come to attend the burial of one of his men who had died suddenly of heart failure. Our load that morning was a very precious one---the bodies of five of our boys which I had watched as they slowly passed out into the future.

We went through the great gates of the old priests' school at Le Mans, now used for Camp Hospital. No 52 along its high stone wall and through the narrow winding streets past the great Cathedral with its ancient tower, its Druid stone and wonderful window glass, on down through the "Tunnel"---a covered stone road descending to the river, passed the old Roman brick tower at the right and on across the river, leaving the ruined stone arches and porticoes of the Romans to guard the river bank at our left.

Soon we came to the Cemetery, the grand Cemetiere of Le Mans. There we were met by an army band, the Chaplin, soldier pall bearers and the firing squad. As the first coffin was lifted from the ambulance to the horse drawn, soldier-ridden, gun carriage every man came to salute. The firing squad presented arms, thus the flag draped coffin on its gun carriage passed tough the gates behind the band and the Chaplain, who walked. Then the others followed, with soldiers marching on either side those we honored went the firing squad and last of all the visiting Chaplin and I.

As the band played softly, we passed down the long tree lined lane of the old French cemetery with its old head wreaths little shrines—on to the soldiers' section. It is a beautiful spot that soldiers' section. As we stood there by our open graves to the left and in front where many American graves each marked by a large white wooden cross with name, date and regiment. Over them was a large flag pole from which an American flag hung at half-mast.

There is something wonderfully sweet to me about that cemetery. It seems as though the True Peace rested there. The French people in all their thoughtfulness keep flowers great wreaths of them—at the base of our American standard. They also plant tiny flowers on the German graves. I know they think of all the mothers and loved ones far away.

And so we stood beside our open graves and as each coffin was lifted and carried to this waiting grave the band played. The Americans stood at salute and the French people back by a row of evergreens uncovered or crossed themselves and then as the Chaplin stood close the flag-draped coffin was lowered. There was a pause when all was quiet, and then another boy was carried to us. Again the band played, again the Chaplain stepped close, and another boy had gone to his last bodily resting place.

When all had been lowered the Chaplin read the burial service, ending with "dust to dust, ashes to ashes, in the hope of the resurrection from the dead, in Christ Jesus our Lord." As he said this he sprinkled a little dirt into each grave. Then the firing squad stepped to the end of the row of graves and *one, two, three* the triple military salute rang out, followed by the beautiful taps, written, so we are told, to bring cheer and peace to the tired American soldier boys many years ago.

As it still sounded softly in the misty air the band began to play "Nearer My God to Thee." Playing softly the band marched away, followed by the others while the Chaplain and I still lingered for a few minutes by the new "American" in the heart of France.

This little description I dedicate to "The Loved Ones at Home."

Mary A. Rolfe
American Red Cross, Home Com. Rep.
Camp Hospital No 52 A.P.O. 762

Ingvold gave a huge sigh as tears streamed down his face. "Belle, he was a true hero. We can find comfort in knowing that. He will be coming home a hero."

"I can't think of him as a hero yet" I said. "How can we give up all the hopes and dreams we had for him? He had such promise to be a great man. I don't understand why God allowed this, I just can't understand."

"Belle, we may never understand, but we have to accept what has happened. I will make sure that he is brought back here so that he can rest next to his brothers in Parker."

Ingvold called the other children, and they were all good at stopping by and seeing if we needed anything. I think it was hardest on Mary. She had so much belief in Tony and knew he would graduate from college. She had taken him under her wing, and she gave him encouragement to work towards his dream of being a pharmacist.

Edith took it hard too. She cried, even though I don't think she fully understood what was going on. She would always remember her Uncle Tony.

1920 - 1921

AUGUST 19, 1920, WAS the day of our Anthony's funeral and burial. I had been dreading this day. Anthony's casket, draped with a United States flag, had arrived on a train that morning, and the funeral service took place on our front lawn at one o'clock.

The American Legion was in charge of the funeral and all the decorations. I hardly recognized our house with all the festive patriotic colors. A large flag was stretched across the front porch with the flag caught up in the center, forming a festoon. That is where all the speakers stood. A bunting was stretched from tree to tree. To the left of the porch sat the casket, while six members of the Legion stood ready to act as pallbearers.

I heard a band playing "Lead Kindly Light," a favorite of Tony's. I heard the speakers talking, but I couldn't comprehend what was being said. I was so transfixed on Tony's casket, and I couldn't take my eyes off it.

I heard someone say, "Our hearts thrill with pride in the glory of the flag, not only my heart, but every heart, that swelled in the breasts of four million who sprang to its defense upon fields of deadly conflict."

How could I feel proud when my Tony was laying there in that casket? I couldn't understand how we could go on from here. I saw my other children wiping their eyes and Ingvold sitting next to me trying to hold it together. I saw it, but I didn't feel anything. I was totally numb.

Now Reverend Brown was reciting the twenty-third Psalm. "Yea though I walk through the valley of death, I will fear no evil, for Thou art with me."

Where is God? Why did he let this happen? I wondered. I couldn't stop thinking of my son, lying there in a casket. Soon we would be putting him in the grave, and then it would be over. But it would not be over for me. I would go on suffering his loss. I could not understand the words being said. I heard bits and pieces, but I could only think of the last time I saw Tony alive when we put him on the train to send him on his way to war.

Suddenly I heard the pastor saying, "Seek portals of this higher bliss, found in communion and companionship with God and then, as recorded in memory of Anthony M. Sletten, the pathway from time to eternity shall be bright, and to be trod in happiness."

Then it was over. A quartet sang "My Faith Looks up to Thee"; then "Taps" was played; then the band, Legion, Relief Corps squad, and other soldiers escorted Tony's remains by car to Fifth Street, where we all joined in the procession to Parker for the burial.

The ride was a somber one. Everyone in our car was weeping, trying to make sense of it. At the cemetery there were more remarks, which I didn't hear. When the pastor was finished, the Canton firing squad fired the last salute, and "Taps" was played again.

Then I watched as Tony was slowly lowered into the grave. Ingvold had to hold me up as I felt like my knees were going to buckle. I was beyond crying. I was in shock and everything seemed like a dream.

When it was over, we were taken back to our home in Canton. All the decorations had been removed, and it looked like our house again. Ingvold helped me up the stairs to bed because I didn't have the strength. Before I went into my room, I went into Tony's room and sat on his bed. There was his trunk he had so proudly packed for his college days. On top of it was a 1917 Hobo Day sticker. I could almost hear him saying. "Ma, I'm going to be a pharmacist someday."

Suddenly, I was so exhausted I could hardly make my way to our bedroom to get into bed. It was all over. There was nothing I could hope for anymore. I prayed to God before I fell asleep, "Lord, I don't understand why this had to happen, but I will trust You. I know you loved Tony just as much—maybe more—than I did. Help me to make it through all this and help Ingvold too. We need Your strength because we don't have it ourselves." Then I drifted into the sweet release of sleep.

God must have answered my prayer because our life went back to a somewhat normal pace after the funeral. We had many happy times with Ellen and her boys and John's two little girls. I loved to spend time with them. I often took their little hands in mine and told them I loved them.

I went through the motions of life, making dinner, going to church, shopping at the store, and reading my Bible, just as I had done since I was a girl. My life had changed so much over the years. I thought a lot about how my life has gone so fast.

I was having almost daily chest pains and relied on nitro to ease the pain. I wondered what would happen to Ingvold if I should die. Would he be able to get along without me? I spent a lot of time lying on the small day bed in the dining room as it was hard for me to climb the stairs. I loved lying there looking at my geraniums in the window with the sun shining in. Even when the days were cold and blustery that winter, the flowers were always a ray of happiness in my life.

Ingvold was very attentive to me. He made soup and brought it to me. He helped me into bed each night, gave me a kiss, and told me how much he loved me. I never had to wonder if Ingvold loved me. I always knew. On April 7 of the upcoming year we would be celebrating our 38th wedding anniversary. I hoped we would have many more years together.

Soon, it was March of 1921. It was a mild month, and John and his family were finally able to come to town to see us. They went to church with Ingvold, but I was not feeling up to going. They came to our house after church, and Nellie fixed something for lunch. We talked, and I watched the girls play with the toys. Edith would give a toy to Mary Ellen and show her what she should do with it. then Mary Ellen would imitate what Edith was doing. Mary Ellen would be three that summer, and she was quite a handful. Edith was reading now, and she read to her sister as they sat in the big chair together.

Before they left for home, the girls came over and said goodbye to me. Edith gave me a big kiss and said she would see me again soon. Then little Mary Ellen came shyly to my side. I took her little hand in mine and told her that she should be a good girl and mind Mama and Papa. She nodded with her eyes big as saucers. "Remember," I said, "you will grow up to be a good mama yourself someday." Then they were gone. The house was so quiet, and Ingvold and I each took a little nap.

When I woke, Ingvold was busy in the kitchen fixing something for our supper, whistling like he used to. It made me happy to hear him, and I remembered the night he stayed with me when Amil was sick. He was such a good husband, and I was so blessed to have him.

We ate our supper together and then I lay down again. We talked about our life and our children and grandchildren. We reminisced about all the things that had happened in our life.

I looked over all the pictures of our children on the wall. There was the picture I had taken after Gus's funeral with my two little boys clinging to my skirt and baby Mary on my lap. That seemed like a lifetime ago. There was the picture of Mary, John, and Tom taken when they were all in school in Nebraska. There was a picture of Ellen and Mary in their beautiful hats. Sam, with his strong jaw, was so handsome. He and Mary had not found their partners yet.

Then my eyes fell on the picture of Anthony taken when he graduated from high school. "He was so handsome and full of life," I said, "I suffered so with the deaths of my children, but Anthony was the worst, Ingvold. Tony's death…"

Ingvold turned to see why she didn't finish her sentence. "Belle. Belle. Belle!" Ingvold called as he looked at her, but Belle was not breathing. He went to her side and took her hand in his; then he lay his head on her chest and wept. His Belle, whom he loved so, was gone.

Epilogue

Ingvold Sletten continued to live in the house on Lincoln St. in Canton, South Dakota, until his death on February 19, 1937, at the age of seventy-four. He was a big part of his children's and grandchildren's lives.

Mary Augusta Anderson was a very well-educated teacher most of her life. She started teaching at the age of seventeen with thirty-seven students in all eight grades and was paid $30.00 a month. She received her BA degree in 1922 from USD in Vermilion, about a year after her mother's death. She was married to Charles John Nelson on March 6, 1925. They never had any children, but she had hundreds of children in her classrooms over approximately 40 years of teaching. Her husband, Charles, died on May 30, 1946, at the age of 67. Mary died on April 2, 1957, at the age of 76.

John Ingvold Sletten lived on the farm south-west of Canton and raised his two daughters, Edith Belle and Mary Ellen, with his wife, Nellie. Nellie had many health problems associated with having the measles when she was a young woman. She died January 8, 1939, at the age of 52. She was privileged to see her youngest daughter, Mary Ellen graduate from college. John continued to farm after Nellie's death.

On April 29, 1941, Mary Ellen married H. Clark Baird, and they made their home at the farm where she had been born. They had eight children, of which I am the sixth. John continued to live with Mary Ellen and Clark until 1943, when he was appointed to fill a vacancy at the Methodist churches at Leola and Westport, South Dakota, when he was 60, fulfilling his dream of becoming a minister. He had kept his preaching license over the years, and in 1947, he moved to Rockham, South Dakota, to pastor that church.

On September 1, 1947, John married Nellie's younger sister Jennie Bixby. They lived in Rockham and Summit and retired in Canton in 1954. They lived in the house on Lincoln St. where both his parents had lived and died. On March 16, 1962, his wife Jennie died at the age of 73, leaving him alone again. In 1963, his daughter Edith, who had never married and had spent most of her adult life caring for people in their homes, moved to Canton, and she remained by his side until his death February 20, 1966, at the age of 83.

Ellen Mable Sletten Yarborough had three sons, Victor, Harry, and Jack. Her husband Fred died February 12, 1938, at the age of 67. Ellen died June 23, 1969, at the age of 80, in Sioux Falls, South Dakota.

Samuel E. Sletten farmed the land that Ingvold had purchased until his death in 1945. He married Lillian Martha Ball on January 1, 1925, and they had two children, Samuel Jr. and Joy Lenore Sletten. Sam died on December 7, 1945, at the age of 54. Lillian died on May 29, 1988, at the age of 93.

Top Left:

Peter August Anderson (1843-1881) and Isabelle Dahl Anderson Sletten (1851-1921), Married 1876

Top Right:

Ingvold's homestead in Turner County, South Dakota, Circa 1887 (L to R): John Sletten, Ingvold Sletten, Thomas Sletten, Isabelle Dahl Anderson Sletten, Mary Anderson Nelson

Bottom Left:

Isabelle Dahl Anderson Sletten with her three children after her first husband, Peter Anderson, passed away. Children (L to R): Amil A. Anderson (1877-1886), Mary A. Anderson Nelson (1881-1957), Peter O. Anderson (1879-1883), Circa 1881

Bottom Right: *Children of Ingvold Sletten and Isabelle Dahl Anderson Sletten (L to R, back row): Thomas Sletten (1886-1905), John Sletten (1883-1966), Mary Anderson Nelson (1881-1957), (L to R, front row): Samuel Sletten (1891-1945), Anthony Sletten (1896-1919) and Ellen Sletten Yarbrough (1889-1969), Circa 1897*

Top Left:

(L to R): John Sletten, Ellen Sletten Yarbrough, Anthony Sletten, Mary Anderson Nelson, Samuel Sletten, Circa 1911

Bottom Left:

(L to R): Ingvold Sletten, Anthony Sletten, Isabelle Dahl Anderson Sletten, Circa 1900

Top Right:

(L to R): Mary Anderson Nelson, Ellen Sletten Yarbrough. Circa 1910

Anthony Sletten
(1896-1919)
Circa 1918

Samuel Sletten
(1891-1945)
Circa 1910

Top Left:

(L to R): John Sletten, Mary Anderson Nelson, Thomas Sletten, Circa 1904

Bottom Left:

(L to R): Mary Ellen (Nellie) Bixby Sletten (1887-1939) and John Sletten (1883-1966), Circa 1911

Top Right:

Home in Canton, South Dakota, Circa 1906
(L to R): Isabelle Dahl Anderson Sletten, Ellen Sletten Yarbrough, Ingvold Sletten, Thora Sletten (Ingvold's father, 1826-1917) and Anthony Sletten

Following Pages:

A letter to John Sletten from his brother, Anthony Sletten, about his experiences in France while serving in World War I

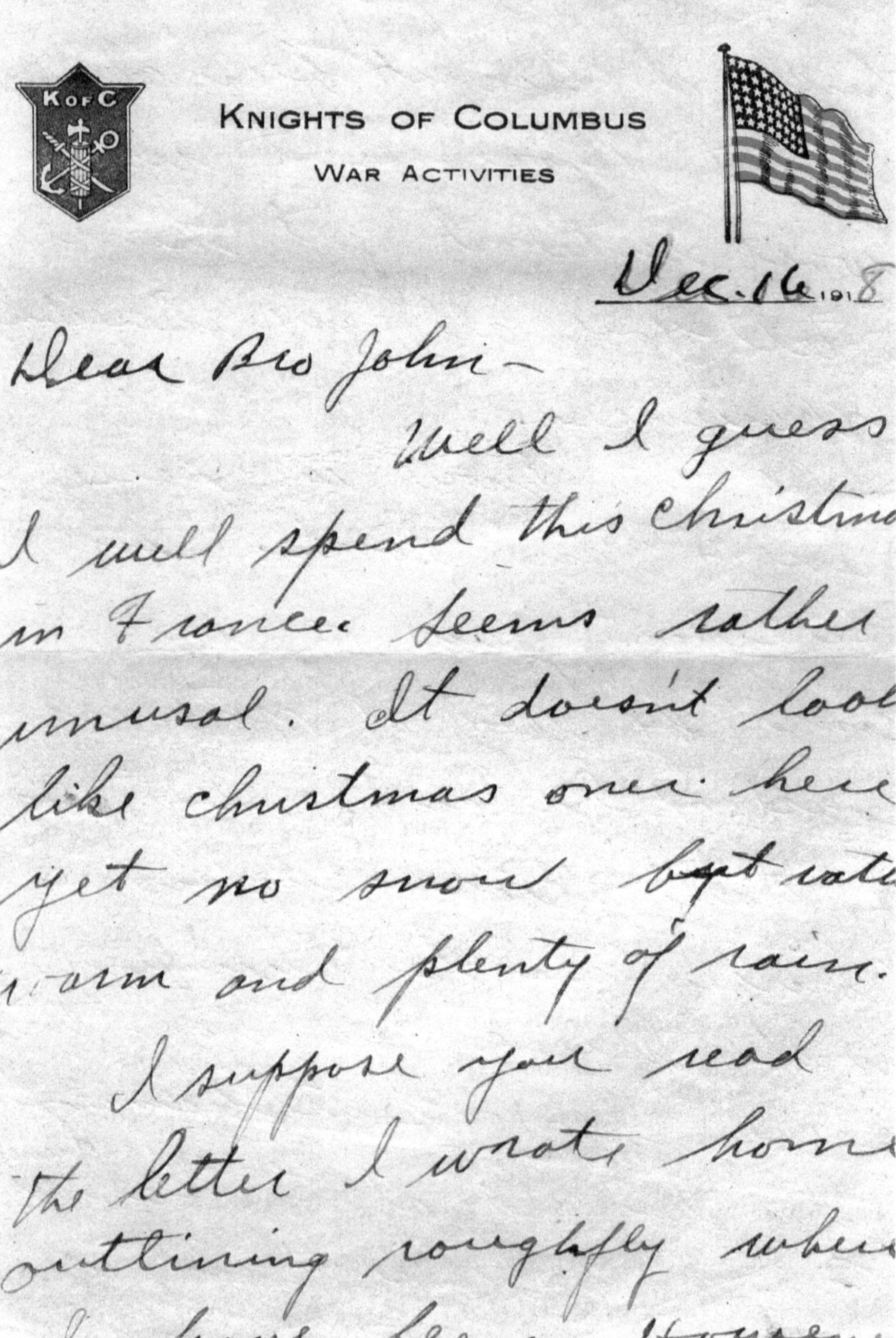

Dec. 16 1918

Dear Bro John —

Well I guess I will spend this christmas in France. Seems rather unusual. It doesn't look like christmas over here yet no snow but rather warm and plenty of rain.

I suppose you read the letter I wrote home outlining roughly where I have been. However

will tell briefly a few
things I haven't been allow
to write before. But will
wait until I get home
to tell you all my interestin
experiences.
As you know we sailed
June 4th and landed in
Liverpool June 15 we
came by way of nothern
coast of Ireland. We took
a train across England to
Romsey (near Southhampton)
where there a few days the
sailed from Southhampton
and landed at Le. Havre [from]
From there we took a
train across nothern France

KNIGHTS OF COLUMBUS

WAR ACTIVITIES

_______________ 191__

to a small town (village) near
Neufchâteau where we
trained nearly a month.
We left for the trenches the
last week in July. On Sept.
12 we went over the top at
5 o'clock in the morning. It
was the St. Micheal drive
toward Metz that you know
don't read ofout. I was
slightly gassed and very
much exhausted so was
taken to a field hospital

was there about 2 weeks
and then returned to my
Co. Was back less then a week
when I became sick so
was sent to a base Hospital
and have been here ever
since as you have seen
by my letters. Am a member
of a casual Co. here now
and expect to move soon.
I don't know where. We
may be kept here in France
for awhile for work or may
be sent home.
    I'm feeling fine and dandy
hoping this finds you the
same. Loving Bro.
                    Tony
            Pvt. Anthony Sletten
                casual Det.
            Base Hosp. # 64

ACKNOWLEDGMENTS

First, to my mother, Mary Ellen Sletten Baird, who came before me and documented many of the stories in this book. She was an author and very wise to have written stories about her parents and grandparents. This is where I first learned about my great grandparents, Ingvold and Isabelle Sletten. I only wish that my mother would have lived to see this book published. I hope I make you proud, Mama.

Second, to my sister, Ruth Baird Pollard, who gave countless hours of editing and mentoring me on this journey. I would never have been able to write this book without her. Thank you, Sis.

I also want to acknowledge Karen Bonneau Hansen and Waneta Krueger, who put together a book on the descendants of Olof Pedersson Dahl and Maria Nilsdotter. I was able to get much of the historical information about Isabelle and her family from that book.

About the Author

MARY BAIRD MAYER grew up with five sisters and two brothers on the farm that her grandfather bought in 1917, in the house where her mother was born. Lucky enough to attend country school for seven years before moving to Beresford, South Dakota, she enjoyed her childhood on the same Dakota prairie as her great-grandmother, Isabelle. After high school, she married her husband, Allen, and had four children. Upon earning an Associate Degree in her late twenties, nursing became her profession for thirty-five years. In retirement, she and Allen are blessed with twelve grandchildren. On any given day, you'll find her busy writing, doing craft projects, attending church-related activities, working on Ancestry.com and making music with her accordion group.